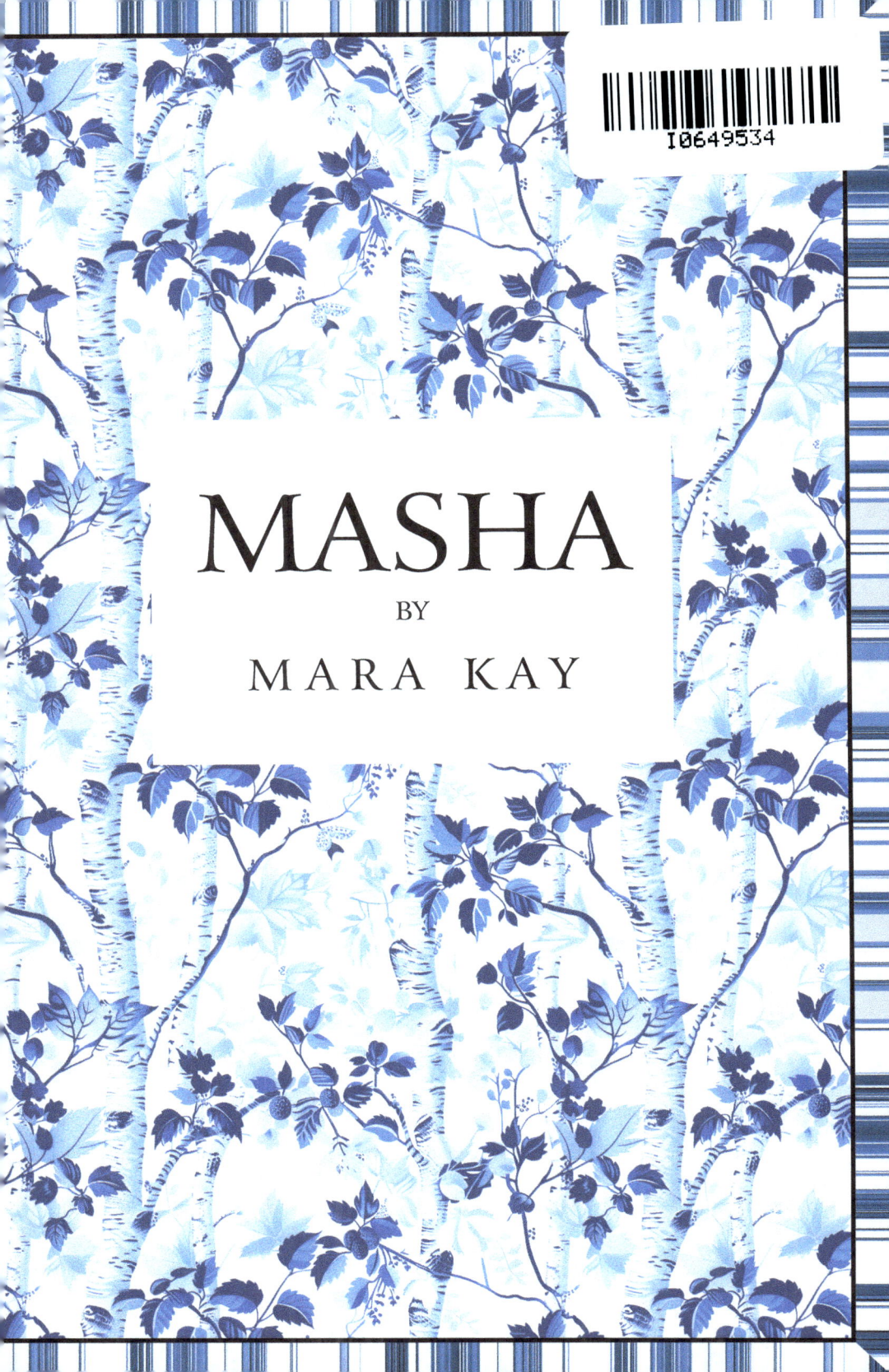

MASHA

BY

MARA KAY

Design and Layout © 2024 Anno Domini Creative

ISBN: 978-1-939689-13-9

Table of Contents

BLUE

WHITE

ANCILLARIES

GREEN

Out of the Snowstorm

T HE WINTER OF 1814–15 WAS UNUSUALLY long, even for the north of Russia. At the end of March, it still snowed every day and as soon as the sky started to clear, cold winds blew up more thick white clouds.

Standing on a footstool, Masha leaned on the windowsill and watched the snowflakes settle on the branches of an old apple tree, cling to the stems of vine over the terrace, and blot out the big flower bed in front of the house.

The garden looked better in winter than in any other season, Masha thought dreamily. The snow hid the weeds, smoothed out the unswept pile of rotting leaves, and turned the tangle of unpruned shrubbery into silvery lace.

It was twilight outside, but the room behind her was getting dark. The china clock under its glass dome struck four thin, quivering notes. Masha turned around. Suddenly, the familiar drawing room with its moth-eaten tapestry chairs, faded brocade curtains, and old portraits on the walls had become strange and unfriendly.

Shadows were creeping cautiously out of every corner, as if ready to close in on the small figure by the window.

Masha put a foot on the floor, ready to run, when a soft light gleamed through the doorway of the small study next to the drawing room. Reassured, she drew her foot back again. Nothing could be really frightening as long as Mamma was at her writing desk, the green-shaded oil lamp at her elbow. The eerie feeling vanished. Masha was back in her safe, dearly beloved world, the only one she had ever known: the old house and the garden outside. She turned back to the window. The twilight was almost gone. One could barely distinguish the dark trunks of the trees at the entrance of the long avenue of cedars. Drifts of snow were whirling here and there like small clouds. She knew what it meant. The storm was rising.

"Masha, where are you?" a voice called from the study.

"In here, Mamma!" Masha jumped off the footstool and ran toward the light. Just as she had expected, her mother was sorting out papers. Masha hated those long sheets of paper with the word "Account" on the top and rows of figures down the page. They came with almost every mail, all addressed to "Maria Borisovna Fredericks, widow of Colonel Vasili Fredericks."

Standing at the door, Masha looked at her mother's head bent over the pile of papers, her light chestnut curls falling in clusters at the sides of the forehead. Was it the green light that put a tinge of gray at the temples? In a sudden burst of tenderness, she rushed across the worn-out rug, her long fair hair flying behind her, and planted a kiss on the small birthmark nestling in a corner of her mother's low-cut neckline.

"What's the matter, dear?" Maria Borisovna asked, taking Masha's cold hands in hers. "Why, you are all chilled! You shouldn't have stayed in the drawing room so long. The stove doesn't hold heat any more. Did you practice your music this afternoon?"

"I did, Mamma, but there must be something wrong with the piano. I know I strike the right notes, but they don't sound right."

Her mother sighed. "I am afraid it needs tuning. I wish we could afford it. The spinet is in much better order, but it is out of fashion nowadays. And now, love, why don't you read to me while I do some mending."

Dragging her feet, Masha went to the bookshelf and took down an old issue of Children's Reading. She disliked the magazine and found each story duller than the next. Settling down in her small armchair, she began. "The Story of a Brick. Bricks are made of clay..." A glance at her mother's face made her realize that she had no listener. Glad of the opportunity, Masha hurried on, leaving out long words and sometimes whole sentences. It was a relief when shuffling steps sounded behind the door and her old nurse, Niania Akulina, walked into the room.

Her small, red-lidded eyes peering from under the black kerchief, Niania approached the white porcelain stove and felt it. "Good so far," she muttered. "Let's hope it will stay warm through the night. A bad storm is beginning."

As if in answer, the windowpanes began to rattle, and a cold whiff of air came from the corridor.

"A... ah!" Niania always intercepted her speech with groans. "It is getting colder and colder." She turned to Masha's mother. "Shall I tell Stepan to bring in another armful of wood, Barinia?"

Maria Borisovna answered quickly. "No! We don't need it. Tell Feklusha not to set the table in the dining room. She can bring us some supper in here."

Niania Akulina shrugged her shoulders. "If you wish so, Barinia." Suddenly, she stiffened and looked up at the ceiling. A creaking sound came from above as if someone was walking up and down the attic.

"The domovoy..." Niania muttered. "He's restless. Hear him walk! Last night he roamed all over the stables. Braided the horse's manes and tails, Stepan tells me."

"Oh!" Masha breathed. "Did Stepan see him?"

"Niania, please see about the supper," Maria Borisovna interrupted. When Niania's stooping figure in the dark calico dress disappeared behind the door, she said severely, "I hope, Masha, you don't really believe all the stories Niania tells you?"

Masha hesitated. "No... But someone does walk in the attic. Listen! There it is again!"

Maria Borisovna shook her head. "It is only the old boards creaking. The house needs repairs. The village folks think there is a spirit, a domovoy, watching over every home, but it is just superstition. We know he does not really exist."

"But I like to imagine him," Masha protested. "I can see him so clearly. He is big, and hairy, and dusty, with dirty long nails and cobwebs in his hair, but his laugh is kind. I think..."

"That will do, Masha." Her mother's tone was firm. "Take your knitting and see if you can manage at least five rows this evening. You will have no stockings left. I will draw the curtains, as the wind is getting up. Move your chair so that you are out of the draft."

Masha obediently collected the long black stocking from her mother's workbasket. Her tongue in her cheek, she applied herself, counting the stitches.

Maria Borisovna adjusted the lamp that was beginning to smoke and replaced the shade. Masha's world became even smaller, confined to the circle of light on the threadbare rug.

Outside, the wind howled and whistled, hurling snow against the windows. In the attic, the steps sounded again. Masha imagined the domovoy crouching in a corner among the cobwebs and wondered if he was very cold up there under the rafters.

"The roads are going to be snowed in."

Maria Borisovna spoke to herself, but Masha looked up quickly, forgetting the domovoy. "Snowed in, Mamma? How nice!"

Her mother's eyebrows went up. "Nice? Why?"

"The Evil Man won't be able to come."

"The Evil Man?" Maria Borisovna repeated helplessly. "Who is he?"

"The one who came last week. He often comes. You send me out of the room when you talk to him, but I watch him from the hall.

He has a gray beard and wears a flowered waistcoat. You said once his boots smell bad. Last time he came, he didn't take his cap off. Niania said no nice person would do that."

Maria Borisovna leaned back in her chair, looking as if she didn't know whether to laugh or scold. "Oh, Masha! I know whom you mean. That man is not at all evil. You mustn't judge people so, my darling. He lent me some money after... after your father never came back from the war. It is only natural that he should want to be paid back. Only I can give him very little at a time, so he gets impatient and comes to remind me."

"Is he rich?"

"He is well-to-do. He owns that big mill by the river."

"Then why doesn't he let you keep the money?"

"There is no reason why he should. You will understand when you are older."

Masha bent over her knitting again. She knew her mother's last words meant the subject was closed.

Niania Akulina's kerchief poked through the door. "Barinia, the ceiling in the yellow room is leaking. I told Feklusha to move the furniture out of the way."

"Oh, no!" Maria Borisovna exclaimed. "Not after Stepan has repaired the roof. He told me he had replaced all the broken tiles."

Niania snorted. "Stepan told you! He knows you are not going to climb on the roof to look at his work. Drinking tea and smoking his pipe—that's all he can do properly. Ah... there is no master in the house. That's the trouble." She trotted away, still groaning.

Masha touched her mother's knee. "Mamma." She hesitated. It was something she had often wondered about but never dared to ask. But this seemed the right moment and she decided to risk it. "Did Papa have to go to the war?"

Her mother did not seem annoyed by the question. "He was not in the army, if that's what you mean. But in 1812 every man in Russia, and I mean every man, Masha, who could carry a rifle, a sword, or even a pitchfork, went to defend his country against

Napoleon Bonaparte. When your father told me he was going, I did not try to stop him. He left at dawn, because he did not want the servants to start crying and lamenting, and you and I went with him as far as the three poplars. You know the place. He led his horse by the bridle, and I walked beside him, holding you by the hand. When we reached the poplars, I kissed your father good-bye and gave him the little ikon of St. Maria of Egypt, your saint and mine. Do you remember it at all?"

"I?" Masha felt bewildered. She hardly ever dared to mention her father's name because it made her mother look so sad, and now she was suddenly asked to remember.

She tried to think, but only a few shreds of memory floated back to her. The blue folds of her mother's gown. She had liked the color... And the brambles, tall prickly brambles on the sides of the road... The horse's hoofs trotting along and the empty stirrup catching at the brambles. Every time it happened, a rainbowy shower of dew came down. "Only brambles," she said, and suddenly burst out crying.

Maria Borisovna patted her daughter's shoulder. "Don't cry, my dear. It was a long time ago, for you at any rate."

At the sound of Masha's sobs something stirred under the desk, making it shake, and a big shaggy head came out to rest on her lap.

Masha gave a watery smile. Trezor was always on hand to console her. Dear, dear Trezor, big and clumsy, with flapping ears and faithful eyes peering through the matted brown hair.

"If Trezor could only talk, he would tell us many a story about the war," Maria Borisovna said, fondling the dog's ears. "I remember how surprised I was coming home and finding his kennel empty, the chain wrenched out with the wood. It only occurred to me later that he had run away to join your father." She went on talking about Trezor, while Masha listened, tears drying on her cheeks. Niania Akulina was never tired of telling her about Trezor's adventures in the army, but now, told by her mother, the story became new: how her father met Trezor running across the fields, his chain dragging after him, how he learned to march with the cavalry horses, how he helped to catch the French spies hiding in the woods.

When the tale was finished, she asked, "Mamma, did the French soldiers ever come here?"

"No, they never reached St. Petersburg County."

"And suppose Napoleon attacks Russia again? He's not dead, is he?"

Maria Borisovna smiled. "You don't have to be afraid. Napoleon is alive, but he is kept in captivity on Elba. It is an island, far, far away from Russia."

"Oh, I didn't know!" In Masha's imagination a cliff was already surging from the foaming waves. On the cliff stood a dark figure of a man, a three-cornered hat on his head, like the bronze statuette in the living room. How tired Napoleon must be to stand like that day after day.

A gust of wind banged the shutters against the wall of the house. The flame of the lamp leaped up and the study door opened with a creak. Maria Borisovna shivered and drew her shawl tighter around her shoulders.

From down the corridor, Niania's voice came shrilly, "Didn't I tell you to get those pillows out of the way before they are soaked? And what are you doing? Preening at the mirror. You make faces at yourself when there is no work to be done."

Feklusha's thin voice answered plaintively, "And I was not looking at the mirror. I was just dusting it." A door banged and there was silence.

Masha murmured, "Niania is angry at Feklusha."

"She is getting old, poor soul," Maria Borisovna sighed. "After all, she was once your father's nurse. She nearly lost her mind when we received the news of Borodino. If it hadn't been for Trezor, your father's body would never have been found among the other dead."

At the sound of his name, Trezor wagged his tail and rolled over.

"That is how it happened that your father is buried here instead of having a nameless grave on the battlefield. Trezor led one of the officers to the place where he had fallen," Maria Borisovna continued.

"Papa was still alive, and the officer was able to catch his last word. Do you know what it was?"

Masha shook her head, her eyes round and fixed on her mother's face.

"It was 'Masha.' He was thinking of both of us." Catching her daughter's surprised expression, she added, "You always hear me addressed as Maria Borisovna, but your father called me Masha. It is a great comfort, isn't it, dear, to have Papa with us?"

Masha answered dutifully, "Yes, Mamma." But for her, "The servant of the Lord, Vasili Fredericks," whose name was written on the white cross under the willow tree, had nothing to do with the tall, broad-shouldered man she could dimly remember, who used to tickle her under the chin and put her astride Trezor's back.

Masha knitted two rows of her stocking before she put her work down. "Mamma, may I ask something more?"

"Certainly, dear. What is it?"

"When you were telling me about Napoleon being on that island, you sounded as if you were sorry for him. Don't you hate him because of Papa?"

"Listen, child," Maria Borisovna said, pushing back her chair and bending down to turn Masha's face toward her. We do not hate a vanquished enemy. Never. At least not in our family."

Rising to her feet, Maria Borisovna folded her sewing and put it into her workbasket. "I think I had better go and see how Feklusha and Niania are managing with that leak," she said. "It is time for supper. We…"

She did not finish, for Trezor suddenly jumped up, nearly upsetting her. Rushing to the door, he started to scratch and whine. The gleam of a lantern flashed between the curtains and the snorting of horses sounded outside.

Feklusha's light feet pattered along the corridor, followed by Niania's heavy tread.

"Guests, Mamma!" Masha cried excitedly, jumping from her chair.

"In this storm?" her mother exclaimed. "Who could it be?"

"Shall I go and see?" Masha offered eagerly, but Niania Akulina was already in the room, Feklusha's freckled face peering over her shoulder. Trezor immediately pushed past them and disappeared with a loud bark.

"Barinia Antonova has just arrived," Niania announced in a tone that conspicuously lacked hospitality.

"What?" Masha's mother asked with surprise. "Olga Kirilovna is here? But she is in St. Petersburg visiting her son. Are you sure, Niania?"

"You come and listen to her talk. You will be sure fast enough," Niania muttered, turning to go.

Maria Borisovna looked down at her shabby dress. "Have I time to change?" she murmured. "Oh, no, maybe I will just get my better shawl. You run ahead, Masha."

Masha was only too glad to oblige. A moment later she was out of the room, the ball of stocking wool still in her pocket and unwinding behind her as she ran.

CHAPTER TWO

The Governess

MASHA REACHED THE FRONT HALL, WHICH was lit by a solitary candle flickering in a wall sconce, just as the door opened, letting in clouds of frozen air and Stepan, a gloomy, middle-aged man with a perpetually bluish-red face, loaded with bags and boxes. Behind him loomed a large, square figure swathed in furs.

It was Olga Kirilovna's habit to begin talking while still outside and to carry on the conversation regardless of the listener's bewilderment. "We were just leaving St. Petersburg when the news came that he had escaped," her powerful voice boomed. "For all we know, he might be coming here any time!" She pronounced the last words on the threshold of the hall and rolled her eyes to the ceiling.

To Masha, this gesture could only have one meaning. "The domovoy!" she gasped, staring at the door from where the uncanny creature was evidently to appear.

Olga Kirilovna gave a shout of laughter. "Domovoy! Ha, ha, ha!"

she spluttered, pressing Masha to her ample bosom. "No, lamb! It is something far more dangerous. Napoleon has escaped from Elba!"

Before Masha could digest the news, her mother walked into the hall. "Olga Kirilovna! I couldn't believe it was you until I heard her voice!" she exclaimed, and Niania behind her snorted, "What's all this about Napoleon?"

"Maria Borisovna, dearest!" Olga Kirilovna leaned over Feklusha, who was trying to help her off with her felt boots and hugged her friend. "Just imagine! That rascal is roaming free again. Of course, he is still in France, and I am sure the Emperor Alexander will give him a beating again."

Maria Borisovna smiled. "I am sure we don't have to worry yet. But you still have not explained why you are here instead of being in St. Petersburg. How is your son getting on at the Cadets' School?"

Olga Kirilovna waved her hand. "Ah, he is getting on as well as he can, poor boy, with all those lessons and inspections and whippings for the slightest prank. He wanted me to stay longer, but I just couldn't stand the city's hustle and bustle any more. So I wrote to my husband to be sure and send horses for us to the stagecoach station on March twenty-ninth. Who would have expected such a storm! You wouldn't grudge us some hot tea and beds, would you?"

"You keep saying 'us,'" Maria Borisovna interrupted. "Is there anybody with you besides the coachman? You don't usually take a maid to the city."

"Never! A glance at the capital makes a good maid impossible for months afterward. I have with me... Heavens! What did I do with her?"

Olga Kirilovna hopped aside with surprising agility, disclosing a slender girl of about eighteen, in a tight-fitting gray traveling cloak and a fur-trimmed bonnet, who was hovering in the shadows by the door.

"Mademoiselle Aglaya Saburova," Olga Kirilovna announced, adding in a loud whisper, "a governess for the girls."

The stranger blushed and curtsied, keeping an uneasy eye on Trezor, who was busily sniffing at the travelers' luggage.

"Don't be alarmed, he's very gentle," Maria Borisovna assured her. "We are glad to see you, Mademoiselle. Niania, help the young lady off with her cloak and boots."

As Niania, muttering, bundled away the visitors' wraps, Masha stared at the girl's blue and white striped shawl and at her brown, high-waisted dress with sleeves puffed at the shoulders and almost reaching the tips of the fingers. The skirt was short, revealing small black slippers with long ribbons crisscrossed to the mid-calf. The girl stared back and looked as if she wanted to say something, then blushed again and started to pat her dark curls disarranged by the bonnet.

The visitors were marched off by Feklusha to wash after their trip, and supper was served in the dining room. Stepan brought in an armful of wood and lit the big stove, which was decorated with blue and yellow ships painted on the porcelain tiles. Masha eyed it with some anxiety. There was not much fuel in the wood-shed. The extra load might mean that one of the trees in the small grove adjoining the garden would be cut down. Disturbed at the mere thought, Masha slipped into the pantry where her mother and Niania were busily conferring about the food to be served.

"I can't talk to you now, dear," Maria Borisovna said in answer to Masha's frantic whisper. She turned to Niania. "Fried eggs, sausage, and perhaps if I sliced the cold meat very thin..."

Niania removed the carving board. "You leave it to me, Barinia," she said firmly. "That young lady from the city will eat what is served to her. Not that I think she is going to be choosy. Looks half starved."

Seated at the round table, under the hanging oil lamp, Masha thought that Niania was right. Mademoiselle Aglaya did look thin and pale compared with the country girls. The visitor must have felt Masha's eyes on her. She smiled, then hurriedly fixed her gaze on her plate.

At the other side of the table, Olga Kirilovna's corpulent figure bulged out of the chair. Her big, pleasant face was flushed after her fourth cup of tea, and she was back to Napoleon. "I can't understand why the Emperor Alexander did not annex France to Russia," she boomed. "He was right in Paris with all his troops. Such an opportunity and he missed it." She puffed and sipped some more tea.

It seemed to Masha that the girl's lips curled up at the corners as if she wanted to laugh, but the next moment the demure expression was back again.

Maria Borisovna looked frankly amused. "Even without making France a province of Russia," she remarked, "it was a glorious day when the Emperor entered Paris at the head of the allied troops. I know there were big celebrations in St. Petersburg at that time." She addressed Aglaya. "Did you see any of it, Mademoiselle?"

Aglaya lifted her eyes. "Yes," she answered almost in a whisper. "I was privileged to watch a magnificent parade from the windows of the Winter Palace. Her Majesty, the Dowager Empress Maria Feodorovna, had graciously invited the whole White Form. It was an unforgettable occasion."

"Mademoiselle Aglaya was a pupil at the Smolni Institute for Noble Girls," Olga Kirilovna explained. "She graduated only two weeks ago."

Masha forgot her shyness. "What is a white form?" she asked eagerly. "Is there a pink one too? Is it a school? A big one?" She paused, out of breath.

For the first time, the girl seemed to be at ease. Her gray eyes lit with warmth as she looked at Masha. "It is a school," she explained, "and a big one too. There is no pink form. The older girls wear white uniforms, the middle school is dressed in blue, and the small girls are in brown."

"Small girls?" Masha became more and more interested. "Do they like being at school? Aren't they homesick?"

A shadow crossed Aglaya's face. "I don't know," she said slowly. "But then I don't remember my parents. An aunt sent me to Smolni. Most girls are homesick for the first few weeks. Then they become used to school life and make friends with other children. It is not only lessons, you know. Pupils are taken out in the carriages sometimes. They give concerts and plays, they sit in the garden. There is not much time to be homesick."

22

"I am afraid you will find the country life very monotonous after the city," Maria Borisovna said.

"Oh, no! I will be too busy teaching my pupils," Aglaya murmured. But Masha thought she did not sound very sure.

Olga Kirilovna, who was peacefully dozing over her tea, suddenly woke up. "Whoever wants to live in St. Petersburg is a fool!" she declared, putting down her cup with such force that tea spilled into the saucer. "Everyone is in a hurry, carriages racing, policemen shouting, people running. You wouldn't believe it, Maria Borisovna, but they have forgotten how to speak Russian in St. Petersburg. If I hadn't had Mademoiselle Aglaya to help me with shopping, I don't know how I would have managed. What did they call the color of that material I bought for a dress, Mademoiselle? That pale gray poplin?"

"La puce evanouie," the girl murmured and this time there was an unmistakable note of laughter in her voice.

"There!" Olga Kirilovna banged her fist on the table. "Flea-in-a-faint! How do you like that? Indecent I call it!"

Masha did not quite understand their conversation about fleas and colors. The school with white, blue, and brown uniforms sounded much more interesting. "Smolni Institute for Noble Girls..." Masha rolled the words around her tongue with the pieces of preserved pears served for dessert. She wished Olga Kirilovna would stop talking so she could ask Aglaya more questions.

But the girl did not seem inclined to talk. She folded her napkin and looked at Masha's mother. "May I retire, please? I feel very tired."

Maria Borisovna nodded. "Certainly, Mademoiselle. Only... I hope you won't mind sharing my small daughter's room. We... we only had time to heat one guest room. Masha, show Mademoiselle Saburova the way."

Masha eagerly jumped off her chair, but Maria Borisovna made her a sign to come nearer and whispered, "I want you to come back here immediately. Give the poor girl a chance to be alone for a few minutes."

Swallowing her disappointment, Masha obeyed. When she came

back, her mother and Olga Kirilovna, over fresh cups of tea, were deep in conversation. Fetching a book, Masha sat down on the rug near the stove. Usually she enjoyed looking at the pictures showing The True Adventures of a Sea Captain, but now she only pretended to turn the pages. The talk at the table was too interesting.

"It is a great responsibility to have a grown-up girl under your roof," Maria Borisovna was saying.

"Of course it is a responsibility," Olga Kirilovna growled. "Expensive too! The Principal of Smolni, Madame Adlerberg, dictated terms to me as if she were doing me a favor, when I was taking an orphaned girl off her hands. The salary first, and to be paid in gold, mind you. And the questions she asked! My daughters' ages, their characters, their habits. She even wanted to know if we had any young men in the house. The audacity of it! It took all my patience not to walk out and slam the door on that woman!"

"You never mentioned you were planning to engage a governess," Maria Borisovna remarked.

Olga Kirilovna snorted. "It was all my husband's idea. I had one foot in the carriage when he suddenly started talking about our daughters being uneducated and empty-headed, and ordered me to find a governess in St. Petersburg. Well, I've got him what he wanted, and if the girls start scribbling love letters, it will not be my fault. Of course, for a boy it is different. I did not object when my son was sent to school. But for girls me. Very well. I let her buy pencils and slates and copybooks and even those new steel nibs, as if we didn't have enough geese in the country to make quills. But when she started on books, I kept my eyes open. And what do I see? She picked up a book full of pictures of naked men and women, yes, naked, only sheets wrapped around them. 'You put it right down,' I told her, 'and if I ever catch my girls reading this kind of stuff, I am going to take a switch to them.' I wanted to add, 'and to you, too,' but of course I didn't."

Masha's mother laughed. "It must have been mythology. They study it in schools now."

"Not my daughters," Olga Kirilovna said firmly. "And that big globe she persuaded me to buy! I had to pay extra so the stagecoach would take it. The money I laid out for all those implements of hers could have paid the feed of ten cows."

Olga Kirilovna continued to grumble, but Masha was not listening any more. The heat coming from the stove made her drowsy and the pictures in the book became all blurred. She pushed the book away and let her head rest against the blue and yellow tiles. The words "Smolni Institute" made her open her eyes again.

"They don't take children older than six," her mother was saying.

"Oh, no, no, no!" Olga Kirilovna was emphatic. "It has all been changed. The late Empress Catherine, may God rest her soul, had some fancy ideas about creating a new woman when she founded the school. That is why the children are separated so young from their families. But now they take them around eight, and the course is only nine years instead of twelve. Much more sensible, I think."

Maria Borisovna did not answer. She sat with her head bent, fingering the tablecloth. "The fee is quite high, isn't it?" she asked at last.

"Not for the pupils whose fathers were killed in 1812," Olga Kirilovna assured her. "They are to be educated at the government's expense. This will be the first enrollment after the war. They take new pupils only every three years. Girls from St. Petersburg County will have preference."

"Masha," Maria Borisovna said suddenly, "go to bed, child, it is almost ten."

Torn between the desire to be with Aglaya and to listen some more, Masha obeyed.

She found Aglaya sitting on the edge of the big four-poster bed, brushing her hair. She looked much younger in her long white nightgown and flannel bed jacket.

"Do you always go to bed so late?" she asked, smiling at Masha.

"No," Masha answered regretfully. "We can't afford to burn the candles," she confessed. "At what time do the little girls in Smolni Institute go to bed?"

"The Brown Form goes to bed at eight," Aglaya answered, "then the Blues, and last of all the Whites."

"Does each girl have her own room?" Masha went on asking.

Aglaya laughed. "Goodness, no! The pupils sleep in the dormitories, big rooms with rows of beds."

Niania Akulina came in and Aglaya frowned when she saw her undressing Masha and putting away her clothes. "At Smolni you would be dressing and undressing yourself," she said, after Niania had left. "And if your clothes were not folded right, you would be punished."

Masha thought it over. "I suppose I could undress myself," she said. "Olga Kirilovna's daughters have two nianias to look after them. Are you going to make them undress themselves?"

"I certainly shall," Aglaya began and stopped. Her face looked tired and anxious again. "I don't know," she whispered, tracing with her finger the design on the bed-curtains. "Are they nice girls?" she asked, looking up.

Masha hesitated. "Yes, they are nice, I think. We don't play together much. They are older than I am. The youngest is ten and the oldest is almost fifteen. They don't like to run outside, or watch the birds, or look at pictures. They help around the house, of course, but mostly they arrange each other's hair or try on earrings in front of a mirror. When they come here, they always go to the kitchen and ask Mavra, our cook, to tell their fortune in cards. She's good at it."

"I see," Aglaya murmured. She put on her nightcap, slipped under the blankets, and blew out the candle. "Good night," she said.

"Good night," Masha echoed, feeling disappointed, as she would have liked to talk more. She lay quietly, staring into the darkness. The wind was not howling any more. Only the snowy branches swished softly against the windowpanes. Outside the door something heavy collapsed on the mat. Masha smiled. Trezor was taking up his watch post. She was just beginning to doze when she heard a sound of muffled sobbing. She gently put out her hand and touched Aglaya's cheek.

The older girl turned her face away. "Please don't pay any attention," she murmured. "It is nothing. I was just thinking about... about that family. Suppose the girls refuse to obey me? I... I wish I could be back at Smolni with all my friends."

"I am sorry," Masha whispered, not knowing what to say. She waited until the sobs were replaced by quiet breathing and soon fell asleep herself, only to wake up again because there were voices in the corridor outside.

"Of course I have given it thought, and many times," Maria Borisovna was saying. "But I just didn't have enough courage. They have no holidays at home during all those long years. It is like giving up one's child forever."

"But it is such an opportunity," Olga Kirilovna's voice boomed.

"Sh... We are disturbing the girls," Masha's mother said, and there was silence. Then Olga Kirilovna's steps could be heard going down the corridor to the guest room.

Half asleep, Masha nestled more snugly in bed, but a strange uneasy feeling she could not understand made her sit up and swing her feet to the floor. Trying to step lightly, she tiptoed to the door. Trezor lifted his head as she stepped over him, then again thrust his nose between his paws.

Maria Borisovna's door was ajar. Masha crept close and looked inside. Most of the room was dark. Only one corner, thickly hung with ikons, was lighted by a small blue oil lamp. Maria Borisovna, in a white wrapper, her hair loose on her shoulders, was kneeling on the floor. Masha could see her mother's face turned imploringly toward the faintly lighted image of Christ and heard her anguished murmur. "Lord, help me to do the right thing. Show me the way."

Holding her breath, Masha crept back into her own room with a vague feeling that her mother's lonely, desperate prayer somehow meant a change in their lives.

The Aftermath of the Visit

WHEN MASHA WOKE UP THE NEXT MORNING, Aglaya was no longer beside her. Niania Akulina drew aside the window curtains, letting in the bleak daylight. "Olga Kirilovna is gone?" Masha asked.

Niania turned around with a groan. "Ah... yes, child, she is gone. Left two hours ago. Came, disturbed people in the middle of the night, made trouble, and left. She and her wagging tongue!"

"Trouble?" Masha asked, sitting up in bed and yawning. "What trouble, Niania?"

The old woman did not answer. Her wrinkled face suddenly became even more crumpled, and the corners of her mouth drooped. Sitting down on the bed, she cradled Masha in her arms, crooning, "My baby, my poor little lamb."

Still sleepy, Masha buried her face in the folds of Niania's shawl, which smelled faintly of dried herbs, soap, and lamp oil. Masha almost went back to sleep again, but remembered her mother praying at night and became wide awake. Wriggling out of Niania's embrace, she asked anxiously, "Is Mamma ill?"

"She is well enough." Niania's tone was gloomy, as if she did not really mean what she was saying.

The uneasy feeling she had experienced in the night clutched Masha's heart once more. In her mind, all troubles were connected with the Evil Man. He must have come early in the morning and upset Mamma, she decided, as she hurried Niania with her dressing.

Maria Borisovna was sitting in her study when Masha rushed in. She looked up at her daughter and tried to smile. Masha's eyes darted around the room. The Evil Man was nowhere to be seen and there were no bills or letters on the desk. Yet her mother looked more tired and worried than usual.

Trezor shook himself and came to rub his head against Masha's elbow. She put her hand on his neck and crossed the room, wondering why her legs were suddenly so limp. "Good morning, Mamma." She stood on tiptoe to reach her mother's cheek.

"Good morning, dear." Maria Borisovna glanced quickly at Masha's face and frowned. "You look upset. Has Niania been talking to you, or Feklusha?"

Masha shook her head. "I haven't seen Feklusha. Niania didn't say anything. She just called me her poor baby."

"I wish she wouldn't listen at doors," Maria Borisovna said impatiently. She put her arm around Masha. "Look here, darling, I intended to have a little talk with you later today, but we might as well have it now. You admired Mademoiselle Aglaya, didn't you? Wouldn't it be nice if you could become as well-mannered and well-educated a young lady as she is?"

"I don't know," Masha whispered. She was sure now that something frightening was coming.

"But I do," Maria Borisovna answered gently. "And situated as we are, there is only one way for you to get a proper education. I have decided to apply for your admission to the Smolni Institute. You are growing up in ignorance here, for there is little I can teach you without suitable books. You are becoming superstitious, like a little peasant girl. This is not at all what your father dreamed for you. At Smolni you will have French and German lessons, music, dancing. There will be books to read and many other girls to play with."

Masha did not answer. She stood with her head bent, her lower lip trembling.

"Masha, dearest." Maria Borisovna's voice was husky. "Above all I don't want you to think I am sending you away because I don't love you. It is just the contrary. Let me explain something so that you may understand better. You see, the man you don't like is holding our mortgage. This means that he can take the house away if I don't pay him on time. It may happen, Masha, it may happen very, very easily."

Masha swallowed hard. "But what are you going to do, Mamma, if the house is sold?"

Maria Borisovna pressed her closer. "That is just what I am trying to make you understand," she said gravely. "Whatever happens to me will be much easier to bear if I know you are safe at school. At Smolni you'll be trained to earn your living later on instead of depending on someone's charity. It will be much better for both of us. Nine years will pass quickly if you study hard."

"I understand," Masha gulped. Leaning against her mother's shoulder, she thought how poor the room looked in the morning light without the soft magic of the green-shaded lamp. Stuffing peeped through holes in the upholstery. The china cabinet was empty of the figurines and the fine teacups that had been sold off one by one. The once satiny-blue wallpaper was faded, except for one big round place above the spinet. Masha swallowed again. She had loved the picture that used to hang in that place: the laughing girl with long dark lashes, holding an apple as if ready to bite into it. She liked to make up stories of how the girl got the apple and what happened to her. One day a man who collected old oil paintings stopped at the house because his carriage had broken down. When he left, the girl with the apple went with him. And now it was time for Masha herself to leave the old house...

"When do I go?"

Maria Borisovna winced at the sound of the strained little voice. "Not for quite a while, dear. I wrote the petition last night. Olga Kirilovna will send it to her cousin in St. Petersburg. He will present it personally. I understand that the list of candidates has to be approved by the Dowager Empress before anyone can be admitted."

Masha looked puzzled. "The Dowager Empress?"

"The wife of our present Emperor, Alexander I, is the Empress Elizaveta," her mother explained. "But I am talking about the old Empress, Maria Feodorovna, widow of the Emperor Paul I. The widowed Empress is usually called dowager. The Smolni Institute is under her care."

"Where does she live?"

"Where?" Maria Borisovna did not seem too sure. "In St. Petersburg, in the Winter Palace, I suppose. And now run and play. Nothing has been changed yet."

"But everything has changed already," Masha thought, walking moodily through the house. "The rooms look bigger than before and much colder. I don't think I've ever seen that chair in the corner, or that grandfather's clock with a crack across the glass." She opened the kitchen door and looked inside. Mavra, the cook, an elderly woman with a big flat face all marked by smallpox, was standing at the table, peeling potatoes. At the sight of Masha, she put down her paring knife and started to wipe her eyes with a dish towel.

Even Stepan growled something about it being a shame to send a child away from home when he met Masha in the corridor.

Masha realized that it would be several weeks before the answer to her mother's petition could arrive from St. Petersburg, but she began waiting for it almost as soon as she was told about going to Smolni.

Twice a week, Stepan mounted Max, the oldest of the two horses, attached a leather bag to the saddle, and rode to the stagecoach station for mail. Standing by the drawing-room window,

Masha watched him go and was back at her post when he arrived home two hours later. She did not protest or complain. She simply waited for the blow to fall.

Maria Borisovna often looked at the small, tense face by the window, sighed, and turned away.

Time passed. The snow became yellow and melted into the ground. Dripping branches swayed in the April breeze. The first pale bunches of lilac opened in the garden by the broken-down fence. Several hens sat on eggs in the barn. The gray kitchen cat had one scrawny black kitten.

Masha was still waiting for the letter. It would be in a big envelope with golden seals, she decided. Anything connected with such a grand person as the Dowager Empress was bound to be gold.

May was just beginning when the letter arrived, but Masha was not by the window when Stepan brought in the leather bag. Niania had lured her away to see the peddler who was displaying his wares on the back porch. She sat, indifferent, on the moss-grown steps, watching Feklusha rummage among the cheap earrings and listening to Mavra bargain for the wooden spoons, until she noticed a thin, paper-bound book with a picture of St. George and the dragon on the cover. She brushed past Niania, who was testing calico between her fingers, snatched up the book, and ran to her mother's study.

"Mamma! Please, please, may I have this? It only costs..." She broke off and stared at the big envelope lying on the writing desk. The seals were red, but she knew it was The Letter. Her fingers opened and the book fell on the floor. "I won't be able to see the chickens hatch now..." she said aloud and wondered why she had thought about the chickens.

"Yes, you will," Maria Borisovna answered.

Masha noticed the strange expression on her mother's face, but the meaning escaped her. "They say I am to go?" she whispered, her eyes glued to the envelope.

Maria Borisovna said slowly, "No, you are not accepted."

Just for a moment, Masha felt a prick of disappointment. It was as if a door had suddenly shut in her face before she had time to see what was behind it.

Maria Borisovna must have noticed the fleeting shadow. "It is not as if they had anything against you, darling," she told Masha, "but so many little girls who lost their fathers in 1812 wanted to enter the Smolni Institute, there was simply no room for them all. So a ballot was taken."

Masha's expression was blank. "A ballot?"

"It means that slips of paper were put into a bowl," Maria Borisovna explained. "On some was written 'Accepted' and on the others 'Not accepted.' As each girl's name was read, a slip was taken out at random. It was all perfectly fair. Olga Kirilovna's cousin was present at the ballot with other girls' parents and relatives. There is a letter from him too."

But Masha was not interested in Olga Kirilovna's cousin. There was an important question she wanted to ask her mother. She knew she could not be happy until she had the answer. Coming closer, she asked in one gasp, "Mamma, are you sorry I can't go?"

"It was a wonderful chance for you. It is only natural I am disappointed..." Maria Borisovna began and stopped. "No, I am not! I am not!" she exclaimed, kissing Masha again and again. "I should be, but I am not!"

That was all Masha wanted. Smolni, the letter with the golden seals, the long waiting, all suddenly became an old, old story, hardly worth thinking about. She picked up the book from the floor. "Mamma? May I have it?"

"You may, dear. Here is some money." Maria Borisovna took a few coppers from her drawer and pressed them into Masha's hand.

Masha carefully counted the coins in her palm. "Mamma, it's too much."

"Never mind. Buy something else you want," her mother answered recklessly.

The old floorboards of the drawing room creaked, the glass terrace door banged, and Masha was out in the garden, running to the back porch. Trezor, digging for something under a tree, earth flying between his hind legs, saw his mistress run and promptly tore after her. They rounded the house and appeared in front of the small group still gathered around the peddler. "I am not going to school! They don't want me!" Masha shouted, her eyes shining.

Feklusha dropped a bunch of bright ribbons and clasped her hands. Niania exclaimed, "God is good!" and started to cross herself. Mavra beamed, the hairy pimple on her chin lumping up and down. Even the peddler, a tall, sunburned young fellow with a ring in one ear, smiled, showing white teeth.

Feeling very rich, Masha bent over a basket filled with cheap sweets. After long hesitation, she selected a pink sugar cock mounted on a stick.

At last, the peddler packed his wares and went away. Mavra hurried back to the kitchen, from which came a smell of something burning. Feklusha and Niania followed her.

Left alone, Masha sat on the stone steps, Trezor beside her, and opened her book. She read slowly, following the printed lines with her finger. Sucking the sugar cock helped her get over long words. From time to time she let Trezor have a lick, then returned to the story. She was too absorbed to listen to the argument raging in the kitchen behind her.

"I am only telling you what is in the cards," Mavra stormed. "Here it is, plain enough even for you two to see: a long road."

"And I am telling you, your cards are wrong," Niania screamed.

"You say what you want. I see what I see," Mavra insisted. "A long road and no return."

The last words floated to Masha, but she shrugged them off, deep in the delights of her book and the pink sugar cock.

CHAPTER FOUR

The Sudden News

THE FIRST WEEKS OF SPRING HAD BEEN gray and rainy, but early in May the sun came out and nature hastened to catch up. Buds became leaves almost overnight, the vine over the porch waved a lacy green curtain, the grass in the meadows was knee-deep, and the apple tree burst into bloom.

Walking in the garden, Masha noticed something blue peeping through the weeds in the big flower bed in front of the house. Squatting down, she peered closer and discovered a small clump of forget-me-nots. After an hour of furious digging at the weeds, she rose, brushed her knees, and proudly surveyed the results. She had cleared quite a big patch of ground. Forget-me-nots, jonquils, and pansies straightened up and reached for the sun.

"Your father loved flowers," Maria Borisovna said after Masha told her about the treasures she had discovered under the weeds. "The grounds were beautiful when we had a gardener."

Masha knitted her eyebrows. "Olga Kirilovna has two gardeners. They are serfs. Do we have any serfs, Mamma?"

Her mother smiled. "Well, let's count. Niania never was a serf. Feklusha's family was set free years ago by your grandfather because one of them saved him from a wild boar during a hunt. We pay her very little, but she would rather work in the house than in the fields. Stepan and Mavra are serfs, but you know that they are both too busy to work in the garden."

"But I can," Masha declared importantly. "At least I can try. May I, Mamma?"

"You may," her mother agreed, "but don't wear your good blue dress while you are gardening. Put on your old gray one."

The next day Masha was back at the flower bed. The gray dress had faded in streaks, and nearsighted Niania had darned the knees of her black stockings with brown wool. But she had a small, rusted shovel Stepan found for her in the barn, and nothing else mattered. Armed with the shovel, she dug and weeded.

A sudden thunderstorm interrupted Masha's labors.

She ran into the house, dripping wet, and cried, "Mamma! There are peonies! And I think the prickly plant in the center is a rose!"

The rain stopped in the afternoon, washing the sky clean of clouds. "The air is so clear one can see almost as far as the end of the earth," Masha thought, sitting in the old swing and flying high above the overgrown raspberry bushes. Her mother explained to her that the earth was round like a ball, but Niania's story about it being flat and resting on the backs of four whales was much more exciting.

From her perch, Masha caught sight of the thatched roofs or the village that had once belonged to her father, but now had been sold along with the green fields stretching to the horizon and the dark woods somewhere beyond them. Only the old house and the grounds immediately around it remained, but it was quite enough for Masha. She swung higher and laughed as the wind ruffled the fine hair on her temples.

The past few weeks had been the happiest she could remember.

To begin with, the Evil Man could not come any more. He slipped on the stairway of his mill and was laid up with a broken leg. "We mustn't be glad about it," Maria Borisovna had said, but Masha could not help noticing that her mother looked more cheerful than usual. Only the night before, Masha had awakened to hear the long-silent spinet singing under her mother's fingers.

There were other joys. The old, once-abandoned birdhouse had a family of starlings this spring. It was fun to watch the yellow beaks peep through the round hole.

Stepan had driven a flock of geese to the fair. He had come back with a sugar loaf wrapped in blue paper, some fine flour, and a skipping rope for Masha.

The thought of the skipping rope made Masha swing slower until her feet touched the grass. She sat for a few minutes trying to decide whether to call Trezor and go skipping down the cedar avenue or to go and help Mavra make cookies.

Trezor was nowhere to be seen, so she went to the kitchen, just in time to see Mavra mix the dough.

When Maria Borisovna looked through the kitchen door half an hour later, she saw Masha, swathed in Mavra's apron, very busy with the rolling pin.

"Oh, here you are!" Maria Borisovna said, entering. "I have been looking for you. Come with me, dear, there is..." Her voice faltered a little. "There is a letter from St. Petersburg. I want to read it to you."

Masha's frightened blue eyes stared from under flour-powdered lashes. "From St. Petersburg? But it is not Stepan's day for mail."

"No, but Olga Kirilovna has had a letter from her cousin which she has sent over. A man on horseback brought it a few minutes ago. You are to go to Smolni after all."

Mavra dropped the baking sheet with a clatter and started to sob. Masha untied the apron and followed Maria Borisovna out of the room. She was aware that her mother was speaking to her as they walked along the corridor, but the words only buzzed in her ears and did not seem to make any sense.

They were already in the study when Masha realized she still had a piece of dough in her hand. Sitting down on a footstool, she kneaded it between her fingers, made a ball, and flattened it out again.

Maria Borisovna stopped talking, looked at Masha's expression, and started all over again. "You see, dear, after the ballot, ten names were put on a waiting list, in case some girls who had been accepted couldn't come. You were sixth on the list, and it seemed such a slim chance that Olga Kirilovna's cousin did not even mention it in his first letter. Five girls in front of you! Yet, it did happen. The parents of the first girl decided to send her to school abroad. The next two turned out to be twelve years old, and no one over nine is admitted. The fourth girl could not read, and candidates are required to read fluently when they enter the school."

Masha threw down her piece of dough. She seemed to have suddenly woken up. "What about the fifth girl?" she asked, her voice trembling with anger. "Why doesn't she enter the Smolni Institute? Why should it be me?"

"Because she is crippled, poor child," Maria Borisovna answered gravely. "Something is wrong with her knee, and she has to use crutches. There are many stairs in the Smolni building. It would be hard for her. That is how your turn came."

But I don't want to go!" Masha cried. She jumped up from her seat, her cheeks blazing, and stamped her foot. "I don't want to! They refused to take me before. Why don't they leave me alone now!"

"Masha!" Her mother's tone was severe, though her hands trembled. "You mustn't talk like that. What has happened to you, child? You have been so reasonable until now."

"Oh, Mamma!" Masha rushed into her mother's arms, tears streaming down her face. "I know I must go, but the first time I was ready, and now it is much more difficult."

Maria Borisovna bowed her head. "Yes," she said gravely, "you are right. It is much more difficult."

Masha was still crying when Niania Akulina walked in. She gave Maria Borisovna a thunderous look out of her faded eyes and putting her arm around Masha's shoulders led her out of the room, murmuring, "Poor child, my poor dear baby."

Going straight to the pantry, Niania unlocked the creaking door with a key she always wore on her belt and began to bustle around opening jars and boxes. Usually, the sight of preserved pears, dried apples, raisins, and nuts would make Masha go wild with delight. Now she stood with huddled shoulders, letting tears fall on the sweets piled in her apron. "There, there, dearie," Niania muttered, stroking Masha's hair and putting a saucer brimming with jam in front of her.

Masha went to bed that night with Niania sitting beside her and telling a tale about Ivan the Fool, something that had not happened since she was five. She was feeling sick from crying and from too much jam. Mania's voice droned on, bringing peace and making her feel safe. She was already asleep when her mother came in and stood for a long time looking at the small, tear-stained face.

Departure

THE HOUSE SMELLED OF TOBACCO WHEN Masha came out of her room the next morning. She knew what it meant. Her mother was looking over the old clothes. They were packed in wooden chests in the storeroom and sprinkled with tobacco to keep the moths away.

Maria Borisovna was seated on the floor surrounded by piles of silk and brocade dresses in all colors. Niania was there too, rummaging in the chests and slamming the lids down with muttered comments about "people who send their own flesh and blood away to live with strangers."

"I can't find anything suitable to make you a traveling dress," Maria Borisovna told Masha, ignoring Niania's remarks. "Everything is red or blue or gold, and you need something dark. Oh, maybe this will do." She held up a gown of brown silk with wide green stripes.

"I don't care," Masha answered, thinking how much fun it would have been to try on all those dresses with enormous, hooped skirts, only she didn't feel like playing any more.

She remained quiet and thoughtful all through the morning. Even the arrival of Mademoiselle Aglaya, sent by Olga Kirilovna to help with sewing, did not make her smile.

Aglaya herself did not look very happy. She confided to Masha's mother that though her pupils were doing quite well, the fifteen-year-old had become too used to liberty and resented having a governess.

"I hope she will learn to obey me little by little," Aglaya said. "In the meantime, it is very difficult." She tried to talk about Smolni to Masha, describing classrooms and dormitories. Met with stony silence, she gave up and turned her attention to the dress problem. "Nowadays dresses are made of light and soft materials," she said doubtfully. "This heavy stuff will not fall right. And those green stripes! Couldn't we find some green silk for a flounce to match?"

"We can't spend too much time contriving," Maria Borisovna reminded her. "If Masha is to go with Olga Kirilovna, she must be ready by next week."

Aglaya nodded. "Yes, Olga Kirilovna is leaving on June fifteenth. Her son had a bad fever, and she is allowed to take him home for the whole summer to convalesce. But..." she looked at Maria Borisovna, "wouldn't you prefer to take Masha to school yourself?"

Masha's mother murmured, "I wish, I wish I could, but it is not possible. There is the stagecoach fare, and I would have to stay at an inn in St. Petersburg. That means more expenses. I couldn't afford it. Besides," she glanced down at her shabby gown, "how could I accompany Masha to the Smolni Institute, a select school, in such clothes?"

Her mother was not going with her! This was a fresh blow to Masha, but she did not want to cry in front of Aglaya. "May I go and play outside?" she asked in a trembling voice.

Maria Borisovna looked doubtful. "You may, but don't do any gardening. You mustn't arrive at Smolni with rough hands."

"She really should wear a hat," Aglaya suggested. "The girls will laugh at her if she is sunburned."

"I don't have any summer hat, only my winter bonnet," Masha

muttered sulkily, but her mother found an old hat of her own and put it on Masha's head.

It was a coal-scuttle bonnet, its brim extending several inches beyond Masha's face. Half blinded, she stumbled out to the porch and sat down miserably on the bottom step. Trezor, who was sunning himself on the grass, approached her cautiously and sniffed the bottom of her dress to make sure she was not a stranger. Masha pushed him away, staring moodily down the cedar avenue.

It was all the fault of that crippled girl, she thought bitterly. She wished she could change places with her and stay home with her mother and Niania and Trezor. She imagined herself lame, hobbling on crutches around the garden, or trailing through the house on her mother's arm. Perhaps, if she wished hard enough, something would happen to her leg so that her mother would have to write to Smolni and explain that she could not manage the stairways. Then, instead of her, the seventh girl would go.

A thrush flew low, almost touching Masha's head, and then vanished in a clump of bushes. There may be a nest, she decided and jumped up to dash after the bird. The leg on which she had been sitting had become numb and Masha felt with terror that she could not move. Her face blanched. The far end of the long cedar avenue suddenly became a magic land she would give anything to reach. Gathering her strength, she lurched forward and ran, stumbling at first, then faster and faster. The trees flashed past her, her heart pounded, her hat flew off and rolled on the ground. She reached her goal and collapsed on the grass just as Trezor came running up, his tongue hanging out. He jumped on Masha, and they rolled over and over, she shrieking, he barking with delight.

Ten minutes later, Masha burst into the room where her mother and Aglaya were working. "I want to help!" She hoisted herself on a chair and put a thimble on her finger.

She hardly took it off for the next few days. After the dress was finished, there were petticoats to be made and handkerchiefs to be hemmed.

Niania Akulina was no help. She steadily refused to have anything to do with the preparations for Masha's departure. "I will not have a hand in it," she would answer, whenever Maria Borisovna asked her to iron or to mend something, and then she would shuffle away, wiping her eyes.

Aglaya left as soon as the last stitch was made, for Olga Kirilovna needed her. Looking at the finished clothes, Masha realized with a sinking heart that the day set for leaving was very near.

Maria Borisovna asked the priest from the village church to come to the house for a short service. Masha watched with interest as Niania Akulina prepared a small table in the drawing room. On it she put a small bowl for the blessed water and the ikon of the Virgin Mary of Kazan that had hung over Masha's bed ever since she could remember. All the household gathered for the service.

When it started, Masha tried to pray, but her thoughts kept wandering. She looked at the priest's long, silvery hair and at the golden cross on his breast catching the sunbeams. Listening to the prayers for "all traveling and navigating," she thought, "But we are not going to navigate. Or are we? Maybe there are rivers to cross?" Catching her mother's eye, she hastily crossed herself in response to "Have mercy on us," sung by the sexton, a slight, elderly man with a surprisingly powerful voice. Trezor, banished to the dining room, whined and scratched at the door.

The service over, Maria Borisovna led Masha to the priest to be blessed and to kiss the cross. Stepan started to tiptoe out, his heavy boots thumping on the floor in spite of his efforts. Niania could not get up from her knees and had to be helped by Mavra and Feklusha.

Masha noticed that Niania had changed during the past few weeks. Her wrinkles were deeper, and her head shook all the time. She no longer bustled around, but spent most of her time in the kitchen, groaning and muttering to herself.

Maria Borisovna asked the priest and the sexton to stay to tea, but they refused, saying that a thunderstorm was coming, and it was better for them to leave quickly. Their horse cart was still rolling down the cedar avenue when a big cloud hid the sun and thunder rolled across the sky.

To everyone's surprise, Niania, who hated to be outside even in fine weather, promptly went out on the terrace and sat on the steps until the first lightning flashed above the apple tree and rain started to fall. "The highway is almost two miles away," she muttered, "too far for our old horses to make it over the dirt roads."

"Masha is not leaving till Friday," Maria Borisovna said sharply, "and today is only Tuesday. Surely it is not going to rain that long."

But the storm turned into a steady downpour, beating the roof and streaming down the windowpanes. Strong winds lashed the trees. The house creaked. Fresh leaks appeared in the ceilings. Footsteps were heard in the attic.

"He never used to wander in the daytime," Niania whispered to Stepan. "No wonder! He doesn't want her to go away." She nodded at Masha, who was standing nearby and listening.

"You'd better watch out," Stepan croaked back. "When he is upset, one never knows what tricks he may be up to."

That evening a heavy picture hanging in the drawing room fell off the wall and crashed into a small inlaid table. "Ah... ah, he is angry about the young mistress leaving," Niania groaned, gathering up the pieces.

"The plaster is old and crumbles away," Maria Borisovna said, but Masha secretly preferred to believe Niania.

On Thursday, the sky became lighter. Standing by the window that evening, Masha watched the long flaming strip in the west, a sure sign of her departure. In her room everything was ready. The new dress was laid on a chair. The bonnet and gloves were on the chest of drawers. The small tin trunk did not close properly and had to be tied with a piece of rope. It did not matter. Nothing really mattered except the frightening thought that this was her last evening at home.

"I have asked Olga Kirilovna to meet us at the stagecoach station instead of picking you up here," Maria Borisovna told Masha, "so that we may be together as long as possible."

GREEN

Masha thought desperately that there were so many things she wanted to talk about with her mother, so many questions to ask, and only a few hours left. But when the darkness came, and the green lamp was lighted in the study, she found she could not talk. Sitting on a footstool, her head on her mother's lap, she cried silently until she was so worn out Maria Borisovna had to help her to bed. Falling asleep, she felt her mother tuck her in for the last time.

A few hours of exhausted slumber and it was time to get up. Feklusha, red-eyed, brought in hot water. Niania arrived with a glass of milk and some bread and butter on a plate. Masha tried to eat, but it only made her feel sick.

Maria Borisovna came in, her bonnet on her head. "We must hurry, dear," she told Masha, "it is getting late."

The new starched petticoats pricked her skin. The shoes, made by the village shoemaker, were heavy and pinched at her toes. At last the new dress went on. Even in her distress, Masha could not help noticing that the waist was almost under her armpits and the green flounce that Aglaya had managed to contrive after all made the skirt look much too long. The bonnet that used to belong to one of Olga Kirilovna's daughters looked better than the rest of Masha's clothes, but the yellow ribbons jarred with the green stripes.

Quite ready, Masha stopped on the threshold of her room and looked back. "I will never forget," she thought, gazing at the wide bed under the sagging pink canopy, the dim mirror between the two windows, the old tapestry screen. The small wooden horse that Stepan had carved for her eighth birthday was leaning forlornly against the leg of a chair.

"We must hurry, love," Maria Borisovna repeated, and Masha moved on.

More faded tapestries and dim mirrors, and the drawing room was left behind. Masha kept her eyes averted from the open doors of the little study. "I mustn't cry," she told herself, "I mustn't." Yet, when the scrawny black kitten rushed up to her and circled her ankle with his paws, she almost let herself go. A murmur of voices coming from the terrace distracted her. She turned around and gasped with surprise. The terrace was full of people. There was Stepan's old mother, who sometimes came to help with the laundry, Mavra's two brothers with their wives and children, all of Feklusha's relatives, and many other people from the village.

"Mamma," Masha whispered, "why are they all here?"

Maria Borisovna looked down into the upturned face. "They came because in spite of everything this is still The House for them," she answered. "They want to say good-bye to the little mistress. You may be proud of it, dear."

There was an unconscious dignity in the small figure who slowly walked across the porch, murmuring thanks for the good wishes and blessings showered upon her.

From behind the house came a muffled howling. Masha had said good-bye to Trezor the night before, her arms around his neck, her cheek against the white spot on his forehead. "I'd rather he did not see you leave," her mother had said. Now he was chained in the back yard. But he knew she was leaving, Masha was sure of it.

It took Maria Borisovna some time to tear Masha away from Niania's frantic embrace and hurry her to the carriage.

The old horses with tangled manes stood with bent heads. The harness hung limply, held together with pieces of cord. Stepan, in a clean white shirt and a baggy gray coat, was squatting on the ground, anxiously tugging at the back axle.

"Is anything wrong?" Maria Borisovna asked.

Stepan slowly raised himself. "The axle doesn't hold too well, Barinia," he croaked, wiping his hands on his trousers.

"It must hold somehow!" Maria Borisovna exclaimed. "The stagecoach is leaving at nine and it's past eight now. Get inside, Masha!"

Masha mounted the rusty carriage steps, her mother after her. Stepan clambered onto the driver's seat and began to gather the reins. Something snapped and one of the reins broke.

An excited clamor passed across the terrace. "The domovoy. He doesn't want her to leave! That's one of his tricks. See if he will not make her stay!"

"Let us go, Stepan," Maria Borisovna ordered. Leaning back on the tattered cushions, she crossed herself. Masha did the same. On the terrace, the men took off their caps. As the carriage slowly turned around the big flower bed, Masha saw her unfinished garden, thick with weeds, the shovel lying on the path beside it.

Suddenly, a loud wail arose in the air. Masha jumped up, and kneeling on the back seat, pressed her face to the window. Niania Akulina was crouching on the terrace floor, crying and wailing. Feklusha and Mavra joined her, and the rest of the women followed. The wailing grew louder and louder, terrifying in its hopeless grief.

Masha had heard women wail once before, at the funeral of Feklusha's grandfather. Frightened, she clutched at her mother's shoulder. "Mamma! It is... it is like being buried. Mamma, I wish they wouldn't."

Her mother pressed the small trembling hand. "Never mind, dear. It is their way of showing they love you. Don't forget, Mavra and Niania have known you since birth."

Masha's terror passed, replaced by a desperate longing to keep on looking at the house, to tuck it deep inside her heart for always.

Dappled sunlight fell on the gray stone walls and reflected in the windows. The terrace was bright with women's blue, red, and yellow kerchiefs. The jasmine bushes were white with bloom. The black kitten was looking at Masha, his triangular face thrust between the columns of the balustrade.

The carriage rolled down the avenue between two rows of cedars, each one familiar and loved. Stepan jumped off the seat to open the gates, but the old wood, swollen by rains, became stuck. "Suppose, suppose it will make us late, so late that the stagecoach will leave without me," Masha thought wildly, watching Stepan lean his shoulder against the gates. Another effort, and they swung open. The old red roof with broken tiles and lichen pushing through every crevice flashed among the trees for the last time and then disappeared.

Masha sat down beside her mother. There was a strange empty feeling in her heart. Everything she loved was left behind, and she knew nothing of what was waiting ahead.

Maria Borisovna put her arm around Masha's shoulders. "We have very little time left," she said, her voice trembling. "Soon, you will be on your own, Masha. There is nothing much I can tell you. Trust in God and believe in people too. Don't forget to pray every day. Study hard and write to me as often as you are allowed to. One day we will be together again."

The horses stopped. Stepan opened the carriage door. The stagecoach was only a few steps away. Olga Kirilovna was at the window. Red-faced, her bonnet askew, she was gesturing wildly for Masha to make haste.

People milling around the station looked with curiosity at the old-fashioned carriage, the neglected horses, and the little girl in her quaint brown- and green-striped dress.

For a moment Masha felt her mother's wet cheek against her own and heard her whisper, "Good-bye, dearest. God bless you. Good-bye!" The next minute she was already in the coach, her trunk at her feet. The horn blew and four strong horses took off.

Dazed, Masha sat still, clutching at her seat.

"Your mother is waving, dear," Olga Kirilovna said. "Why don't you wave back?"

Masha sprang to the window. Her mother's handkerchief fluttering in the air was rapidly becoming a white dot in the distance. She was desperately looking at it, tears swelling in her eyes, when there was a metallic noise and Trezor appeared on the road. He was running madly, but unevenly, in zigzags, hampered by the long chain dragging after him.

"Trezor!" Masha screamed.

The dog must have heard her voice in spite of the rumble of wheels. With a loud bark, he dashed forward, panting, his sides heaving.

At the same time, a heavy carriage drawn by six horses rolled from a side road. It was heading straight at Trezor.

"Stop! Stop!" Masha cried wildly, beating the glass with her fists. "You are going to kill him! Please, stop!"

The carriage passed the stagecoach, clanging and raising clouds of dust. Masha closed her eyes, but Olga Kirilovna behind her gasped, "Stepan! Look at him!" and she dared to look again.

Trezor was still running, but slower, his strength giving out. Behind him Stepan was galloping, riding bareback on one of the horses he had probably unhitched from the carriage. His cap was off, and his gray hair fell over his forehead. Catching up with Trezor, he bent down, almost lying across the horse's back, and snatched at the chain.

The stagecoach rounded a bend and Masha could see no more. She sank on the seat, murmuring, "He was with Papa to the very end. He wanted to be with me too, but..." she ended in a sob, "we didn't let him."

"There, there, dearie," Olga Kirilovna soothed Masha. "He is needed at home to look after your mother and the house. You lie down and rest. What a blessing, there will be no other passengers till the next station, and that is almost two hours away. That's better! Let me take off your bonnet. Now close your eyes and rest."

Masha lay quietly, covered with Olga Kirilovna's shawl. The stagecoach swayed and shook. White clouds flew past the windows. The wheels rumbled over and over again, "Nine years, nine years!"

BROWN

In St. Petersburg

MASHA CAUGHT HER FIRST SIGHT OF ST. Petersburg early in the morning, from under the dripping hood of a cab.

Warm summer rain fell in sheets, making soft thudding sounds against the wooden sidewalks and gathering into rivulets between the cobblestones. To Masha's dazed eyes the city appeared just a blur of white pillars against the dusky reds, pale yellows, and soft grays of the palaces and buildings. Dark embankments of the Neva and shadowy arches of the bridges floated by. Dim outlines of monuments rose and disappeared. The almost-deserted streets stretched on, curved, and seemed never to end.

The leather cushions of the cab seats were clammy, and the dampness crept under Masha's black velvet cape, made up from her mother's mantlet. She shivered and drew her head back, nestling close to Olga Kirilovna. Now she could only see the wide back of the driver, made even wider by the thick folds of his shabby gray coat, gathered with a belt at the waist.

Olga Kirilovna looked down. "Feeling tired, dearie? And sleepy too, I suppose? Those stagecoaches! The idea of traveling at night and arriving in the city in the small hours of the morning! Just be patient a little while longer, child. We'll have a nice long rest as soon as we reach our furnished rooms. Won't it be nice to have a hot meal after the last mess they served us at the inn?"

Masha did not answer. Closing her eyes, she pretended to doze. It was easier than explaining to Olga Kirilovna that she was too numb to feel tired and that all food had tasted the same since they left home.

The cab turned a corner with a creaking of brakes. Masha's head nodded and came to rest against Olga Kirilovna's shoulder. She was really asleep now, all huddled in her green-striped dress, the yellow ribbons of her bonnet hanging limply under her chin.

A jolt of the cab woke her up. They were in front of a two-storied frame house with a gabled roof. It was not raining any more. A big patch of blue was slowly spreading across the sky. A few doors down the street, a man was opening the shutters of a small grocery store. Two boys ran by, stacks of newspapers under each arm.

"Are you awake, dear?" Olga Kirilovna asked as she shook Masha's shoulder. "Let's get out."

Feeling as if her feet were made of lead, Masha stumbled out of the cab and realized for the first time that they had been followed by another cab carrying Olga Kirilovna's bags and Masha's own small trunk. Standing on the pavement, she rubbed her eyes and looked at the house. It was painted a dirty blue. A few wooden steps led to a tiny porch that seemed out of proportion to the rest of the house. Above the narrow front door was a circular window and underneath it a large sign announced in faded red letters, The Furnished Rooms of Widow Iziumova.

Somehow, the whole structure reminded Masha of a bird-house. Her brain still fuzzy with sleep, she wondered if the door would open, and the widow Iziumova would peep out and say "Qweek!" like the starlings at home. Her dress would probably be black since she was a widow. Only of course she wouldn't be wearing a dress, not in a birdhouse. She would have feathers instead, glossy black feathers...

And then a young woman with a round, smiling face came out on the tiny porch. There was nothing bird-like or black about the woman. Tall and rather plump, she was dressed in a pink calico dress, with a brown shawl crossed at the high waist and tied behind in a bow.

Olga Kirilovna, after paying the drivers and counting the luggage on the porch, came over. "Couldn't find that carpetbag," she boomed, "but it was right there after all. Masha, this is Katerina Ivanovna Iziumova. I always stay in her rooms while in St. Petersburg. She will take good care of both of us."

Masha tried to curtsy, but her foot caught in the green ruffle that had become unstitched, and she nearly fell on her face.

"Well now!" Katerina Ivanovna exclaimed, catching her. "The idea of making a child's dress that length! Careful, dear. Just follow me."

Entering the dimly lit hallway, the landlady stopped and called, "Mitia! Come here! There is luggage to be taken upstairs."

A high-pitched voice answered something from the depths of the house.

Masha wondered who Mitia could be, but Katerina Ivanovna was already ushering her up the narrow stairway, along a corridor with doors on each side, and into a fairly large room with geraniums flaming at the window and an enormous bed in the middle.

"Here we are!" Katerina Ivanovna announced. "And now, let's get out of these dusty clothes."

In a moment, Masha's bonnet and cloak were off and her dress was whisked over her head. She sat on the bed, with the landlady's dimity wrapper thrown over her shoulders, feeling rested already. As Katerina Ivanovna was leaving to see about breakfast, Olga Kirilovna burst in, followed by a boy loaded with luggage.

Masha guessed it was Mitia. He looked about ten or eleven, with thin arms and legs, and an even thinner neck emerging from the high collar of his baggy gray shirt. His long, freckled face did not express any interest at the sight of Masha. He pocketed the coin Olga Kirilovna gave him, sniffed, wiped his nose with the back of his hand, and slipped out before Masha could think of something to say.

"Resting, dearie?" Olga Kirilovna asked, collapsing on a small sofa. "How do you like Katerina Ivanovna?"

"I like her very much," Masha answered with conviction. "She is kind."

"Yes, yes, an excellent woman," Olga Kirilovna agreed. "Her husband was a clerk in the Senate. Killed in the war like your father. It is fortunate she could set up these furnished rooms. Just a few, but it helps. Pensions are small."

The door opened again and a snub-nosed maid, in a flowered calico dress, brought in a tray loaded with breakfast.

For the first time since she left home, Masha felt hungry. She sat at the round table in front of the sofa, trying not to spill her hot milk and listening with interest to the conversation between Olga Kirilovna and the landlady, who came in to see if everything was in order.

"You eat your fill, dearie," Katerina Ivanovna coaxed Masha. "At the Smolni Monastery, they'll feed you like a bird."

Masha choked. "Monastery?"

"The school was founded in the Smolni Monastery," Olga Kirilovna explained, "and the first teachers were nuns. That was a long time ago. There are no more nuns there now, but the old name is still used."

Relieved, Masha returned to her milk.

"I am not going to see my son today," Olga Kirilovna declared, putting her cup down at last. "It will only excite him. Tomorrow, after Masha is settled in Smolni, I will pick him up and we will set off for home immediately. This afternoon, I am going to do some shopping. There are several things I want to buy, but with these high prices, I wonder how far my money will go."

Katerina Ivanovna sighed. "Ah, it is because the country still can't get over the war. It is not too bad now, but you should have seen the prices three years ago. Meat was worth its weight in gold, and one was lucky to get a bag of flour--not the best kind either. That's why fashionable ladies started to go to market to buy victuals, though some people say they were simply aping the English custom. It seems that during the war even the wealthiest English ladies turned housekeepers, and thrifty ones too."

"Sounds like a good idea to me, whatever the reason," Olga Kirilovna approved.

Katerina Ivanovna began to laugh. "I really don't know. Maybe the Englishwomen understood marketing better than our grand ladies. I remember seeing one, all fuss and feathers, buying fish and holding a perfume bottle under her nose at the same time. How she expected to smell out bad fish, I can't imagine."

The meal over, Katerina Ivanovna insisted that Masha stretch out on the sofa and catch up on her sleep. In another moment, the springs of the bed groaned under Olga Kirilovna's weight.

Masha dozed for some time, then woke up and became restless. Getting up, she tiptoed to the window and lifted the lace curtain.

She was in the same place when Olga Kirilovna discovered her a full hour later.

"My goodness!" Olga Kirilovna boomed, "I thought you were lost. What are you looking at?"

"The pictures," Masha whispered mysteriously.

"The pictures? Where?" Olga Kirilovna peered out.

"Over there." Masha pointed at a big horn of plenty, brimming over with rolls and cookies, painted above the bakery door. "And there, near the corner! See the big ham and the fork sticking in it? Isn't it pretty? Just like a real one. Oh, and there is a pair of scissors, all shiny, only you can't see it well from here."

"Bless the child! Haven't you ever seen the shop signs?" Olga Kirilovna bent down and kissed Masha. "I will show you even nicer ones when we go out presently."

Masha found her dress spread out on a chair, all cleaned and the ruffle mended. Even the ribbons on her bonnet were ironed. She was ready first and waiting for Olga Kirilovna in the hall when Mitia appeared, an enormous pair of freshly shined boots under each arm. At the sight of Masha, he put the boots down. The two children stared at each other.

Masha stepped closer. "Those are very big boots," she ventured as a conversation starter.

Mitia shrugged his shoulders. "They belong to the lodger in the corner room. He is big."

The conversation seemed to stop there. Masha tried again. "Why don't you live with your family?" she asked.

Mitia passed his hand under his nose. "I don't have no family. I am from the orphanage."

"Oh?" Masha felt sorry for Mitia. "Do you like working here?" she asked to change the subject.

His head to one side, Mitia seemed to consider the question. "It isn't bad. Barinia is kind. She let me go to the Easter Bazaar. It's like a fair," he added, seeing Masha look puzzled.

"A fair?" Masha flushed with excitement. She had once been allowed to attend a fair with Mavra and Stepan. It remained a never-to-be-forgotten day for her.

"Were there trained bears?" she asked eagerly. "And merry-go-rounds? And tents? Did you see a show?"

"Of course there were tents," Mitia answered with a lofty air. "Big ones too. Me and Egorka, he works next door, we saw three shows. About a Turkish sultan, that was the best one.

"Three shows!" Masha exclaimed, amazed. "Where did you get so much money? You can't just walk into a tent..."

She did not finish speaking. Mitia's cheeks began to puff out until his eyes became mere slits. He covered his mouth with his hand and snorted with laughter.

"Ee, ee, ee! Walk! The man at the entrance would give you a bash on the ear if you tried. You go on all fours. Like this." He bent down and made a motion of crawling under the tent. "That's how it's done."

The novelty and the wickedness of the idea made Masha gasp. She was trying to find a suitable answer when Olga Kirilovna appeared at the top of the stairs. At the sight of her, Mitia picked up the boots and fled.

Still perplexed, Masha followed Olga Kirilovna into the sunshine.

New Faces and New Sights

THE CITY THAT HAD SEEMED SO QUIET IN the early morning hours was now teeming with life. Keeping a tight hold on Olga Kirilovna's hand, Masha walked along, shrinking from the dark portes cocheres and narrow stone steps leading to wine cellars, their entrances decorated with tin bunches of grapes. She looked with curiosity at the shops and listened with mingled interest and terror to the drunken singing coming from behind the doors of the taverns.

Soon the streets became wider and Nevski Prospect came into sight, with a double line of lime trees forming an avenue in the middle. Carriages drawn by four or six horses rolled by, shiny crests on the doors, liveried footmen clinging behind. Peacock feathers on coachmen's caps waved in the breeze. Whips cracked, accompanied by cries of "Make way! Make way!" Modest cabs pushed on as best they could. People came out of the shops, filled the pavements, crossed the streets under the horses' noses. Street vendors threaded their way through the crowd, loaded with fruit, wicker baskets, potted flowers, waffles or cakes. Their shrill voices carried above the rumble of wheels. Beggars held out their hats, singing prayers and asking for charity.

Dazed and a little frightened, Masha looked up to see if her companion was scared too. But Olga Kirilovna's fat round face was placid under the lavender dome of her parasol. Reassured, Masha began to enjoy the sights. Everything was fascinating, from the small Negro grinning from his place beside the coachman and the red-liveried footman walking two beribboned dogs to the old organ-grinder chased by a policeman. The ladies were disappointing. Masha had imagined that in St. Petersburg everyone would be wearing bright silks and brocades, like the clothes in the old chests at home. Instead, they were all dressed in plain gowns of white or pale colored muslin and lawn, falling in straight lines almost from the throat. "Like walking pillars," Masha thought. Many of them were followed by a footman loaded with packages, which was just as well. It would have been difficult for them to keep their shawls gracefully draped and at the same time clutch their purchases.

The gentlemen looked much prettier than the ladies, Masha decided, with their shiny top hats, flyaway jackets, and tight breeches. Their enormous neck scarves billowed and their silver-topped canes swung gaily as they walked. A few even had their hair curled and their cheeks were very pink. But when Masha expressed her admiration, Olga Kirilovna only said, "Shame on them! Behaving like women, frizzling their hair and rouging their faces. Anything to follow a stupid fashion!" and she stepped into a doorway.

"Is this the Winter Palace?" Masha whispered, following Olga Kirilovna through the glass door and staring at the blue carpet and mirrors.

But it was a French hat shop, and the lady in a black silk gown was Madame Rose, the owner, and not the Dowager Empress Maria Feodorovna, as Masha had at first thought.

"I couldn't face your future Principal, Madame Adlerberg, without a new hat," Olga Kirilovna declared. "Now which one shall I take?"

"This one," Masha whispered with deep conviction, pointing at a tall pink cylinder tied diagonally with a wide mauve ribbon. "It is beautiful!"

"Oh, ho, ho!" Olga Kirilovna spluttered. "Do you really like that old-fashioned thing, dearie? It used to be popular during the war, but I don't suppose anyone wears it now."

Madame Rose looked hurt. "The military hat is not our latest model," she said primly, "but many ladies still wear it. So patriotique! However," she flashed a smile at Olga Kirilovna, "if Madame wishes our dernier cri..." With the last words, she picked up an enormous turban of green velvet and presented it to Olga Kirilovna.

Masha mentally christened the turban "cabbage head," but Olga Kirilovna beamed at herself in the mirror and asked Madame Rose to have the turban delivered the very same day. "Those foreign shops are so elegant," she told Masha, walking out of Rose Bonnets. "Our Russian shops are much plainer. We might as well go to Gostinni Dvor now, since we are on Nevski. I want to buy some lawn for the girls' summer dresses."

Masha was not sure just what Gostinni Dvor was until they entered the stone arcades housing row upon row of shops. There was nothing of the quiet, perfumed atmosphere of Madame Rose's shop about this place. Wares were piled in mounds, spilled out of boxes and barrels, hung in bunches above the entrance. Ladies in embroidered shawls elbowed with peasant women. The smell of sweat and tobacco mingled with the strong, gluey odor of bolts of cloth.

"I don't like it here," Masha protested, but her voice was lost in the hubbub of talking and bargaining. A husky salesman stood at the door of each shop, praising his wares and calling in customers at the top of his voice. As soon as one of them saw Olga Kirilovna, he barred her way and almost forced her into his shop. Olga Kirilovna had barely pronounced the word "lawn," when one clerk was already taking piece after piece off the shelf, while another clerk deftly unrolled the material. Soon the counter was piled high with lawn of all colors, and more was coming.

Pressed close to the counter, Masha looked at the billowing folds until it seemed to her that they were going to rise to the ceiling and engulf her.

"What's the matter?" Olga Kirilovna asked, peering under Masha's bonnet. At the sight of the pale little face, she hastily paid the clerk and led Masha out of the shop.

Fresh air helped. Masha took a deep gulp and felt better.

"Brigands!" Olga Kirilovna puffed, patting her face with a perfumed handkerchief. "All out to drag a customer into their lair." She bent over Masha again. "What would you like to do now, dearie? Go back to Katerina Ivanova or do some shopping yourself? What about buying a gift for your mother? A ganezou maybe. It is a little scarf. One always needs it with these low-necked dresses. And we could get a few gifts for your servants and a collar for Trezor and some paper for yourself to write letters home."

Masha's face dimpled, then became sober again. "I can't. I haven't any money."

"Never you mind that," Olga Kirilovna said comfortably. "I will lend you some money and you can pay me when you graduate from Smolni." She put her hand on Masha's shoulder and guided her back into Gostinni Dvor.

It took Masha a long time to make her purchases. It was a delightful agony to decide between the lace-trimmed and the ruches-edged ganezou, and between the blue and the pink notepaper. Choosing Trezor's collar was even more difficult. The clerk wanted to know what kind of dog Trezor was, but Masha could only describe him as "the best kind in the world." At last even the collar was bought. There were also kerchiefs for Niania Akulina and Mavra, a high comb for Feklusha, and a new tobacco pouch for Stepan.

Flushed and smiling, her arms full of packages, Masha sauntered beside Olga Kirilovna. They were just leaving Gostinni Dvor when a strange procession appeared from around the corner. An old horse was dragging a long peasant cart on which lay an upturned coffin lid. An elderly man walked beside the cart, reins in one hand

and his cap in the other. Two women in black kerchiefs followed, moaning and chanting in mournful, singsong voices.

Masha paled and pressed herself against the wall.

"Don't be afraid, dearie," Olga Kirilovna soothed her. "Those poor people have had a death in the family. They have no money for a proper burial, so they ask for help. See how everyone is throwing coins into the coffin lid? Here, I will throw two coppers, one for you and one for myself."

"I... I am not afraid," Masha managed to blurt out, as she watched the crowd part in front of the cart, men taking off their hats and women nodding in sympathy.

Suddenly, the heads turned in a different direction. Two street urchins who were peacefully playing on the sidewalk fled, throwing fearful glances over their shoulders. People were craning their necks and standing on tiptoe as if to see something.

"What is it now?" Olga Kirilovna grumbled, taking Masha's hand. "Let's..."

She was interrupted by a high nasal voice chanting, "God have mercy on us. God have mercy on us."

A young girl standing beside Masha murmured, "Annoushka" and made a hasty sign of the Cross under her shawl.

Masha saw a short, thick-set woman in a shabby black dress emerge from the crowd. She seemed to be walking straight toward them. As she came nearer, Masha noticed that in spite of the gray locks hanging from an old-fashioned black bonnet, the woman's face showed almost no wrinkles. It was round, very white, and quite expressionless, reminding Masha of the paper dolls her mother used to cut out for her. The woman held a big bag filled with victuals in one hand, while with the other, she kept fingering the large brass cross hanging on a chain around her neck.

"Welcome to St. Petersburg, little girl," the woman called out. "Welcome!" She was now so close Masha could see her eyes, dark and extraordinarily vivid compared to the rest of the face. She advanced and stood in front of Masha. "Pretty child," the woman went on, touching Masha's arm. "Do not be afraid. You will live in a palace, a beautiful palace."

Masha shrank back, almost too terrified to cry out.

"Go away!" Olga Kirilovna ordered the woman, but the usual assurance was missing from her tone. "Go away!"

But the woman did not retreat. "How dare you not believe me?" she screamed at Olga Kirilovna. "If I said she is going to live in a palace, that is how it is going to be."

The people crowding around began to whisper and nudge each other. The woman cried, "You had better believe me!" She shook her finger at Olga Kirilovna, and then turned and disappeared around a corner,

Olga Kirilovna hastily adjusted her bonnet, then gathered Masha into her arms. "The woman is gone, dearie. Don't cry," she admonished. Masha would have liked to stop crying, but the minute she swallowed a sob, another one mounted in her throat.

At last, a salesman from a nearby shop sent out his boy to fetch a cab. Olga Kirilovna bundled Masha in and held her close all the way back to Katerina Ivanovna's furnished rooms.

Katerina Ivanovna herself was in the hall when they arrived. "Well, you've been away a good long time! I was just going to send Mitia out to look for you," she exclaimed. At the sight of Masha's tear-stained face, she added, "My goodness, what has happened to the child?"

Five minutes later, Masha was seated on the sofa, sipping tea from the cup Katerina Ivanovna was holding to her lips. Olga Kirilovna sat in a chair, fanning herself with a handkerchief, and telling the landlady about the strange "Annoushka" who had scared Masha. "She spoke like an educated person," Olga Kirilovna ended her tale. "Who is she?"

Katerina Ivanovna put the empty cup on the table. "No one really knows," she answered. "There is a story that she comes from a noble family and that she was engaged to a wealthy young man, who jilted her on the eve of her wedding. She disappeared from St. Petersburg, then turned up again some years later, looking as you saw her today. She is strange, but people respect her. They say that she can predict the future just by touching someone. There is also a rumor," she lowered her voice to a whisper and glanced at Masha, "that Annoushka was once a pupil at Smolni."

Masha did not care. Tired out, she spent the rest of the evening nestled in a corner of the sofa and was only too glad to obey Olga Kirilovna's order to go to bed early.

At nine o'clock it was still daylight outside, but Olga Kirilovna drew the curtains and lit a candle. "Can't stand those white nights," she declared, "so unnatural! Shall I draw the bed-curtains, dear, so the candle doesn't disturb you?"

Masha sat up in alarm. "Oh, no, please! I like the candle." She glanced around and asked in a whisper, "That woman... she couldn't come here, could she?"

"Of course not," Olga Kirilovna soothed, patting Masha's pillow. "You go to sleep fast so that you will be all rested in the morning. I will glance at the paper, since you don't mind the candle."

Snug under the blanket, Masha watched Olga Kirilovna turn the pages of the Northern Bee, muttering to herself, "Napoleon! Turning the world upside down again! Duke of Wellington... Hm, let's hope he knows what he is doing. What? Nevski Prospect is to be called 'Street of Tolerance' because there are churches of all denominations? Nonsense! Ha! Velvet is coming back into fashion."

Masha's mother used to read the Northern Bee too. "My only luxury," she called it. Stepan brought it with the mail from the stagecoach station. Masha turned toward the wall. "I want to go home," she sobbed noiselessly. "Oh, Mamma! I want to see you and Niania and Trezor, I want to be with you all."

She fell asleep, murmuring, "I want to go back," and dreamed that she was going home. She was sitting beside Olga Kirilovna in a carriage driving up the cedar avenue. Only they could not reach the house. The avenue seemed endless. The tree trunks flashed past mile after mile, but the house with the loved ones was still not in sight.

CHAPTER EIGHT

Smolni Institute for Noble Girls

MASHA LEFT FOR SMOLNI EARLY THE NEXT morning. A rented carriage was waiting at the door of the "birdhouse." "A cab would never do," Olga Kirilovna declared, smoothing her best lavender dress and draping a white lace shawl over her shoulders.

Katerina Ivanovna helped Masha lace the ribbons of her shoes and fasten the hooks of her green-striped dress. "I wish I could visit you," she told Masha, "but Smolni is too grand for me."

Mitia brought Masha's small trunk. Olga Kirilovna opened her brown plush purse for the tenth time and closed it again with a snap. "I'm so afraid of losing her birth certificate," she complained to the landlady, nodding at Masha. "Madame Adlerberg is quite capable of sending her home if I don't bring it."

Masha listened indifferently to Olga Kirilovna's anxious exclamations. Her head felt heavy and everything seemed uncomfortable. Her clothes were too warm, the ribbons of her bonnet tickled her chin. She stood by the window, looking at the horn of plenty above the bakery door and wondering why it looked so dull today.

"Come, dear. The carriage is waiting," Olga Kirilovna said.

Katerina Ivanovna murmured, "Oh, the poor child," and started to wipe her eyes.

Masha did not cry. With a stony expression she descended the stairway and let Olga Kirilovna help her into the carriage. They were already seated when Mitia dashed out of the front door, past Katerina Ivanovna standing on the porch steps. He ran to the carriage window and thrust an apple into Masha's hands. In spite of herself, Masha smiled. But before she could thank Mitia, the horses moved on.

There was a long way to go. Smolni was located on the outskirts of the city. Masha sat very straight, taking tiny bites out of her apple. Olga Kirilovna tried to point out sights to her, but Masha turned away from the windows.

The horses' hoofs click-clacked against the cobblestones, changed to soft thumping on the wooden paving, then click-clacked again.

The streets ended at last, giving way to isolated houses surrounded by vast gardens, empty lots, orchards, vegetable gardens, groups of trees, and empty lots again.

"Suppose we never arrive," Masha thought. "Suppose we just go on driving for nine years, and then turn around and head for home. Suppose..."

"Smolni!" Olga Kirilovna announced.

Masha sprang to the window. The carriage was crossing a vast square toward the white and pale-yellow building of Smolni. "Oh, it is big!" Masha gasped, staring at the majestic pillared portico in the center, supported by an arcade. The two wings of the building ended in similar porticoes, but on a somewhat smaller scale.

The carriage rolled up a raised, semicircular approach and stopped.

"We are late!" Olga Kirilovna lamented, climbing out of the carriage and ordering the driver to wait for her. "I sent a note to

Madame Adlerberg yesterday saying that we would be here at nine, and now it's almost ten."

"Perhaps she won't take me," Masha suggested hopefully. As they entered the hall, they were confronted with an imposing figure in a green uniform, his chest decorated with a row of medals. Masha stepped back fearfully.

"A general," she whispered, full of awe.

Olga Kirilovna snorted. "General indeed! He is simply a doorman. Must have served in the army before." But her tone was respectful as she asked the man to announce her to Madame Adlerberg.

He gave Masha a kindly glance from under his gray eyebrows, but before he could speak, a lady appeared in the hall. Tall and thin, she was dressed in a high-waisted gown of deep blue, trimmed with white ruches at the throat and cuffs. Her hair, so blonde it looked almost white, was brushed upward and into a crown of large curls, topped by a small white bonnet that looked like a butterfly.

"Madame Antonova, I presume?" the lady asked, approaching Olga Kirilovna. "We received your note and were expecting you..." she glanced at the watch pinned to her shoulder, "about an hour ago. I am Mademoiselle Neigardt, the Inspectress." Icy blue eyes swept Masha from head to foot. "So this is the child?"

Masha felt Olga Kirilovna's hand press her shoulder. She curtsied, narrowly avoiding stepping on the unfortunate flounce again.

"Don't put your foot forward so far and you won't be hampered, no matter how long your gown may be," Mademoiselle Neigardt said briskly, "and always keep your back straight."

Masha murmured a frightened "Yes," felt Olga Kirilovna's hand press her shoulder again, and added, "Mademoiselle."

The Inspectress nodded and turned to Olga Kirilovna. "Madame Adlerberg is ready to see you. In the meantime, I will have the child put through an examination. She must have some knowledge of reading and writing before she can be admitted."

"Masha reads very well," Olga Kirilovna began, but Mademoiselle Neigardt did not let her go any further.

"Monsieur Aranov, who teaches Russian to the younger pupils, will be the best judge of the matter," she said dryly. "Ah, here is one of our student teachers. She will take you to Madame Adlerberg's rooms."

At a sign from the Inspectress, a young girl of about nineteen or twenty, clad in a gray dress with a wide black bertha collar and a small black apron, came nearer. She dropped a curtsy to the Inspectress, another one to Olga Kirilovna, and waited respectfully.

Walking beside Mademoiselle Neigardt along a corridor, and trying hard not to slip on the polished floor, Masha stole a glance at the woman and thought, "I am afraid of her."

"In here," the Inspectress said, opening a door.

Masha saw a big room with rows of desks painted dark green with black tops. Behind the windows, tree branches were swaying in the breeze.

An elderly gentleman with a cone-shaped bald head was sitting at the teacher's desk placed on the dais, a pile of copybooks in front of him.

Mademoiselle Neigardt thrust Masha forward. "Monsieur Aranov, this is Maria Fredericks, ready for the examination."

To Masha's relief, the Inspectress left the room. Feeling more at ease without the searching eyes watching her movements, she managed to write on the blackboard the few words Monsieur Aranov dictated, even though the chalk broke twice and the letters were all crooked.

He corrected a spelling error, said "Mmm..." and handing her an opened book said, "Please read."

Masha began in a shaking voice, but soon became interested in the story and read fluently. It was about a prince who traveled all over the world in search of a rose without thorns. There was a picture of the prince on the next page. Masha was about to look at it when the teacher said, "Enough," and tried to take the book away from her.

"But I want to see the picture," Masha protested, clutching the book with both hands, "And did the prince find the rose after all?"

"Fredericks!" Mademoiselle Neigardt suddenly appeared beside Masha, her mouth set in a thin line of disapproval. Masha let the book go and froze in her place. "I'm sorry," she murmured.

The Inspectress ignored her. "How did the child do?" she asked Mr. Aranov.

"Satisfactory, quite satisfactory," he muttered. "And now, if you will excuse me..." He gathered the copybooks under his arm and vanished.

The next moment the door opened again and an agitated voice called something Masha did not catch.

Mademoiselle Neigardt exclaimed, "What? The Whites refuse to do their sewing task?" and darted out of the room. "I will be back presently," she called to Masha over her shoulder.

Left alone, Masha began to look around. There were many interesting things. Pictures of birds and animals hung on the walls; a big globe stood on a small table.

Crossing over to the rows of desks, Masha sat down at the nearest one. It was much too high for her and she decided that the classroom was probably used by the older girls. She opened the lid of the desk and looked inside. It was full of books and papers. Masha took a book at random and studied the title. Advice to My Daughter did not sound exciting, but inside the pages another book was tucked. Thin and paper bound, it had a bright picture on the cover. Masha admired the dashing young man leaping over a high wall, a young girl in his arms. A big red heart pierced by an arrow and a half-moon surrounded by flames decorated the background.

Masha read a little, but there were too many strange words. She put both books back into the desk and began to fidget. It seemed like hours since the Inspectress left. The big classroom was rapidly becoming a very lonely place. Masha longed for Olga Kirilovna's cheerful face. She walked to the door and opened it.

The long corridor was deserted. Closing the door softly behind her, Masha took a few steps, then stopped. Which way to go to find Olga Kirilovna? It was very quiet, except for a muffled sound of music coming from behind a door at the far end of the corridor. Masha reached it and peeped inside. She saw a small room, almost entirely filled by a piano. A brown-clad girl of her own age was seated on the high stool, furiously banging at the keys.

"Go away!" she screamed, without turning around. "You are too early. I still have ten minutes left, and I must learn this exercise for tomorrow's lesson. Go away!"

Frightened, Masha banged the door shut and started to run, forgetting the polished floor. Rounding the corner, she slipped, lost her balance, and sprawled almost at the feet of a slim girl in a white uniform and green apron, carrying a pile of books.

"Oh!" the girl screamed, jumping back and dropping the books that scattered in all directions. "How you scared me! Who are you? And why don't you look where you're going?"

"I am sorry," Masha mumbled, scrambling to her feet and picking up the books. "My name is Masha Fredericks," she explained, handing the books back to the girl, "and I am to stay here for nine years."

"You mean you are a new pupil?" the girl asked. "But surely you have not been left on the doorstep? Who brought you in?"

"Olga Kirilovna, my mother's friend, brought me." Masha's voice was beginning to shake. "Then she went to the Principal and... and I can't find her."

"But someone must have been in charge of you," the girl insisted.

Masha glanced around. "A lady called in-spect-ress," she whispered, "only someone called her and she had to leave in a hurry."

The girl smiled. "I know why she was in a hurry. The White Form refused to sew with rusty needles. Never mind, we will find your friend. I saw a lady talking to the doorman a few minutes ago. She had a big feathered hat and a pink dress. Could that be the person who brought you in?"

"Oh, no!" Masha was ready to cry. "Olga Kirilovna's dress is lavender and she has a cabbage hat, not feathers."

"A what?" the girl exclaimed.

"A cabbage," Masha repeated, tears trembling on her lashes. "I mean it is green and big and round."

"I understand," the girl said soothingly. "Don't cry. I will look after you. My name is Anna Wulff. I am in the White Form." She took Masha's hand. "Come with me. We are going to Maman."

Masha looked up with a puzzled air. "Maman?"

"It is what we call Madame Adlerberg," Anna said in a matter-of-fact tone. "Come on." But Masha refused to move.

"I cannot call the Principal 'Maman.' I have my own mother," she said in a choking voice.

Anna bent down and peered into Masha's face, her dark gray eyes under the straight brows tender and serious. But if she was going to speak, she thought better of it, and only gently pulled at Masha's hand, urging her on. "Let's hurry," she said, glancing at the books under her arm. "I was supposed to take these to the library, but I'd better see you safely to Maman first. Mademoiselle Neigardt may be looking for you, and then you will be in trouble."

They walked down a stairway, along the corridors again, and at last stopped in front of a tall door. Anna knocked.

A voice from within answered, "Hierein."

Anna quickly opened the door and pushed Masha inside, announcing, "This is a new pupil, Maman. She lost her way." Then she curtsied and disappeared.

At Masha's entrance, Olga Kirilovna, seated in an armchair near the fireplace, exclaimed, "Here she is!" and clasped her hands.

Masha rushed forward only to stop abruptly as she came face to face with Madame Adlerberg sitting on the other side of the fireplace.

Middle-aged, with a plain, careworn face, the Principal of Smolni did not look as awe-inspiring as Masha had imagined she would. But there was quiet dignity in every line of the short figure, clad in a simple black dress with a wide lace collar, and the blue eyes were sharp and penetrating. The gray hair was crowned by an enormous bonnet of white tulle, with a big bow on the top of the head and two long streamers hanging behind.

After the long corridors and bare classroom, Madame Adlerberg's study, though fairly large, looked small and homelike. A bronze clock stood on the mantlepiece beside the fireplace. There was a desk near the window, with a pile of sealed letters beside a thick register in green leather covers. The crimson velour curtains matched the rug. Masha noticed several miniature portraits painted on ivory and china standing on the tops of bookshelves and on small inlaid tables. From each one a girlish face smiled. She guessed these were portraits of old pupils.

Several minutes seemed to pass before Madame Adlerberg spoke. "Why did you not wait in the classroom for Mademoiselle Neigardt to come back?"

The tone held no reprimand, only a question. Masha breathed easier.

"She did not tell me to wait. Truly."

"Never say 'she.' It is most disrespectful. Very well, we will suppose it was a misunderstanding. You have caused a great deal of anxiety. We were afraid you might have wandered out of the building. Mademoiselle Neigardt is still looking for you. I am going to send a maid to tell her you are here."

The Principal was reaching for a small silver bell on the table beside her when the door opened and the Inspectress came in, looking hot and breathless.

Her eyes lighted upon Masha and immediately two red spots flamed on her cheeks. "I expected you to stay exactly where I left you," she said sharply. "Such behavior..."

Madame Adlerberg held up her hand. "The child misunderstood you, Mademoiselle. She is sorry she has caused trouble." She beckoned to Masha. "Come here, my dear."

Masha came nearer.

"I have learned that you did very nicely in your examination," the Principal said kindly, "especially in reading."

Masha dimpled. "It was a very interesting story, all about a rose without thorns. Only the teacher didn't let me finish."

Th older woman smiled. "The story was written by her late Majesty, the Empress Catherine," she said. "It is an allegory. Your teachers will explain to you what it means."

"The other book was not interesting," Masha commented, encouraged by the Principal's smile. "I couldn't understand it."

"What book are you talking about, my dear?" Madame Adlerberg asked with a surprised air.

"The one with a picture on the cover," Masha explained. "It is called..." she made an effort to remember, "Beautiful Elenora... and... and the Harem," she ended in triumph.

Mademoiselle Neigardt came nearer. "Where did you find this book?" she asked.

"In one of the desks," Masha answered simply, and was surprised to see a deep frown appear on Madame Adlerberg's face.

"Later," the Principal said quickly as Mademoiselle Neigardt started to speak. There was an awkward pause and Masha felt that somehow she had done something wrong.

At last Madame Adlerberg cleared her throat and addressed Olga Kirilovna, wilting in her chair, her turban a little askew, her big round face tired and strained.

"Has the child had any instruction in foreign languages?" she asked.

"Her mother taught her a little French," Olga Kirilovna answered, "but you know, in the country..." Her voice trailed into silence under the Inspectress's disdainful look.

"We consider languages very important here," the Principal told Masha impressively. "When Her Majesty, the Dowager Empress Maria Feodorovna, visits us, she usually talks to the pupils in French or German. You must work very hard on these subjects."

"Yes, Madame."

"You will call me 'Maman,' since I will be taking your mother's place while you are at school. If you study well and behave yourself, I will be proud of you, and it will grieve me if you give cause for complaint."

"I will try to do well, Madame."

"Say, 'Maman.'"

"I will try to do well... Maman."

The Principal smiled approval and shifted her attention to Olga Kirilovna. Taking up Masha's birth certificate and other documents from the table, she slid them into an envelope and sealed it. "We will keep these and return them after the child graduates," she told Olga Kirilovna. "I am very glad you were able to bring her at this time of the year. We like the children to arrive during vacation, so that they can get used to the school before beginning their studies on the first of August. Music lessons and practicing are, of course, continued all through the summer. Needlework lessons are taken in the garden. It is Her Majesty's desire that the pupils spend as much time as possible outside for the benefit of health. Which reminds me, I must ask you to let me see if the child has been vaccinated against smallpox. Bare her arm, please."

The tight-fitting sleeves of Masha's dress were not made to be rolled up. After some struggle, Olga Kirilovna had to undo the hooks at the back of the dress and lower the whole bodice. Madame Adlerberg put up the lorgnette hanging on a slender gold chain around her neck, and scrutinized the mark. "It is of utmost importance for us to protect the pupils from epidemics," she said, while Olga Kirilovna hooked Masha's dress up. "We had several cases of measles this spring. A few girls are still in quarantine."

With the last words, the Principal rose and bowed to Olga Kirilovna. "Everything seems entirely satisfactory, so I am not going to detain you any longer," she said. "I know you are anxious to see your son. We will leave the child alone with you for a few minutes to say good-bye." She bowed again and sailed out of the room, followed by the Inspectress. Masha heard her say in a low voice as she passed Olga Kirilovna, "Do not be distressed if the child is upset. I can assure you that once you are gone, she will settle down quite happily."

It turned out, however, that Olga Kirilovna was the more upset of the two. Masha sat on the edge of a chair, very pale, with dry eyes, wondering if there could be something wrong with her chest, it hurt so.

"My poor baby," Olga Kirilovna wailed, rummaging in her reticule for a handkerchief. "To think that I brought you here while my own daughters are safe at home! But I only had your interests in mind, dearie, believe me."

Masha nodded. "I know."

"How can I leave you here alone with all these high-and-mighty persons?" Olga Kirilovna went on lamenting, wiping her eyes on her shawl, since the handkerchief failed to turn up. "Cold as a stone they all are." She took a deep breath and whispered mysteriously, "Listen, dearie, what about going back with me? The carriage is waiting. We will pick up my son and take the stagecoach home before they can catch up with us. I will tell your mother... Oh, merciful heaven! What am I going to tell her, old fool that I am?"

Masha looked at Olga Kirilovna's face, all red and glistening with tears. Jumping up, she threw her arms around the sobbing woman. "Please don't cry," she whispered, "I would love to run away with you, but I can't. I promised mother to stay here and learn all kinds of things. Tell her I love her, and Niania, and... everybody." She felt her own eyes fill and hastily whispered, "Good-bye."

"Good-bye, dear child, I will visit you in the autumn, when I bring my son back to school," Olga Kirilovna promised, kissing Masha several times. She left at last, wiping her eyes with one hand and trying to adjust her shawl with the other.

Standing by the door, Masha watched Olga Kirilovna walk down the corridor, followed by her distorted reflection in the gleaming floor. When the familiar heavy figure in the lavender gown disappeared around a corner, she went back and stood looking at a big oil painting above the sofa until the picture stopped being a shapeless blot and became a monastery, black against the pale evening sky.

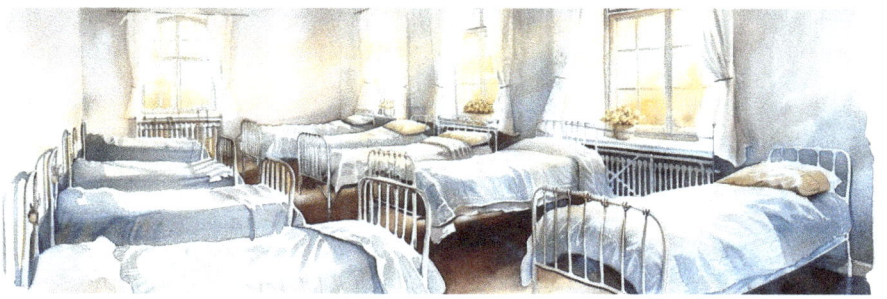

Getting Acquainted

THE SOUND OF MAMAN'S LIGHT STEP MADE Masha turn around. The Principal entered the room in the company of a young woman with a merry face, her wide mouth spoiled by prominent teeth. Her gown was of the same blue shade and the same pattern as Mademoiselle Neigardt's, but somehow it looked more coquettish. There was no bonnet on the curly auburn hair and the few freckles seemed put on to make the skin look whiter.

"This is your Form Mistress, Mademoiselle Souchet," the Principal told Masha. "She will take you to the linen room to be fitted with our uniform, and will appoint your bed in the dormitory. I expect you to respect and obey her."

Masha curtsied mechanically, her thoughts following Olga Kirilovna. She would be leaving the building now, getting into the carriage, telling the driver...

"Fredericks," the Principal's voice cut through Masha's thoughts.

"Go with Mademoiselle now, and remember that I expect to hear about your good progress."

Masha curtsied again. "Yes, Madame."

"Yes, Maman."

"Yes, Maman." Masha wondered if the word would ever become familiar to her.

"Come, my dear. You will see how nice it is to work and play with little girls of your own age," the Form Mistress said, giving Masha a pat on the shoulder.

As they were walking to the door, Mademoiselle Souchet stopped for a moment, and glancing at the silver-framed mirror above the mantlepiece, fluffed the curls on her temples.

Instinctively, Masha turned her head. The Principal was watching the mirror with a frown on her face. Masha realized that the frown was not meant for her; nevertheless, she was glad to dart across the threshold, out of Maman's presence.

Unsuspecting, Mademoiselle Souchet tripped lightly along the corridor, showering Masha with questions. Did she have a governess at home? How advanced was she in music? Had she ever taken dancing lessons?

Masha answered, yes, or no, sometimes at random, for she found Mademoiselle Souchet's Russian difficult to understand.

"Most of the new girls arrived a month ago," the Form Mistress chattered as they mounted the stairway. "However, one pupil arrived this morning, just before you did. Here is the linen room. Walk in."

The linen room was very large and lined with cupboards. Two maids, sewing at a long table, did not even look up at Masha's entrance, but a little white-haired lady, busily counting sheets, smiled and asked Masha's name.

"Take good care of your clothes," she admonished, bringing out a brown dress with a bunchy skirt, a low, round neckline, and elbow-length sleeves. "This is an expensive material and had to be ordered from England." She shook her finger. "And don't forget, clean aprons are given only once a week. You won't get a fresh one before that, even if you soil yours."

The dress over her arm, and carrying a small pile of underwear, stockings, and shoes, Masha followed Mademoiselle Souchet into the dormitory.

It turned out to be twice as big as the linen room, with three long rows of beds covered with gray blankets. At the head of each bed stood a small bedside table with two drawers, and at the foot a stool. Stiff white cambric curtains framed the windows. The walls were bare, the floor spotless.

One of the beds was occupied. A small girl in a brown uniform was lying flat on her back, kicking her feet in the air. At the sight of the Form Mistress, her face puckered and she let out a long wail.

Mademoiselle Souchet paid no attention. "This is the Browns' dormitory and this is your bed," she told Masha, pointing at a bed in the middle row near the center of the room. "That's your trunk standing on the stool. You may unpack and put your belongings into these drawers. After you have changed into the uniform," she went on, ignoring the wails that became more and more strident, "pack your own clothes into your trunk. It will be sent back to your mother. I will send a maid in presently to cut your hair."

"Cut my hair?" Masha faltered.

The Form Mistress looked sympathetic. "It has to be done," she said gently. "You are too young to wash and comb long hair properly. You will be allowed to let it grow when you are in your third year here." Without leaving Masha time to answer, she said firmly, "Please start unpacking," and left the room.

As soon as the door closed, the girl on the bed stopped wailing and lay quietly, watching Masha out of her large, blue-green eyes. But when Masha made a step in her direction, the girl turned toward the wall and buried her face in her pillow.

Discomfited, Masha walked to her trunk and started to take out her possessions. They were not numerous: a brush and comb, her handkerchief case, the notepaper Olga Kirilovna had given her, a copy of the New Testament her mother had had when she was a little girl, a small workbasket. There was plenty of room left in the drawers after she had unpacked.

It was difficult to get into the uniform. After a long struggle with hooks and with the apron strings, Masha managed it, thinking with terror that this would have to be done every morning. The skirt reached her ankles, the thick woolen stockings were too short and the shoes, obviously already worn, were too big. She folded her green-striped dress and put it into the trunk with the rest of her clothes, wondering why it was necessary to return them. Suddenly she realized that she would never wear the green dress again. "I will be grown up when I graduate," she murmured, lifting the lid of the trunk to have a last glimpse of the dress. It did not look discarded; it looked dead. Masha hastily dropped the lid again.

"What are you making such a face about?" a sullen voice asked.

Masha jumped and turned around. The girl was sitting up on her bed, clasping her knees, a heavy mass of bronze curls tumbled over her shoulders.

"You look as if you were going to cry," she remarked, staring at Masha.

"I only..." Masha stammered, then decided to tell the truth. "I was thinking that I will be too big for that dress when I am out of school," she explained, nodding at the trunk.

The girl snorted. "Of course! Besides, the. fashion is sure to be different. What's your name?"

"Masha Fredericks."

"Mine is Sophie Brozina. Do you like Smolni?"

"I don't know yet," Masha answered cautiously. "Mademoiselle Neigardt seems very strict, but Mademoiselle Souchet is kind, only I don't understand her when she talks to me."

Sophie shrugged her shoulders. "That's because she is French. Madame Adlerberg and the Inspectress are German. Didn't you know?"

"No," Masha admitted. "I only thought they spoke in a funny way."

Sophie fidgeted impatiently. "I don't care how they speak. I hate school, and I am not going to let that Frenchwoman or anyone else touch my hair. I will scream and scream until they give up."

Such daring astonished Masha. "You may be punished," she warned.

"I suppose so," Sophie agreed indifferently. "My last governess tried to make me stand in a corner."

"And?" Masha prompted, deeply interested.

"I bit her," the girl announced triumphantly. "She rushed to Papa and told him she was leaving. That's how I came to be sent to Smolni. Did you bite your governess too?"

Masha shook her head. "I did not have a governess. Mamma couldn't afford one. She taught me herself."

"Lucky you," Sophie said heartily. "I've always had a governess, two sometimes, one French and one German. Only they never stayed long," she added with a laugh.

Masha opened her eyes wide. "Two governesses! Your father must be rich."

"Rich?" Sophie knitted her eyebrows. "I never thought of it. We live in a big house, right here in St. Petersburg. There are many servants—I mean footmen and maids. Does that mean being rich?"

Before Masha could answer, the door opened and Mademoiselle Souchet appeared, followed by a maid in a blue and white striped uniform and armed with scissors and combs.

"Begin with her," Mademoiselle Souchet ordered, and Masha realized she was the victim. In a moment, she was seated on a stool, a towel around her shoulders. The scissors clicked and the long fair locks fell on the floor. Setting her teeth, Masha looked at the wall, while the maid trimmed the hair just below the earlobe and drew it off the forehead with a large round comb.

Sophie gave one look at Masha's head and began to draw air into her lungs. But the Form Mistress did not give her time. "Spare yourself!" she cried shrilly. "No one is going to cut your hair if you don't want to. In a few days it will become so dirty, it will have to be shaved off. Voila!"

Sophie changed color. "Shaved? Oh, no!" She scrambled off the bed and sat on the nearest stool. "Cut it," she murmured, closing her eyes.

"Oh, mon Dieu!" Mademoiselle Souchet exclaimed, exasperated. She took the scissors away from the maid and pounced on Sophie. In a few minutes the hair was cut with just enough ringlets left to curl at the nape, and the comb was placed so that it looked almost elegant.

"And now, enough nonsense," the Form Mistress said briskly. "Your classmates are coming from the garden. You have half an hour before dinner to get acquainted."

Masha felt the palms of her hands become moist as she listened to the sound of voices and steps in the corridor outside the dormitory. Even Sophie looked uneasy.

"Quiet! Quiet!" Mademoiselle Souchet clapped her hands as the brown-clad, white-aproned girls poured into the dormitory. Behind them walked a student teacher. At the sight of Masha and Sophie, the girls stopped short and stared.

"Here are two new girls," Mademoiselle Souchet announced. "This is Brozina and this is Fredericks. Tell them about life at Smolni, and mind, no noise!" She made a sign to the student teacher and they both vanished behind the door.

There was a rush, and the girls crowded around the newcomers, perching on beds, stools, and even on bedside tables.

"How old are you?"

"What's your first name?"

"Where are you from?"

"Do you like Maman?"

"Are you German?"

At this last question, addressed to her, Masha suddenly bristled, "I am not. I'm Russian."

"Of course you are," soothed a slender, brown-haired girl with serious eyes and a small black mole on her cheek, sitting down on the bed beside Masha. "I have a German name too— Meller, Natasha Meller—but I'm Russian. I suppose our ancestors came from Germany years and years ago. Now Katish Muffle over there is German and a baroness as well. Aren't you, Katish?"

A blonde, dimpled girl, sitting on Masha's bedside table, nodded and said in a sleepy voice, "You are probably going to be my pair."

"Your pair?" Masha asked.

"Yes, I mean when we walk two by two. I'm the odd one."

"She may be paired off with Lena," Natasha Meller contradicted. "Lena is due back from the hospital any day now."

"She is too short to walk with Lena," a voice shouted from behind Masha. "The other new girl is more likely to be Lena's pair."

Sophie, who was talking with two girls who looked like sisters, turned around. "I'm not going to be paired off with anyone that I don't like," she declared.

A strikingly pretty raven-haired girl with enormous black eyes, sitting on the bed opposite Masha's, her arm around a fairy-like creature with golden locks, laughed unkindly.

"That's Sasha Rossett," Natasha Meller whispered into Masha's ear. "We call her Sashette. She's a little older than the rest of us. The tiny girl beside her is Stephanie Radzivill. She's Polish and an awful crybaby. The girls who are talking to the other new girl are Ellie and Mary Vuich. Their father died a hero in 1812."

Masha liked the Vuich sisters. Dark-haired, with velvety brown eyes and timid faces, they looked like frightened deer. "Why do they have such funny names?" she whispered to Natasha.

"Funny names?" Natasha looked surprised. "Oh, you mean Ellie and Mary? That's English for Elena and Maria. It's fashionable to turn Russian names into English or French. We have plenty of Dollies and Betsies too."

A tall girl with a haughty expression and prominent gray eyes pushed her way through the crowd. "I know you," she told the new girl Sophie. "You're General Brozin's daughter. My name is

Marie Divova. We met at a children's party last Christmas. You tied several girls to their chairs by their sashes at supper. There was a commotion!"

One of the Vuich sisters pulled Sophie's sleeve. "Marie Divova has a cousin who is a lady-in-waiting to the Empress Maria Feodorovna," she whispered with awe.

But Sophie did not seem impressed. "I remember you too," she answered Marie Divova in a clear voice that carried through the dormitory. "You kept stuffing yourself with sweets until you were sick and your governess had to take you home."

The girls tittered and Marie Divova blushed angrily. "Well, I was only trying to be friendly," she said, turning away.

The blonde, dimpled girl called Katish asked Masha, "Is your home in St. Petersburg too, or do you live in the country?"

"Really, Katish, need you ask?" said the black-eyed girl, Sashette, looking at Masha's tanned arms.

"Don't be nasty, Sashette," Natasha Meller rebuked good-naturedly. "We country girls are not afraid of the sun. Not everyone can be pink and white like Stephanie."

At the sound of her name, the fairy-like Stephanie lifted her blonde head from Sashette's shoulder. "When I was at school in Paris," she said, "we were never allowed in the sun, and we washed our faces with rose water, and..."

"And you had a room to yourself," interrupted an untidy-looking girl with a mop of brown hair and a mischievous face, perched at the foot of Masha's bed. "And you all wore silk stockings," she went on, imitating Stephanie's fluty voice, "and you had cafe au lait every day, and everything was so elegant. Even the rod was tied with blue ribbons,"

"It was not," Stephanie protested tearfully. "You're always making fun of me, Nadia."

"Because you make me tired, singing praises to that Paris school of yours," the other answered crossly. "I like Smolni, and don't you dare say anything against it."

"If I had lived here for as many years as you have," Stephanie began peevishly, but the other girl ignored her and turned to Masha. "I am Nadia Maslova," she said. "Was it you who came into the music room this morning while I was practicing? Sorry if I screamed at you. I thought it was someone else coming too early and I simply had to learn that exercise."

Masha would have liked to talk to Nadia Maslova, but a bell rang loudly outside the dormitory. At the same time, Mademoiselle Souchet appeared and said something in French.

Masha caught Nadia's hand. "What did she say?"

Nadia looked at her with surprise. "She said we must hurry and wash our hands. Dinner is at twelve and it is a big crime to be late. You mean you did not understand?"

Masha reddened. "No."

"Better start learning fast," Nadia advised. "We are supposed to speak French one day and German the other. Form Mistresses make allowances at first, but then they simply pretend they don't understand Russian."

"And on Sundays we speak Turkish," Sashette said, coming up beside Masha.

"Turkish?" Masha repeated, feeling her heart sink. "But..."

"Oh, never mind! Sashette is only joking," Nadia interrupted her. "It is a stupid joke too," she added, looking at Sashette. "Can't you see the new girl is frightened?" She took Masha's hand. "Let's go and wash, and stop worrying."

Following Nadia and the other girls, Masha entered the lavatory with its rows of basins and towels.

Hands washed, the girls formed ranks. Masha was paired off with Katish, the blonde girl who had guessed Masha would be her pair. Sophie, the odd one, walked behind them, a sullen expression on her face.

"Silence! No talking in the ranks," Mademoiselle Souchet kept repeating as the procession wound its way through the corridors toward the refectory. But whispered conversations still ran from rank to rank.

"Milk soup again today. I hate it."

"Where do you think the new girls are going to sit?"

"At our table, I suppose."

The last remark came from Nadia, and Masha hoped it would prove true. She felt lost and frightened among so many unfamiliar faces—some friendly, some indifferent, a few mocking.

They reached the refectory, and Masha saw rows of tables and benches, painted green with black tops, just like the desks in the classroom.

Blue-uniformed girls were streaming in through another door, followed by the White Form.

Grace was sung and the meal began.

The Brown Form had three tables allotted to them. To her joy, Masha found herself between Nadia and Natasha, the friendly girl with the black mole on her cheek.

"We may talk," Natasha said, "but not loud, or Mademoiselle will come over and scold us. See the staff table? Thank goodness Maman takes most meals in her rooms."

"In old times," Nadia said solemnly, "there was no talking at mealtime. A nun used to read a holy book, and pupils had honey mixed with hot water for breakfast instead of tea or milk."

"From the way you talk," Sashette said crushingly, "one would think you were here fifty years ago."

"Well, I was practically born here," Nadia giggled, plunging her spoon into her milk soup.

"What does Nadia mean?" Masha whispered to Natasha. "She couldn't really have been born here, could she?"

Natasha lowered her voice. "No, of course not. But she's not new like the rest of us. She has been at Smolni for... let's see... about four years. Both her parents died when the Bolshoi Theater burned down in 1811. She had no relatives, so she was sent to Smolni. She was so young her nurse had to come along to look after her."

The tall girl whose cousin was a lady-in-waiting craned her neck to take a better look at the Whites' tables. "There are several missing," she remarked.

"Oh, they were probably delayed practicing," Natasha answered airily.

"I can't eat this meat. It tastes like a fried rag," Sophie muttered, dabbing at her plate with her fork.

"But the turnips are nice," Natasha consoled. "They are from the Empress Maria Feodorovna. She likes us to eat plenty of vegetables."

"She brought all these?" Masha exclaimed, staring at the long rows of plates and thinking of how Olga Kirilovna used to bring a basket of peaches from her greenhouse.

Giggles ran around the table. "I only meant the turnips were sent from the palace," Natasha explained, trying not to laugh.

Sashette leaned toward Masha, her black eyes flashing. "Do you like geometry with or without gravy?" she asked.

Someone nudged Masha, but it was too late. "I have never eaten geometry. Does it taste nice?" Masha answered innocently.

This time the giggles were so loud Mademoiselle Souchet at the staff table turned her head. Immediately, there was dead silence.

Masha forced herself to eat, her eyes on her plate. She realized that Sashette was only teasing, but it hurt.

"There are five Whites missing," the tall girl began again.

Suddenly, she gave a loud gasp and announced in a dramatic whisper, "Here they are! Just LOOK!"

Five girls in white uniforms entered the refectory. They walked in one by one, their heads bent, traces of tears on their cheeks.

"Mercy!" Natasha murmured. "They have no aprons on!"

"I think they look nicer without," Masha said sincerely, and was rewarded by a thunderous look from Sashette.

"You little stupid," Sashette hissed. "Being deprived of your apron is the greatest disgrace that can happen to you at Smolni."

Frightened by Sashette's outburst, Masha huddled in her seat and watched the five disgraced ones cross the refectory. When they reached their table, they did not sit down, but picked up their plates and began to eat standing. One of them, Masha noticed with dismay, was Anna Wulff, the girl who had led her to Madame Adlerberg's study. She was making an effort to eat, but tears kept dropping into her plate. Her neighbor, a beautiful olive-skinned girl, was not eating at all. Her face in her hands, she was sobbing aloud. The next two Whites had their backs turned toward Masha, but the fifth, a big, healthy-looking blonde, was obviously enjoying her food and did not seem upset.

The tiny girl with the golden curls sniffed, dropped her fork and burst into tears.

"What's the matter with her? She isn't being punished," Sophie asked scornfully.

Every face at the table looked shocked. "Stephanie should cry," Natasha told Sophie reprovingly. "She has a crush on Clementine Del Pardo—the dark girl. Her father is a Spanish general. He had to leave Spain because of polit... political something. That poor girl is sobbing hard enough. But look at the tall blonde girl, Mania Suvorova. She seems to be enjoying herself."

"Suvorova!" Masha exclaimed. Her mother had told her many a story about the heroic deeds of Marshal Suvorov, stories that were already becoming legends. "You mean she is his daughter?"

"No," Nadia said. "His daughter, Natasha Suvorova, graduated from Smolni years ago. Mania Suvorova is his grand-niece."

"We have a big painting of Suvorov at home," Natasha said. "My brothers always salute when they pass it. Mania is a very nice girl."

"Oh, never mind Suvorov," Nadia interrupted. "What do you think has happened? It takes a big crime for the Whites to be punished publicly,"

Before anyone could offer guesses, the staff rose from their table and the girls followed.

"What? No dessert?" Sophie grumbled under the cover of grace being sung.

"We wash our hands and clean our teeth now," Masha's pair,

Katish, told her as they mounted the stairway, "and then we do our needlework tasks in the garden."

"Silence! Silence! No talking in the ranks!" shouted Mademoiselle Souchet

The "Tattletale"

MASHA LIKED THE SMOLNI GARDEN. BIG and shady, it spread itself between the back of the building and the Neva. She was a little disappointed that a high wall separated it from the river, but the tree-lined avenues, the paths between groups of bushes, the flower beds, the fountains were enchanting.

"We are allowed to wander around," Nadia explained to Masha, "but each class has a special place to sit and read or sew. See those stone benches near the pine trees? That's for the Whites. The Blue Form's place is under the limes. Our corner is by the lilac bushes, over there."

"Are we allowed to run sometimes?" Masha asked anxiously, thinking of her races with Trezor at home.

"Of course," Nadia assured her. "Maman likes us to run. She says it is healthy. We play all kinds of games. There is a swing too and ninepins."

97

Mademoiselle Souchet's voice came from across the fountain. "Come, come, girls, it is needlework hour."

"Oh, bother! Let's go." Nadia pulled Masha by the hand.

The lilac bushes enclosed a sanded quadrangle lined with wooden benches. Most of the Browns were already seated, their workbaskets beside them.

"Our needlework teacher, Frau Udam, will assign you a task tomorrow," Mademoiselle Souchet told Masha. "In the meantime you can help Katish Muffle hem this towel. Yes, take the other end." She turned to Sophie. "As for you, you can work on the stocking one of the pupils had started before she went to the hospital. Can you knit?"

"Yes," Sophie mumbled, eyeing with distaste the long black stocking the Form Mistress dangled in front of her.

Her tongue in her cheek, Masha applied herself to making small stitches. Beside her, Nadia hemmed furiously at something crumpled that looked like an apron. "I'm always behind with my sewing and practicing," she said, sighing, then glanced at Masha. "I overheard Natasha telling you about me at dinner."

"That's true," Masha admitted. "But don't talk about it if you'd rather not," she added hastily.

"Oh, I don't mind." Nadia went on making stitches half an inch long. "I hardly remember my parents, or anything else really. I only know that my nurse woke me up in the middle of the night and I was frightened because the windows were all red. Our house was not far from the theater. My nurse had me dressed in case we had to leave the house. Then, suddenly, there was Smolni. I don't recall what happened in between."

Sophie, who had been listening, wanted to know, "Did you wear the uniform when you were little?"

Nadia put her sewing on her lap and stretched herself. "The first year I wore my own white dresses with a black apron for mourning," she answered. "Then my nurse was sent away and I had to wear the uniform, but I was called sub-Brown and a teacher gave me lessons all by myself. This is the first year I am really a member of the Brown Form."

"I believe I wore a black apron too after Papa was killed in the war," Masha said, as Nadia's tale seemed to bring back memories.

"Borodino?" Nadia asked.

Masha nodded.

Ellie and Mary Vuich said in chorus, "Our father died at Borodino too."

"Father commanded a regiment during the war," Sophie said proudly. "He has ever so many decorations."

"You speak only about your father," Nadia said. "Is your..." She stopped awkwardly.

"Mother died when I was a baby," Sophie answered. Her tone was calm, but there was a wistfulness in her eyes.

Several girls laid down their sewing to join in the conversation.

Masha looked in Mademoiselle Souchet's direction, expecting her to say something, but the Form Mistress seemed far away from her charges. Seated in a wicker chair in the middle of the quadrangle, she was reading and rereading a long letter, a dreamy smile on her face.

Beyond the bushes, Masha could see the Blues gathered under the lime trees, listening to their Form Mistress read aloud. Only the stone benches reserved for the Whites remained unoccupied.

Natasha followed Masha's gaze. "The Whites are in Maman's rooms," she whispered.

Sashette craned her neck to hear. "How do you know?"

"Marie Divova found out somehow. Oh, here's Lena Mandrika back from the hospital."

A small girl with a sallow face and a high forehead, blue veins standing out on her temples, was coming down the path. Going straight to Mademoiselle Souchet, she curtsied, assured the Form Mistress that she was quite well, and joined the girls.

"Over here, Lena!" Natasha called, waving her sewing. "This

new girl, Sophie Brozina, was helping with your stocking. Oh, and here is another new girl, Masha Fredericks."

Lena's eyes opened wide at the sight of her stocking that had taken a strange shape in Sophie's hands. "I will have to undo most of it," she said. There was no blame in her voice, only patience, but Sophie flared up immediately.

"Then start undoing it," she shouted, flinging the stocking at Lena. "As if I wanted the ugly thing!"

Without a word, Lena took the stocking and sat down beside Masha.

"I'm sorry you have been ill," Masha ventured, feeling bound to say something.

Lena pursed her lips. "It was God's will," she answered primly, beginning to undo Sophie's handiwork.

Stephanie giggled. "Sophie is to be your pair," she informed Lena with a sly smile.

Lena gave Sophie a long look. "She will be a cross, but I will bear it," she answered with resignation.

Sophie remained speechless, but the rest of the girls did not look surprised. Katish murmured under her breath. "There she goes again!" and Nadia whispered to Masha, "She always acts funny. Her only relative, an older sister, is a nun and brought her up in a convent. Lena wants to be a nun too when she grows up."

A pale girl named Varia Bikova, who spent most of her time reading, suddenly exclaimed, "The Whites!" With a snap, she closed the book she was reading under the cover of a half-finished scarf.

A throng of white-uniformed girls appeared from the building and headed toward the stone benches. At the same time, Mademoiselle Souchet folded her letter and rose. "Go on with your needlework. 1 will be back in a few minutes," she said, walking away.

Everyone's needle was immediately put down and all eyes became fixed on the Whites who stood under a tree surrounded by a double wall of Blue pupils. The Spanish girl seemed to be the center of attention. She talked and gestured, wiping her eyes from time to time.

"Pity we can't hear," Natasha remarked. "Shall we go over to them?"

"No," Nadia said. "They will only chase us away. Let's send Stephanie. The Whites won't mind her. They think she is as sweet as she looks. Run, Stephanie, and find out why Clementine Del Pardo is pointing at us. Quick!"

Stephanie did not wait to be asked a second time. Ignoring Nadia's doubtful compliment, she streaked across the grass and stood at a respectful distance from the older girls, her head to one side, listening avidly.

The Browns craned their necks and waited.

"Goodness, how long she takes," Marie Divova said impatiently. "Surely she has had time enough to gather what it is all about."

"Look, Madame Legarpe is coming!" Varia Bikova exclaimed. "See that gray-haired lady, Masha? She is the Whites' Form Mistress. Oh, the Blues' Form Mistress is waving to them to go back to their sewing. Look, Stephanie is coming back!"

Stephanie came running, her comb off her hair, her blue eyes popping out of her head.

"What do you think?" she cried, collapsing on the nearest bench. "Neigardt searched the White Form classroom this morning and found five books in the desks. You know, wicked books. Clementine said that Maman was simply furious. She punished those to whom the books belonged, then gave a lecture to the whole class and burned the books in the fireplace in front of them."

Nadia giggled. 'They must have been hot, especially Maman. Imagine fire in this fine weather."

Sashette glowered at Nadia. "It is not a laughing matter. How did Neigardt find out about the books, Stephanie? Do you know?"

Stephanie lowered her long lashes with a mysterious air. "The Whites gave some money to one of the maids to buy the books at the market. They were sure no one knew about it, but Neigardt found out because..." She made a dramatic pause and pointed at Masha. "Because she told her exactly where to look."

There was a general gasp and every girl turned in Masha's direction.

Stunned and bewildered, Masha rose from her seat without realizing she was still holding her end of the towel. "I didn't know..." she began, but Sashette interrupted her sharply. "Did you or didn't you tell the Inspectress about the books?"

"Yes, but..."

She did not finish. Katish pulled the towel out of her hands. "Tattletale!" she shouted, and several voices screamed after her, "Tattletale! Tattletale!"

"And I thought you were such a nice girl!" Nadia told Masha in a trembling voice. She gathered her sewing and went to the opposite bench.

Immediately, there was a wild scramble to get as far away from Masha as possible. Natasha murmured, "Oh, how could you?" then followed the rest. Only Sophie stayed. Her eyes flashing defiance, she moved closer to Masha. "I don't believe a word of that stupid story!" she declared.

"She admitted it!" Sashette cried, followed by shouts of, "Tattletale! You have disgraced the Brown Form! The Whites will never speak to us again!"

Masha sat still. She did not try to defend herself any more. She knew no one would listen and, after all, she did tell about the book she saw in the Whites' classroom. "But I didn't know," she whispered to herself miserably.

Mademoiselle Souchet came back a few minutes later and the girls paired off to go inside. Masha walked with Katish, but Katish kept her face turned away and her arms stiffly at her sides.

Tea was served in thick white cups, and each girl received a slice of white bread.

"You may have a second slice if you want," Nadia told Sophie, ignoring Masha.

"I would never ask for one anyway," Masha thought, choking over her portion.

"I wonder how she found out about the books," Varia Bikova remarked conversationally.

"Oh, her kind always ferret out everything," Sashette answered over Masha's head.

After tea, the Brown class went to the garden again, but to Masha's relief, she was ordered to stay behind.

"The dentist is here this afternoon, and he wants to examine your teeth," Mademoiselle Souchet said.

"Is he going to pull them out?" Masha asked, so alarmed she forgot her disgrace for a moment.

"Certainly not," the Form Mistress answered surprised. Then she said severely, "I hope you have always cleaned your teeth at home, Fredericks. It is a most important habit."

"Mother made me clean them," Masha answered regretfully, "but Niania thought it unhealthy."

After the dentist, there was a music lesson for Masha and some practicing. It was suppertime when she rejoined the Brown class.

"You have been away a long time," Sophie said, but before Masha could answer Nadia and Varia began to tell Sophie something and make her laugh.

Masha did not try to speak to Sophie any more. She sat over her plate of macaroni and cheese that seemed bottomless and prayed that supper would soon end.

At last it was bedtime. The girls trooped upstairs to the dormitory. Varia read a chapter from the Gospel and said a prayer in French, making Masha wonder whether God understood.

She undressed, fumbling with hooks and buttons, followed the girls to the lavatory, and tumbled into bed. The pillow felt wonderful to her tired head. She closed her eyes, only to open them again as the Form Mistress's voice said, "You are not lying in bed correctly, Fredericks. Turn on your right side, please, and put your arms outside the blanket."

The unexpected remark chased away Masha's sleep. She lay quietly, looking around and listening to the conversations. Natasha Meller was folding her clothes and placing them neatly on a stool beside her bed. Lena Mandrika was kneeling on the floor, saying her prayers. Marie Divova was patting on her face something white from a bottle.

"What witch's brew are you using now?" Nadia called.

"It is only almond milk," Marie answered in an offended tone. "Since you know everything that has ever happened at Smolni, you should also know that in old times the school provided French whiskey for the pupils to wash their faces with. It was supposed to be good for the skin."

"But where did you get the almond milk from?" Nadia wanted to know.

"My cousin Zinaida gave it to me last visiting day," Marie answered loftily. "All the ladies-in-waiting use it."

From Sophie's bed came a sound of argument. "I don't want to wear a nightcap. It gives me headaches," Sophie was saying.

"But you must," Varia Bikova insisted. "It is a rule."

Masha was trying to forget her disgrace by imagining ladies-in-waiting, all in silks and velvets, washing their faces with almond milk. Why didn't they drink it instead? Almond milk was good. She thought about Feklusha pressing the almonds in a small china mortar. The bittersweet smell from Marie Divova's bed reminded her of home.

A white-uniformed girl appeared in the dormitory and began to make the rounds, checking to see if the garments were folded neatly on stools.

"That is Katia Sankina," Natasha told Sophie. "The Whites take turns on dormitory duty. Sit down, Katia, and tell us a story."

"You don't deserve any stories," Katia Sankina answered severely. "As for you, new girl," she said, coming close to Masha's bed, "I hope your classmates will teach you not to rummage in other people's desks. Telling tales to Maman. How disgusting!" She turned around and left the room, slamming the door behind her.

"Is he going to pull them out?" Masha asked, so alarmed she forgot her disgrace for a moment.

"Certainly not," the Form Mistress answered surprised. Then she said severely, "I hope you have always cleaned your teeth at home, Fredericks. It is a most important habit."

"Mother made me clean them," Masha answered regretfully, "but Niania thought it unhealthy."

After the dentist, there was a music lesson for Masha and some practicing. It was suppertime when she rejoined the Brown class.

"You have been away a long time," Sophie said, but before Masha could answer Nadia and Varia began to tell Sophie something and make her laugh.

Masha did not try to speak to Sophie any more. She sat over her plate of macaroni and cheese that seemed bottomless and prayed that supper would soon end.

At last it was bedtime. The girls trooped upstairs to the dormitory. Varia read a chapter from the Gospel and said a prayer in French, making Masha wonder whether God understood.

She undressed, fumbling with hooks and buttons, followed the girls to the lavatory, and tumbled into bed. The pillow felt wonderful to her tired head. She closed her eyes, only to open them again as the Form Mistress's voice said, "You are not lying in bed correctly, Fredericks. Turn on your right side, please, and put your arms outside the blanket."

The unexpected remark chased away Masha's sleep. She lay quietly, looking around and listening to the conversations. Natasha Meller was folding her clothes and placing neatly on a stool beside her bed. Lena Mandrika was kneeling on the floor, saying her prayers. Marie Divova was patting on her face something white from a bottle.

"What witch's brew are you using now?" Nadia called.

"It is only almond milk," Marie answered in an offended tone.

"Since you know everything that has ever happened at Smolni, you should also know that in old times the school provided French whiskey for the pupils to wash their faces with. It was supposed to be good for the skin."

"But where did you get the almond milk from?" Nadia wanted to know.

"My cousin Zinaida gave it to me last visiting day," Marie answered loftily. "All the ladies-in-waiting use it."

From Sophie's bed came a sound of argument. "I don't want to wear a nightcap. It gives me headaches," Sophie was saying.

"But you must," Varia Bikova insisted. "It is a rule."

Masha was trying to forget her disgrace by imagining ladies-in-waiting, all in silks and velvets, washing their faces with almond milk. Why didn't they drink it instead? Almond milk was good. She thought about Feklusha pressing the almonds in a small china mortar. The bittersweet smell from Marie Divova's bed reminded her of home.

A white-uniformed girl appeared in the dormitory and began to make the rounds, checking to see if the garments were folded neatly on stools.

"That is Katia Sankina," Natasha told Sophie. "The Whites take turns on dormitory duty. Sit down, Katia, and tell us a story."

"You don't deserve any stories," Katia Sankina answered severely. "As for you, new girl," she said, coming close to Masha's bed, "I hope your classmates will teach you not to rummage in other people's desks. Telling tales to Maman. How disgusting!" She turned around and left the room, slamming the door behind her.

June 23, 1815

CHAPTER ELEVEN

Sophie Intervenes

FOR A MOMENT NO ONE SPOKE, THEN Sashette said scornfully, "Teach her indeed! As if she cared. She could at least cry to show she is sorry!"

Masha swallowed a sob that was coming up in her throat. "I won't cry," she whispered to herself. "I didn't know about the book. I didn't really tell tales."

Sophie began to shout something in answer to Sashette, but Mademoiselle Souchet came in and wished "Bonne nuit" to the girls.

The two oil lamps standing on the tables at each end of the dormitory were extinguished. Only the feeble night-lights were left burning.

"I won't cry," Masha whispered again before falling asleep.

The sharp ringing of a bell awoke Masha the next morning. Around her girls were tumbling out of beds, yawning, untying their nightcaps, and talking in sleepy voices.

Her mind blank, the bell still ringing in her ears, Masha got up and dragged herself to the lavatory. At her approach, Nadia seized her soap and moved to another basin, while Katish pretended to be very busy cleaning her nails.

Masha quickly bent over the nearest basin, splashing cold water into her face until her cheeks cooled and the few furtive tears were washed away.

It would have been nice to linger in the speedily emptying lavatory, but Masha remembered her struggles with the uniform and went back to the dormitory. Another dismal thought suddenly struck her. Mademoiselle Souchet would be speaking only French today. The one day of grace granted to new girls was over.

To her surprise, instead of Mademoiselle Souchet, a heavy, broad-shouldered figure in a blue gown was towering between the rows of beds.

Disconcerted, Masha stopped, vaguely remembering hearing that each class had two Form Mistresses. This one, with a plain, square face and a slight moustache on her upper lip, looked quite a bit older than the Frenchwoman. Her graying hair was arranged in two neat pincushions on each temple and was crowned by a large ruched bonnet.

Gathering her courage, Masha walked up to the blue figure, curtsied, and murmured, "Bonjour, Mademoiselle."

A brisk "Guten morgen, mein kind" made her look up in alarm.

"I am Fraulein Knappe," the Form Mistress said in heavily accented Russian. "You must speak German to me."

"But I don't know German," Masha protested in a shaking voice.

An unexpected twinkle appeared in Fraulein Knappe's gray eyes. "Come, come," she said. "We all say this and then we learn fast. Are you Fredericks or Brozina?"

"Fredericks," Masha murmured.

"Speak up. I can hardly hear you. Well, where is Brozina?"

There were giggles and a group of girls parted, disclosing Sophie sitting on the edge of the bed, her dress hooked the wrong way, her apron askew, her comb over one ear.

At this sorry sight, Fraulein Knappe exclaimed "Himmell" in a deep bass and took one long stride in Sophie's direction. "Such a big girl and can't dress herself. Schandel," she scolded, straightening Sophie's clothes.

"It is not my fault," Sophie defended herself. "My nurse dressed me at home."

Fraulein Knappe folded her hands and addressed the whole dormitory. "Her late Majesty, the Empress Catherine," she said, "used to get up at six in the morning, light the lamp and the fireplace in her study, and work till eight without disturbing any of her attendants. With such an example to follow, I trust there will be no more disgraceful occurrences in this respect."

When the speech was over, the girls curtsied and Masha curtsied too. The Form Mistress smiled and ordered the girls to form ranks.

The Principal, accompanied by Mademoiselle Neigardt, was waiting for the girls in the large hall. There were prayers and then breakfast in the refectory.

Except for a sleepy "Good morning" from Sophie, no one spoke to Masha. She tried to look indifferent as her table neighbors talked across her as if she didn't exist.

"In my boarding school in Paris," Stephanie was saying plaintively, eyeing with distaste her cup of milk, "we had coffee and crusty rolls for breakfast."

"Oh, you've told this to us at least ten times already," Nadia interrupted. "We know all your French menus by heart."

"And talking about rolls makes this slice look even thinner," Natasha complained, holding up a wafer-thin slice of bread and butter.

"Ask for more," Katish suggested.

"One more slice won't help me," Natasha sighed. "I need a whole loaf."

"Must you be so vulgar?" Marie Divova asked disdainfully, taking tiny sips of milk.

"What's vulgar about a good loaf of bread?" Natasha wanted to know. "I can assure you, Marie, that you wouldn't turn up your nose at our country bread, all warm from the oven, Mmm..." She closed her eyes and sniffed. "I can smell it!"

The last remark was too much for Masha. "Mavra used to bake bread for breakfast too!" she exclaimed. "She has a special recipe and..." She met the hostile gazes fixed on her and stopped.

Natasha said coldly, "I was not talking to you" and at the other end of the table someone hissed, "Tattletale!"

"I shall talk to Masha if I want to!" Sophie cried, but Marie Divova turned on her with, "Be quiet, Brozina. After all, you are only a new girl." Her tone was so sharp even Sophie looked subdued.

It took every effort for Masha to put down her untouched cup without splashing the milk.

Varia Bikova said wistfully, "When we had breakfast at home, Father always let me dip a lump of sugar into his coffee."

Sashette gave a short laugh. "I can't say I have such fond memories. Every meal in our house was a nightmare—my stepfather sitting straight as a rod and clinking his spoon against his cup if any of us children dared to whisper a word. My brothers cringing in their seats... The baby was always at the table, too, with her nurse, spilling milk and blubbering—disgusting little thing."

"Your sister?" Marie Divova asked.

"My half sister," Sashette snapped.

Immediately after breakfast several girls were sent to the music rooms for practicing, Sophie among them.

"Your turn will be in the afternoon," Fraulein Knappe told Masha. "Mind you work hard. Mademoiselle Absolom was not pleased with your music. You must have practiced very little at home."

Masha wanted to explain that the piano was out of tune, but decided it did not matter. She said only, "No, not much," and was made to repeat the sentence in German before being allowed to join the rest of the Browns in the garden.

A game of Cat-and-Mouse was going on, accompanied by shrieks of laughter as Nadia, with Lena Mandrika in pursuit, ran in and out of the circle formed by the girls.

Masha did not attempt to join the game. Instead, she skirted the lilac bushes, darted past a fountain, its water rippling in the sunshine, and headed for a small bower surrounded by fir trees. It seemed like a safe place to be alone for a while. But two Blues appeared on the path and went in the same direction. Masha promptly turned back, passed between two tulip beds, pushed aside a low-hanging branch of an acacia tree, and suddenly stopped short. In front of her, in the middle of a small lawn, stood another inmate of the Smolni Institute, one that seemed even newer and more miserable than she.

Her face lighting up, Masha stared at a small birch tree. It looked newly planted, the soil still upturned around the roots. The tree was a poor sight, with its pitifully thin trunk and its small leaves hanging forlornly from scrawny branches.

Masha pushed through the shrubbery and came close to the birch tree. They were of the same height, but she knew enough about trees to realize that they could not be of the same age. A nine-year-old tree would be much taller than a nine-year-old girl.

Masha caressed the drooping leaves with her finger. "Now look here," she whispered, "don't be so unhappy. You feel uncomfortable because you are new, but it will pass. Did you live in the woods before? I suppose the city trees look down on you. But at least they don't call you 'tattletale' I made a terrible mistake, you know, and now the girls will never speak to me again. Here, I am going to tell you exactly what I did. Listen ..."

It was wonderful to tell someone the whole wretched story. Masha hurried on, hardly pausing for breath, the words running into each other.

She ended her tale with, "You see, I have more reason than you to be unhappy. We both feel lonely, so why shouldn't we be friends, special friends? I will come to visit you and I will tell you all my secrets. Wait! I have an idea!"

Stepping on the path, Masha picked up a sharp stone and scratched on the bark "June 23, 1815."

"Now we will never forget the day we first met," she explained to the birch tree. "Please take root and grow. I will do my best too, even though it is hard. I'd better go now. They may miss me. Good-bye!"

As she turned away, to her surprise, she heard someone call her name. Sophie appeared, crashing through the bushes. At last she reached Masha, all breathless, with scratched arms.

"I've been looking for you everywhere," she panted. "Where have you been hiding? Come along! They are in the garden. This is just the right moment because their Form Mistress is not there."

"The right moment for what?" Masha asked, backing away. "I don't want to go anywhere, Sophie. The girls…"

"Do you want to have the whole school against you for the rest of your nine years here?" Sophie cried impatiently. "Come on!"

"I tried to explain…"

"I don't mean to the Browns. They are just a bunch of ninnies. You must explain it to the Whites."

"The Whites?" Masha's eyes became round with terror. "I couldn't."

Sophie stamped her foot. "You must!"

But Masha's temper was roused too. "I am not going anywhere!" she declared, digging her heels into the ground. "So there!"

Sophie did not answer. She simply pounced. The next moment Masha found herself being dragged through the shrubbery, Sophie firmly grasping her arm. They trampled a flower bed, stumbled over a pile of sand, and crashed into the midst of the Whites who were peacefully installed on the stone benches with books and sewing.

Anna Wulff cried out. Clementine Del Pardo dropped her sewing and waved a pricked finger in the air. Two girls jumped off the bench and collided with each other, scattering the contents of their workbaskets. There were several exclamations. "What's the matter? What are you two doing here? Those Browns!"

Sophie pushed Masha forward. "Speak," she hissed into her ear.

But Masha stood silent, blushing furiously and doing her best not to burst into tears.

"Just what do you two children want?" Mania Suvorova asked, a frown on her good-natured face. "Can't we have a moment of peace even during vacation time?"

A fat, freckled girl, eating sweets out of a paper bag, clapped her hands and cried, "Shoo! Shoo!" as if she were chasing away chickens.

"Oh, be quiet!" Clementine Del Pardo snapped. "It's not enough just to shoo them away." She marched up to Masha and seized her by the shoulders. "How did you dare to come here?" she asked angrily. "Do you know what you have done? Anna Wulff has had 100 for conduct all the year through. She was sure of graduating with a gold medal. You may have spoiled it for her. You brat!" She shook Masha, repeating, "You brat!"

"Clem, don't!" Anna Wulff cried, and Sophie shouted, "She did not report you!"

The Spanish girl let Masha go and turned to Sophie. "Prove it!"

"Prove it?" Sophie cried, beside herself. "Just look at her. Look at her face and you will see she didn't, and if you can't see it, then you are stupid, stupid, stupid!" She glared at the astonished Whites and took a step nearer Masha.

"Of all the cheeky little…" Del Pardo began, but Anna Wulff said quickly, "Wait, Clementine. There is no harm in letting the child explain." She bent down and looked into Masha's eyes. "Just tell us exactly what happened," she said gently.

"I was waiting for Mademoiselle Neigardt in your classroom," Masha began in an almost inaudible voice. As she went on, she became more and more sure of herself. "The picture was so pretty. I didn't know it was a wicked book and we were not supposed to talk about it," she pleaded.

Anna glanced at her classmates. "It is not really a wicked book," she said, "just silly, and we were silly to read it."

"Perhaps we were foolish to believe the child deliberately

reported us," the Spanish girl said, studying Masha's dejected figure and imploring expression. "I said all along…"

"Oh, come, Clem," Mania Suvorova protested, "you were the first to scream about 'the little sneak.'"

"Well, it was Sankina who made a scene in the Browns' dormitory."

"A scene! It was because you said…"

"I think," said Anna Wulff in her gentle voice, "that we should have known better than to accuse someone without even asking. The child didn't know what she was doing, that's quite obvious. And we have turned her form against her. It was cruel and thoughtless of us, and now we must put the matter right."

"That's easy. I'll explain everything to the Browns this very afternoon," Suvorova promised. She was going to say something else, but the fat girl mumbled through the sweets in her mouth, "Madame Legarpe!"

"Better run away, children," Anna advised as Madame Legarpe sailed majestically up the path.

The two girls raced toward the Browns' territory. Just outside the lilac bushes, they stopped, took a long breath, and looked at each other.

Masha spoke first. "But I never told you anything about it. How could you be so sure I was not a tattletale?" she asked.

"How?" Sophie mimicked Masha's anxious tone. "Because I am your friend, and a friend always knows."

CHAPTER TWELVE

An Unexpected Visit

THURSDAYS AND SUNDAYS WERE VISITING days at Smolni. During her first few months at school, Masha used to hope that someone would come to visit her. She would sit at her desk, tense, waiting for her name to be called to go downstairs. After all, Olga Kirilovna had promised to visit her in the autumn. It was a big disappointment to receive a letter in September saying that Olga Kirilovna was laid up with rheumatism and could not travel. She was sending her son back to school with a trusted manservant. "I hope to see you sometime in January, dear child," she ended her letter.

At that time January had seemed very far away. Now, in spite of the cold November wind hurtling itself against the classroom windows, it did not seem much nearer.

Masha glanced at the wet snowflakes clinging to the windowpanes and shivered. She could not get accustomed to the low temperature maintained at Smolni. The classrooms and dormitories were cold and the long corridors drafty. It had often been cold at home too, but at least there she was warmly dressed. The low-necked, short-sleeved uniform offered no protection. The pupils were allowed to wear short capes of white linen tied with a bow at the throat, but only in the dormitories and corridors, never in the classrooms.

"The temperature is just right and healthy," Fraulein Knappe would say, looking at the thermometer hanging near the classroom door. For a long time, Masha did not know what the little glass tube meant. After it was explained to her, she came to regard the thermometer as something magic and evil, responsible for the goose pimples on her arms.

The snowflakes became denser. Masha hoped the snow would cover the birch tree and make it warm. It had taken root and was growing. Even now, with only a few yellow leaves clinging to its branches, it looked sturdy and upright. Masha often thought how lucky it was that Maman wanted the girls to run in the garden in almost all kinds of weather. This made it possible for her to snatch a minute or two for a visit with her friend. It was wonderful to have someone to whom she could tell all her secrets, especially since it was not always safe to confide in Sophie. Everything depended on Sophie's moods, and her moods changed so rapidly. Only a few minutes ago she was scowling because she had been deprived of her visiting privileges for drawing a caricature of the Inspectress. Now she was laughing and playing ticktacktoe with Emilia Agte, a relative of Mademoiselle Neigardt. "A very distant relative," Emilia always insisted.

"There won't be any visitors today. No one will come in this weather," Nadia remarked. Her tone was cheerfully indifferent for she never had any visitors herself. "My parents' friends used to bring me sweets and pat me on the head," she had once told Masha. "But after a while, I suppose, they got tired of driving all the way to Smolni, and besides I grew too big to be patted on the head."

In spite of Nadia's gloomy predictions, a student teacher appeared at the door and announced that Marie Divova's cousin was waiting for her downstairs.

"She comes in a court carriage," Marie informed the girls, making them open their eyes wide with wonder and envy.

Katish Muffle went next. The Vuich sisters followed, excited at the prospect of seeing their mother who did not often favor them with a visit. "Mamma is always so busy with dressmakers and hair-dressers," they often remarked sadly.

Sashette was called downstairs to see her godmother. Even Lena Mandrika had a visitor, her uncle who had arrived from Moscow for a few days. "He is very nice but very worldly," Lena confided to Masha as she left the classroom.

Trying not to feel left out, Masha settled down more comfortably at her desk and opened a book. It was a German tale about two girls who chose to help their mother with housework on a holiday instead of playing. Knitting her brows, Masha was trying to figure out whether the girls were washing themselves or helping with the wash when the student teacher came again. Very agitated, she rushed to Fraulein Knappe and instead of speaking German blurted out something in forbidden Russian.

Masha fully expected Fraulein Knappe to draw herself up and say, "I don't understand what you are saying." Instead, the Form Mistress exclaimed, "What?" and dropped her knitting.

Masha tried to listen, but the other girls were talking hard and she could only hear snatches of the conversation. "No, no, there is no rule against it," Fraulein Knappe was saying. "However, it is most unusual… No, it is better to have Mademoiselle Neigardt's approval." She rose and left the room, the student teacher at her heels.

She was back a few minutes later. "Fredericks," she called.

Masha did not move, certain that the Form Mistress was making a mistake. Anything connected with visitors had nothing to do with her.

Fraulein Knappe raised her voice. "Fredericks! I am talking to you!"

Masha came forward.

"Your family's… er… manservant is in St. Petersburg and would like to pay his respects." Fraulein Knappe's tone sounded as if she was not quite sure this was proper. "You may go down."

"Stepan!" Masha forgot to curtsy. She ran to the door in a swish of long skirts, heedless of Fraulein Knappe's, "Gently, gently! Young ladies don't run."

Visitors were received in the big white ballroom encircled with columns. Between every pair of columns was a low wooden balustrade, painted white, with chairs placed on each side. The girls were allowed to talk to their parents and relatives only over the balustrade, and a Form Mistress on duty walked up and down the floor to make sure no letters were passed in either direction. The girls were allowed to accept gifts, but only with the Form Mistress's approval.

A long mirror on the wall caught Masha's reflection as she entered the ballroom. In spite of her haste, she stopped. There was no mirror in the dormitory and only very few girls had hand mirrors. It gave Masha a shock to see herself taller and thinner than she was at home. Her chin looked sharper and her face paler. "Suppose Stepan has changed too," Masha thought in terror. "What if we don't recognize each other?"

She hurried on, past the Brown, Blue, and White girls, who were talking to their visitors. Sashette was talking to a lady in furs and a feathered bonnet. Nearby, Lena Mandrika was sitting primly on the edge of a chair, while a white-haired, ruddy-faced gentleman on the other side of the balustrade seemed to be having a hilarious time. At the farthest end of the ballroom, Masha found Stepan.

At the sight of Masha, he blinked and stared.

Masha stared too, her face slowly breaking into a wide smile. She needn't have feared—this was the same Stepan she had known ever since she could remember, with his calloused hands, the gray lock of hair always falling on his forehead, no matter how well smoothed down with oil. He croaked a greeting and his perpetually hoarse voice brought the echo of the old, low-ceilinged rooms of home into the immense ballroom. It took Masha some effort to persuade him to sit down. He finally obeyed, wiping his hands on his trousers before touching the chair and placing a big gray bundle carefully on the floor beside him.

Clearing his throat between sentences and covering his mouth apologetically with his hand, Stepan explained that his eyes had begun to bother him lately. It got so bad, he couldn't even repair the harness properly any more. Well, one had to get old some day. He was not complaining, but he decided to buy spectacles. It was Mavra who gave him the idea of getting them in St. Petersburg. The nearest town was miles away anyhow and the doctor there was an old rascal, who had sold Mavra's sister-in-law a pair of spectacles made of ordinary windowpane glass and at a good price, too. So, he packed a clean shirt and set off. It was a long way, to be sure, but people with wagons gave him a lift here and there. Now he was staying with his niece, a good girl, married to a carpenter. First thing to do was to visit Masha of course and bring her greetings from home.

"They… they didn't make it difficult for you at the door?" Masha asked, trembling at the idea that Stepan might have been turned away.

"Yes," Stepan admitted, the doorman had refused to let him in at first, but he had explained that he served Masha's family and was allowed to enter. "People usually listen when one talks reasonably to them," he said.

Masha was aware that the girls and their visitors were glancing with curiosity at Stepan, but she ignored the whispers and raised eyebrows. Sitting as close to the balustrade as possible, she was drinking in every bit of home news, resisting the temptation to hurry Stepan as he rambled on at his own slow pace.

He told Masha that the Barinia was in good health. Of course she was sad sometimes. No wonder, with her husband in his grave and her only child far away, but those are God's ways. Mavra was grumbling as usual. Wouldn't let anyone into the kitchen at baking time, thinks too much of herself. Feklusha was getting married. Found a nice man, who just finished his apprenticeship at the blacksmith's in the village. She had begged an old silk gown from the Barinia and was making herself a wedding dress out of it. Imagines that being married in silks will make a barinia out of her. Ha! Stepan was ready to spit, but restrained himself just in time.

"And Niania? How is she?" Masha asked eagerly. "Mamma writes so little about her, just 'Niania is as well as can be expected at her age.'"

Stepan nodded, scratched his head, and remained silent. Only after much pressing did he finally admit that Niania was getting a little queer. She would go to the gates every evening and watch the road, hoping that Masha would return. Then she would go back, moaning, "'I will never see her again. My heart tells me I will not see her again!'"

Masha sat still, looking at the floor. It seemed to her that she could see the cedar avenue in the cold winter twilight, and Niania's gaunt figure wrapped in her black shawl, shivering by the gates. Only she would not be alone. Trezor would be there too, anxiously looking down the road, then back at Niania.

Barely moving her lips, Masha asked, 'Trezor goes to the gates with Niania, doesn't he?"

Stepan mumbled something that sounded like "Yes," and taking an enormous red handkerchief out of his pocket, wiped his face with it, as if he were hot. He took a long time folding the hand-kerchief and putting it away. By the time he finished, Masha was able to speak again. "Tell me every little bit of news," she pleaded. Stepan cleared his throat and launched into the village news. The church was getting a new roof. The shoemaker's widow had married off her youngest daughter. Feklusha's father bought a new plough...

Then it was Masha's turn to tell Stepan about her school life. She was not sure at first that he would understand, but he listened with such deep attention and murmured "Fancy that!" with such feeling that Masha became more and more excited telling about Maman, the Whites, Sophie, and even about her friendship with the birch tree.

Stepan did not look a bit surprised. He said that trees were wise, they knew things. When the fruit trees bloom for a second time in one year, it is a sure sign that their owner is going to die. It is their way of saying good-bye to him. And did anyone ever tell Masha about the fallen oak tree just outside the garden fence? It had crashed down on the eve of Borodino.

Yes, indeed, the trees know...

It was heartbreaking to say good-bye to Stepan when the visiting time was over. He was going to buy his spectacles the next day and start for home immediately after. Before taking leave, he picked up the gray bundle and handed it to Masha over the balustrade.

"This is a gift from Mavra. And this," he said, taking a small flat package from inside his jacket, "is from the Barinia."

Masha glanced around to ask Madame Legarpe's permission, but the Form Mistress only nodded from a distance. Delighted, Masha peeped inside the bundle. "Prianiki!" she exclaimed. "And shaped like animals too! It must have taken Mavra ages to cut them."

"Yes," Stepan agreed. "Mavra spent a whole afternoon cutting the prianiki out and crying. That's the way women are."

He said farewell abruptly and left—a dear familiar figure in his peasant clothes, with slightly stooping shoulders and an uneven gait.

The ballroom was almost empty. Only a few girls lingered, saying good-bye to their visitors over the balustrade.

Masha opened the gray bundle and taking out a prianiki stuffed it into her mouth. It smelled of honey and spices and was surprisingly fresh, considering that it had been baked several days ago. Mavra must have used her special recipe. She picked up the bundle and left the ballroom. She slipped her mother's package into her pocket unopened. She would open it after lights-out, when everybody would be asleep.

On the stairway she met Lena Mandrika, her lower lip thrust out, a big box tied with ribbons under her arm.

"Did you have a pleasant visit with your uncle?" Masha asked.

"He called me 'funny little woman,'" Lena answered in an offended tone.

"But he gave you a lovely box of sweets," Masha pointed out and ran lightly past Lena, hugging her bundle. It was nice of Mavra, she thought, to bake such a lot of prianiki. There will be enough for two rounds. The girls will love them.

She pushed the dormitory door with her shoulder and entered, crying joyfully, "Guess what I have for all of us! Prianiki! We..." She stopped, realizing that nobody could possibly hear her in the noise and laughter that rilled the dormitory.

Sashette was standing in the center of the floor surrounded by a circle of girls, all laughing uproariously at something Sashette was telling them. Moving closer, Masha listened too.

"Honestly, I saw the man myself," Sashette was saying. "Madame Legarpe was on duty downstairs and she almost swooned when she saw him. She glared through that lorgnette of hers as if she expected him to jump the balustrade and attack her. It was so funny!"

"And the man? What was he doing?" several voices cried.

"Oh, he just marched on, like that," Sashette hunched her shoulders, drew her head in, and began to walk, lifting her feet high as if afraid to take a step.

Masha put down her bundle. With two strides she was in front of Sashette, her face drained of color, her blue eyes wild with anger. "Stop that!" she shouted. "How dare you? Stepan came all the way from home to see me, and you... you are mocking him. But you will be sorry for it, you will!" She clenched her teeth and rushed at Sashette. The first blow hit Sashette's shoulder, the second landed smack on her chin.

With a shrill squeal, Sashette jumped back. "You little stupid!" she screamed. "Don't you dare touch me again or I will tell Fraulein!"

Without paying any attention to the threat, Masha fell on her again.

This time Sashette did not wait to be attacked. With a loud scream she ran and stood behind the nearest row of beds. "Take her away!" she shouted. "Don't let her come near me! Call Fraulein Knappe! Call Maman!"

"Masha, don't! You mustn't!" Nadia caught Masha's arm.

Masha tried to wrestle free, but her strength suddenly gave out. She stood with heaving chest and shaking knees.

Nadia turned to Sashette. "You never told us the man was Masha's visitor," she said reproachfully. "You made it sound as if it was someone coming in by mistake."

"How could Sashette know who is visiting whom?" Marie Divova argued in Sashette's defense.

A few girls murmured, "Of course Sashette couldn't really know," but the majority shouted, "Nadia is right. Why didn't you tell us, Sashette? You shouldn't have made fun of him! This is quite different!"

"I don't care," Sashette muttered, "my chin hurts. I am going to report that wildcat to Fraulein right now."

"No you won't," Sophie said, as she pushed her way through the crowd, vaulted the bed, and came close to Sashette. "Not after I am through with you. Masha did not hit you hard enough, but I will."

"Just try and I will report you too!" Sashette screamed, dodging in and out between the beds.

"Sashette! You can't go to Fraulein Knappe! It is not done!" Katish cried, as Sashette ran toward the door.

"Well, what is she expected to do? Wait to be assaulted again?" Marie Divova cried.

"Yes, yes, go ahead, Sashette!" cried the girls in Marie's group, while Masha's supporters yelled, "You daren't! Come back!"

Suddenly, a shrill voice cut through the din, "Tattletale!"

Everyone turned around. Lena Mandrika was standing by the door, her box of sweets under her arm. Her face was prim as usual, and she pointed an accusing finger at Sashette.

Someone began to titter, and in another moment the whole dormitory was rocking with laughter.

Natasha said quickly, "Why don't you say you are sorry, Sashette, and have it over?"

Sashette shrugged her shoulders. "Oh, well, I am sorry, though I don't know what Masha is making such a fuss about."

Masha knew it was her turn to apologize, but she felt it would be a disloyalty to Stepan. "I hope I didn't hurt you badly," was all she could say, to which Sashette retorted angrily, "You did though."

"Oh, don't start it again!" Nadia broke in impatiently. "What have you got in that bundle, Masha?"

The question made Masha promptly put aside the fight. Pink with pleasure, she dipped into the bag and brought out a prianiki shaped like a cat. "See! Isn't it pretty? And there are horses, dogs, pigs, everything! Here, choose, take two," she held the bag out to Stephanie, who happened to be the nearest.

Stephanie shot a quick glance at Sashette, who indicated "No" with her head. "Thank you, but I don't want any," Stephanie said.

"Can't you even decide for yourself?" Emilia Agte cried scornfully, but Sashette had already thrown her arm around Stephanie's shoulders and was leading her away.

"Leave her alone and mind your own business," she flung at Emilia without turning back.

"And don't try to offer any of your stale delicacies to me," Marie Divova called from a safe position behind her bed.

"They are not stale!" Masha cried, tears in her voice. "How can you say so when you have not even tasted them."

"She will find out soon enough!" Sophie snatched a prianik out of the bag, and jumping on the bed, began to stuff it into Marie's mouth. "Eat it! Eat it! Eat it!" she repeated.

With a shout of glee, Nadia also grabbed a prianik and attacked Stephanie. Sashette flew to her friend's rescue, but Varia promptly hung on her arm. In no time, the dormitory became a battlefield. Most of the girls forgot what they were fighting about in the sheer joy of forcing the prianiki into each other's mouths. Lena Mandrika flung herself into the thickest of the melee, using her box as a shield. Even the serious-minded Natasha joined in the skirmish. Terrified, Mary and Ellie Vuich fled and hid behind the window curtains.

Standing aside, the empty bag at her feet, Masha watched through a blur of tears her precious prianiki being trampled underfoot and flung from one end of the room to the other,

It took Fraulein's powerful voice to stop the commotion. At the sight of her, the girls froze in their places, flushed, disheveled, with torn aprons and crumpled skirts. Katish said sheepishly, "It was only in fun. Masha had some goodies sent from the country, and…"

The Form Mistress interrupted her. "A poor idea of fun!" she said. "I am not interested in knowing what it was all about. I only want to ask two questions: First, are you street urchins or young ladies? Second, do you realize that the supper bell is about to ring? Go and tidy yourselves up as best you can. The whole class will stand at suppertime." She ended her speech with a resounding "Schandel" that made even Sophie look ashamed.

Masha did not follow her classmates to the lavatory. Crouching by her bed, hidden from Fraulein Knappe's eyes, she sobbed into her apron. In her hand she clutched the only prianik she had managed to salvage. It was shaped like a dog and reminded her of Trezor, which only made her sob harder.

When the girls started to form ranks to go to the refectory, Masha scrambled to her feet, rubbed her eyes so hard it hurt, and took her place beside Katish.

Katish, looking red and uncomfortable, began, "Masha, we did not mean…"

"Please don't talk to me." Masha's voice was tense with pent-up tears. "Please let me be."

Sophie, who was walking in front, muttered, "It is all Sashette's fault. She started it."

"Oh, Sophie, how can you say so?" Natasha protested. "It was you…"

"No talking in the ranks!" Fraulein Knappe commanded, and everyone became silent.

"Move on, children! Move on!" Madame Legarpe, who was leading her White Form to the refectory and found the way barred by Browns, called impatiently.

Masha took advantage of the confusion. She stepped out of the ranks and started to run down the corridor in the opposite direction from the refectory.

She had barely turned a corner when there were steps behind her and someone caught her sleeve. "Why are you running away?" Anna Wulff asked. "I saw you leave your form a minute ago. You will be in trouble."

Masha looked up, tears streaming down her face. Gulping and swallowing hard, she managed to tell Anna what had happened in the dormitory.

Anna listened attentively, and when Masha finished, she drew her close. "Of course it hurts," she said. "Doubly, because you feel for Mavra as well as for yourself. But do you know something? The girls feel bad now too. In a way they feel worse than you. "Masha shook her head. "They don't care."

"Oh, yes, they do," Anna insisted. "Just give them a chance to say it. And now come with me. I will explain everything to your Form Mistress."

Anna put her hand on Masha's shoulder. "Just promise me you will let the girls say they are sorry," she said. "Remember, you are all going to live together for many more years, and there will be many more times when you will have to forgive each other. Believe me, I have had six years to find this out."

Masha straightened up. "I promise."

She never found out just what Anna told Fraulein Knappe, but she was the only one in her form who was permitted to sit down at supper. All the other Browns had their meal standing. "And we deserve it," Nadia whispered to Masha. "I am so sorry."

It was only the first apology. When the girls came back to the dormitory, Masha found herself surrounded by contrite faces, everyone saying that they did not really mean to spoil the prianiki, that they were sorry...

But the best apology came from Sophie. With a "May I?" she took the last prianik from Masha's bedside table and divided it among the whole form, each girl getting a few crumbs. "Now," she said, "you can write home, Masha, and tell how much we enjoyed your prianiki. This one was delicious and the other ones must have been just as good."

Masha's tear-stained face cleared. "But Mavra, our cook, can't read."

"Your mother can read the letter to her," Sophie consoled, and even Marie said, "Your Mavra is a very good cook, Masha." Sashette did not say a word, but she looked uneasy.

The long day was over at last, and Fraulein Knappe had said "Gute Nacht." Masha waited until her neighbors were asleep and getting out of bed, she crept close to the night-lights. Trying not to make the paper rustle, she took out of the package a square piece of cardboard with a small silhouette-likeness of her mother's head. Aglaya Saburova, the governess for Olga Kirilovna's daughters, must have drawn it for there were the initials A.S. in one corner. The picture was enclosed in a narrow carved frame, probably Stepan's work.

Masha looked at the little black image for a long time, filling the contour with the living features she remembered so well, then bent and kissed it.

A ray of light appeared under the door. The Form Mistress on night duty was making her rounds. Masha kissed the picture again and ran to bed, stumbling on her long nightgown.

CHAPTER THIRTEEN

The Royal Visitors

TOWARD THE MIDDLE OF DECEMBER, HEAVY snowfalls and cold winds made it impossible for the girls to walk in the garden. Breaks were spent in the large recreation hall instead. The Whites walked in couples, talking, the Blues practiced a new step for their dancing class, and the Browns darted across the floor, chasing each other, or trailing the adored ones at the risk of being shooed away.

Masha stood by the window, thinking how cold and lonely the birch tree must be, and repeating the multiplication table at the same time. "Three times seven makes twenty-one," she murmured. "Four times seven…"

"What are you doing all alone?" Nadia asked, coming up to Masha, arm in arm with Katish and Natasha. "Multiplication table? Why? There is no arithmetic class today."

"I know, but it takes me such a long time to memorize all these figures," Masha answered with despair. "They just won't stay in my brain."

"And German verbs won't stay in mine," Natasha sighed. "It is easy for girls like Sophie and Marie Divova, who had governesses at home. My older sisters had a governess too, but my father could not afford one for me. Napoleon's troops took away our horses and cattle and burned our house when they were retreating along the Smolensk road. We are poor now."

"Where do you live now, if you have no house any more?" Nadia asked.

"Father had another one built," Natasha answered. "I hardly remember the old house, but I know it was much bigger than the new one. The foundations can still be seen. Mother always cries when she passes the place."

"Never mind, you are avenged now," Katish consoled. "Wasn't it exciting when Maman told us about Waterloo!"

Masha did not join in the conversation. After almost six months at Smolni, she knew only too well that although many girls called themselves "poor," their families had well-heated houses, many servants, and plenty of clothes. She remembered how surprised Frau Udam, the needlework teacher, had been at her simple remark, "I could not learn embroidery at home. Mother has no money to buy silks."

Frau Udam had said, "Tut, tut," and the girls looked at each other.

It was still worse when she had once said that it was nice to have meat every day. It was not often served at home since it was too expensive. Sashette had remarked in a loud whisper that she did not know "paupers were accepted at Smolni," and the rest of the girls seemed embarrassed. From that day on, Masha stopped talking about home.

"Masha! Nadia!" Sophie appeared, running across the recreation hall, and joined the group, breathless, her apron askew as usual. "I've been looking everywhere for you," she told Masha reproachfully. "Come and listen to something funny, all of you. And you too!" she waved to Lena Mandrika and Varia. "Over here!"

"What is it?" Katish asked curiously, following Sophie into a corner.

Sophie grinned and pulled a creased envelope out of her pocket. "It is a letter from a cousin of mine," she explained. "We played a lot together until he was sent to Cadets' School and I to Smolni."

"You are not supposed to receive letters from boy cousins," Lena Mandrika said virtuously.

"But it is not forbidden to receive a box of caramels from a boy cousin," Sophie answered triumphantly. "Is it my fault that the letter was at the bottom? Now listen, all of you!"

Sophie unfolded the letter and scanned the lines. "Dear Cousin," she read, "mm... Ah, here is the place!"

"Last week, His Highness, the Grand Duke Nicholas, honored us with a visit. He entered our classroom quite unexpectedly, picked up Boris Riabov (he is the youngest in the class and very slightly built), seated him on the teacher's desk, and took off his shoes and socks to see if his feet were clean. The Grand Duke also made several boys open their collars, and he looked at their necks and behind their ears... Thank goodness, my desk is in the back row, so he didn't get to me. I think that on the whole His Highness was pleased with the inspection because he complimented our director on keeping us neat."

Sophie stopped reading and put the letter back into the envelope. Katish and Lena shouted with laughter. Natasha smiled too but said, "Poor little Boris, he must have been terrified."

"Oh, yes," Masha agreed with feeling, remembering a French fairy tale Mademoiselle Souchet had read to the class a few days back. It was all about a terrible ogre. The Grand Duke Nicholas sounded just like him! Tall, reaching the ceiling probably, with a black, furry face and horns, and maybe even wearing the seven-league boots that Niania often mentioned in her tales. "Does the Grand Duke visit Smolni sometimes?" she asked in a small voice.

"I think so," Katish answered indifferently. "Nadia says he often accompanies his mother, the Empress Maria Feodorovna. He is the Emperor's youngest brother."

Masha trembled.

"Are you cold?" Katish asked, rubbing her hands. "I am. It is chilly in here. I hope they are not going to chase us into the garden this afternoon. The sky is clearing."

"They couldn't possibly. The garden is buried in snow," Lena objected.

"They'll lay planks over the snow and we'll be made to walk round and round, like prisoners," Nadia predicted gloomily, warming her hands under her apron.

In spite of Nadia's forebodings, there was no walk in the garden that afternoon. The sky cleared, but the cold wind blowing from the Neva became even colder, so the girls trooped into the recreation hall again for the three o'clock break before study hours.

They were inside for barely a few minutes when Madame Legarpe burst in, followed closely by the Blues' Form Mistress and Mademoiselle Souchet at her heels.

Very agitated, waving her lorgnette, Madame Legarpe cried, "The Empress Maria Feodorovna is here! Order! She is coming with Maman!"

Mademoiselle Souchet tried to collect her Brown flock, who were scattered all over the room, but it was too late. The door opened wide, and the girls nearest the entrance swayed in a deep curtsy.

Pressed against the wall, Masha could not see anything but the backs of two Blues in front of her. She heard voices, a swish of skirts, and a steadily rising murmur, "Nous avons l'honneur de saluer votre Majeste Imperiale."

The Blue girls moved slightly, and Masha saw the Dowager Empress Maria Feodorovna for the first time. Round-eyed, she stared. Somehow, she had always imagined that a dowager Empress would be old and wrinkled, maybe leaning on a stick, like a picture in a book of legends at home. To her surprise, Maria Feodorovna's round, pink face looked quite young under the highly dressed blonde hair that was crowned with an ostrich feather. Around the Empress's neck was a pearl necklace. Tall, sturdily built, and somewhat stout, Maria Feodorovna held herself rigidly erect. One could easily visualize iron-stiff stays under the pale-blue, high-waisted dress. She took short mincing steps, obviously hampered by high-heeled blue shoes that looked too tight for her.

Behind her walked a tall man with somewhat bulging blue eyes and reddish sideburns, dressed in a green and gold uniform with white breeches.

An officer of the Guards and a pretty young girl in a gray silk dress edged with fur brought up the rear.

"Is she a princess?" Masha gasped, her eyes passing from the Empress to the girl and back to the Empress.

Varia, who happened to stand near, laughed. "That is Marie Divova's cousin—the one who graduated from the Catherine Institute in Moscow last spring and has been made a lady-in-waiting. You know... 'my cousin!' Marie is always talking about her."

"But what does a lady-in-waiting do?" Masha asked curiously. "Just walk behind the Empress all the time?"

Varia looked a little vague. "Well, yes, I suppose so. She also reads to the Empress and goes to the theater with her. It is a great honor to be a lady-in-waiting, and just imagine living in a palace! Look at Marie—how she is preening! One would think she was a lady-in-waiting herself."

"Quiet!" hissed Mademoiselle Neigardt, appearing suddenly behind Varia, and the conversation stopped.

Maria Feodorovna reached the middle of the room and addressed the girls. "My dear children," she said, "I am so glad to see you all again." She spoke in French and Masha noticed with interest that the Empress dropped her r's. "I have been indisposed ever since I arrived from abroad, otherwise I would have visited you several days ago. I trust you are studying hard and giving satisfaction to your dear Maman and to your teachers." She smiled and sat down in an armchair that seemed to have appeared by magic.

Immediately, the White and Blue girls rushed forward and made a tight circle around the Empress, who called them by their names and asked them about their studies and news from home.

Masha saw Sophie and threaded her way toward her friend. "Who is that man with the Empress?" she asked in a whisper.

"Nadia just told me it is the Grand Duke Nicholas," Sophie whispered back, and added with a giggle, "Do you think he is going to take off our shoes?"

"The ogre?" Masha gasped. To her terror, the Grand Duke took a step in the direction of the Browns, saying gaily, "And here is our new crop! Any war orphans among you?"

The group of girls around Masha stepped back, leaving her exposed. She realized that the dreaded moment had come. The ogre would pick her up and take off her shoes and stockings. For a second she stood transfixed. But when the Grand Duke asked, "What is your name?" and bent over her, she whirled around and with a shriek started to run, pushing her way through the crowd of girls.

Anna Wulff stepped out to grab Masha as she ran past her, and the situation would have been saved if Mademoiselle Souchet had not lost her head and dashed after the fugitive.

Hearing steps behind her gave Masha wings. She had no doubt at all it was the ogre, chasing her in his seven-league boots. Wrenching herself free from Anna, she tore madly across the recreation hall, Mademoiselle Souchet after her, both heedless to calls and exclamations, "Masha, stop! Fredericks! Mademoiselle!"

In the middle of the hall, Masha stepped on her long skirt and fell down just as Mademoiselle Souchet was about to catch her. Carried away by her own speed, the Frenchwoman almost fell on top of Masha, but was caught and supported by Mademoiselle Neigardt's iron hand.

The Inspectress gave Masha a look that was quite sufficient to make her swallow her sobs and hastily scramble to her feet. Mademoiselle Neigardt led her by the hand, while the Form Mistress followed, breathing heavily and pushing stray hairpins into place.

Masha was sure that Maman would be outraged, but there was nothing except endless patience on the Principal's face. She calmly told Masha to use her handkerchief, then she straightened her round comb, and presented her to the Empress.

Out of a corner of her eye, Masha could see the Grand Duke talking to Sophie and laughing at something she was telling him. It did not look as though he would be taking off Sophie's shoes after all.

"Come here, my dear," Maria Feodorovna said, extending a chubby hand and drawing Masha closer.

Masha looked at the dimples on the Empress's pink cheeks and at her kind blue eyes. But ill at ease under the serious gaze of Maman, and feeling the Inspectress's eyes on her back, she answered Maria Feodorovna's questions almost in a whisper. Yes, she was nine years old; yes, her father was killed at Borodino; no, she had no brothers or sisters.

The Empress smiled, gave Masha a light pat on the head, and said, "I know that little by little you will become used to the life here, my dear, and Smolni will become your real home."

Masha was not of the same opinion, but before she could answer, the Principal made her a sign to curtsy and give her place to Stephanie.

As she backed away, Masha heard Maria Feodorovna say to the Principal in German, "I see what you mean. A nice child, but very countrified. No wonder she became intimidated to the point of running away."

The Grand Duke Nicholas made no attempt to come near Masha again. He only smiled at her from a distance and playfully shook his finger at her.

Masha was pondering the Empress's words when two Whites standing near her nudged each other and whispered, "Look! Nelidova!"

Fascinated, Masha watched a small woman, with a slight, almost childish figure, dressed in an old-fashioned gray dress with hoops, slip into the hall and creep along the walls in the direction of the Empress. She passed close to Masha, giving her a serious look out of enormous black eyes that seemed to take up half of the plain little face.

Maria Feodorovna seemed very pleased to see the strange woman. She kissed her warmly and made her sit on a footstool near her chair. Marie Divova was introducing her cousin to a few selected schoolmates. Masha did not attempt to join the group. She knew only too well she would not be welcome. But she listened eagerly from a distance as the girl described a ball in the palace. It did sound like a fairy tale!

The royal visit soon ended. As Maria Feodorovna was leaving, the pupils ran after her, kissing her hands and pleading with her to come again soon.

"I certainly will," the Empress said, smiling. Then, standing in the doorway of the hall, she waved to the girls and called, "And now good-bye, the Browns, the Blues, and the Whites!" She waved again and was gone, the Grand Duke, Maman, and the others in her wake.

The girls gave poor attention to their lessons that afternoon. Whispered conversations kept running behind the opened books. Mademoiselle Souchet only made a slight effort to keep discipline. She sat at her table, red-eyed, pressing a handkerchief soaked in aromatic oils to her temples. She disappeared as soon as the girls went to the dormitory for their free hour from five to six.

"Did you see my cousin Zinaida? Isn't she attractive? And her dress! Did you notice that ruche at the throat?" Marie exulted.

"Oh, yes, she is beautiful!" several voices answered, but the girls were really more interested in the mysterious lady called Nelidova.

"Why didn't you tell us about her before, Nadia? You must have known all along," Natasha reproached.

"I simply forgot all about her," Nadia defended herself. "She only appears in public when Maria Feodorovna is visiting. She has an apartment in Smolni and her meals are brought to her. Her first name is Katerina. She used to be a pupil. Her class was the first to graduate from Smolni."

"She was one of the first pupils?" Sashette exclaimed. "She couldn't be. She is not old enough."

"She looked as old as the hills to me," Katish argued.

Several girls joined in, saying, "To me too!" while the others protested, "No, no, she looked quite young!"

Looking back, Masha could not decide whether Nelidova looked young or old to her. She was just a gray shadow. "How strange," Masha thought, "if Nelidova should never die, but continue to live in Smolni forever and ever…"

"But why didn't she leave the school after she graduated?" Sophie wanted to know. "Why would she stay on here?"

Nadia took her favorite and strictly forbidden position on the top of her bedside table. "Nelidova left with the rest of her class," she explained, "and became lady-in-waiting to the Emperor Paul's wife, Natalya Aleksievna, who died very young. Then Nelidova became lady-in-waiting to Maria Feodorovna, Emperor Paul's second wife."

Masha did not know much about the Emperor Paul. She listened fascinated.

"I think I remember my father talking about Nelidova one day," Marie Divova remarked. "She was a great friend of the Emperor Paul. People used to call her his guardian angel. It seems that many a time when he was about to commit an injustice, she stopped him."

Varia murmured, "He was assassinated, wasn't he?"

Nadia lowered her voice. "Yes. A girl in the White class told me the whole story. Her uncle was among the conspirators. They wanted him to renounce the throne, but he wouldn't sign an abdication, so they strangled him. It happened in 1801. Not so very long ago really."

"Oh, how horrible!" Stephanie squeaked.

"She also told me," Nadia went on with relish, "that… that…" she stammered and became silent as Mademoiselle Souchet suddenly appeared in front of her.

"What is the meaning of this conversation?" she screamed at Nadia. "You know very well that it is forbidden to mention this subject. And climbing on the table in the bargain! Take off your apron. Immediately! You will go down to supper without it."

Nadia opened her mouth to protest, but looked at Mademoiselle Souchet and changed her mind. Slipping off the table, she silently untied her apron and laid it on a stool.

She stood at supper and the rest of the form found it difficult to eat. There was no usual rampage when the girls went to bed that evening.

Nevertheless, it became a habit in the Brown Form, after lights-out, to talk about the Emperor Paul, Nelidova, and the assassination—whispered stories passing from bed to bed.

Christmas at Smolni

WHEN NADIA TOLD MASHA THERE WOULD be a Christmas tree at Smolni, Masha looked blank. After Nadia had described the beauty of the tree, she said firmly, "I don't believe it."

"But why not?" Nadia asked, astonished. "Haven't you ever seen one?"

Masha shook her head. "No, I haven't. Niania used to tell me about a tree with golden apples growing on it, but that was a fairy tale. You are telling me a fairy tale too."

Nadia laughed good-naturedly. "Oh, well," she said, "you will see for yourself."

On Christmas Eve the girls spent a long time in the dormitory cleaning their nails and brushing each other's hair.

"In the times of the Empress Catherine, the pupils wore silk uniforms on festive days," Stephanie remarked longingly, looking at herself in a small hand mirror.

"And they were invited to the palace for dances," Sashette put in. "They were not locked up like in a convent."

"Well, who would want silk uniforms?" Nadia objected.

Masha knew this was the beginning of the usual argument. The form was divided into two camps—the admirers of Maria Feodorovna, and those devoted to the memory of the Empress Catherine. The second group was mostly made up of girls whose mothers or aunts had been pupils at Smolni.

Varia looked up from her reading. "And they studied The Rights of a. Human Being and Citizen instead of our silly Advice to My Daughter," she said resentfully. "And had lessons in natural history. But Maria Feodorovna considers it unsuitable for girls."

Natasha Meller spoke from her bed, where she was sitting, a dreamy look on her face. "I wish I could be with my family," she said. "It used to be such fun preparing gifts for our parents. Once my oldest sister made up a play and we all acted in it. Neighbors came and brought their children…"

"My cousin Zinaida told me," Marie Divova said, "that in the palace each member of the imperial family has a personal tree with gifts underneath it. She also said that the ladies-in-waiting get such beautiful gifts, bracelets, and brooches."

"How wonderful!" Stephanie sighed. "I love pretty things."

"We always had a beautiful Christmas tree in our family," Katish told the others, while she brushed her thick blonde hair. "We danced and ate so many sweets I was often sick the next day."

Masha thought about her own Christmas at home. There was no dancing, but there was a spicy smell in the kitchen and little gifts on her bedside table—a pair of pretty knitted mittens from her mother, a ribbon from Feklusha…

She was deep in memories when Katish nudged her. "You haven't been listening. Marie Divova says that last Christmas her parents gave a children's ball for her."

"Just like for grown-ups," Marie was saying. "Flowers, favors, everything, and then supper. Boys, I mean gentlemen, led the ladies to the table. What about you, Sophie? Did you have a children's ball too?"

Sophie did not answer immediately, and when she spoke, her voice had none of its usual gay bantering tone. "No," she said. "Papa always sent me out to parties with my governess, but I don't remember having a party at home. I just can't imagine a children's ball in our house. It is…" she frowned, "I don't know how to describe it… It is a hushed house, heavy curtains and draperies everywhere, dark paintings on the walls, big, heavy furniture. Oh, my rooms were gay enough, but the rest of the house was always half dark and… and smelled lonely, somehow. A maid told me that when my mother was alive, there were always guests and music, but after she died, my father kept to his study, or was away with his regiment." She rubbed her forehead. "Strange how far away it all seems already. Maybe it is just my imagination and the house was not so dark after all."

"Well, I remember our house in Odessa only too well and it certainly was not dark." Sashette kicked a stool with the toe of her shoe. "On the contrary, there was much too much light. My stepfather considered curtains unhealthy. It seems to me there was always a glare, of sun in summer and of snow in winter." She kicked the stool again. "How I hated those bare rooms. This dormitory seems cozy compared to them."

"Cozy?" Natasha exclaimed. "You can't mean it, Sashette."

"Oh, yes, I do." Sashette spoke vehemently. "No rugs, no knick-knacks, no pictures, no toys. They all accumulate dust. That was my stepfather's rule, and my mother obeyed it too, because she admires every word of his."

Masha noticed the girls exchanging surprised glances. Sashette very rarely spoke of her family. Masha almost felt sorry for her, but Sashette did not let the feeling last long.

"How do you feel in festive shoes, Fredericks?" she asked, admiring her own slender foot in the black satin slippers the Browns had been issued for the party. "You ran barefoot at home, didn't you? Or did you wear shoes on big occasions?"

Before Masha could answer, the door opened and Fraulein Knappe appeared, very dignified in a rustling blue silk dress, an orange bow pinned to her left shoulder.

Nadia nudged Masha. "Look! The bow means she has served twenty-five years. Isn't it nice?"

"Ye... yes," Masha answered doubtfully. It seemed a long time for an orange bow.

Mademoiselle Souchet came in too, though not on duty that day. Her gown was not the regulation blue, but much paler, and her hair was arranged in such intricate ringlets and puffs that the girls gasped.

"Now you will see..." Nadia whispered to Masha as they were walking down the stairway.

The ballroom doors were wide open. Masha saw something green and tall, ablaze with candles, smelling of pine, resin, and melted wax.

"I told you!" Nadia hissed, almost stepping on the back of Katish's shoes as she walked behind her. "Isn't it lovely?"

Masha did not answer. Clasping her hands, she went down on her knees in front of the tree. Her mother had often told her the story of how the Three Wise Men came to Bethlehem and adored the infant Christ. She was never sure just what the word "adored" meant. Now she knew.

Fraulein Knappe exclaimed, "Fredericks!" The Browns stopped short, falling over each other to get a better look at Masha. The Blues and the Whites, who entered the ballroom later, kept asking, "What is it? What has happened?"

It was Mademoiselle Neigardt, appearing from nowhere, who jerked Masha up, not too gently. "You really should teach that child more restraint," she snapped at Mademoiselle Souchet, and was going to say something more, but at the sight of the Frenchwoman's elaborate coiffure, words seemed to fail her.

Fraulein Knappe did not look really annoyed. "Is it the first time you have seen a Christmas tree?" she asked Masha, and answered herself, "Yes, I can see it by your face."

The girls formed two large semicircles around the tree. Masha took her place beside Katish just as the Principal came in, dressed in a silvery gray gown and lace bonnet, so big and airy it seemed ready to fly away. She wished the girls a "Very Happy Christmas" and announced that the Empress Maria Feodorovna had graciously sent gifts for the pupils. At these words, two maids entered carrying an enormous hamper piled with pretty bonbonnieres. Behind them came two more maids with an even larger hamper, full of golden yellow balls.

Masha could not believe her eyes. Here were the golden apples Niania had told her about. She touched Mademoiselle Souchet's sleeve. "It is not a fairy tale then?" she asked.

"Comment?" Mademoiselle Souchet bent over Masha. "What is not a fairy tale?"

"The golden apples." Masha pointed at the hamper.

Mademoiselle Souchet rolled her eyes in despair. "These are oranges, Fredericks, not apples. Oh, dear me, I know you lived in the country, but still…"

"They did not grow in our garden, truly," Masha tried to explain, but the Form Mistress only waved her hand and started to laugh.

The school chorus sang a Christmas prayer and Maria Feodorovna's gifts were distributed. Masha's bonbonniere was shaped like a small basket, made of pale green velvet, and filled with sweets. She put it on a small table beside her and bit into her orange, wondering why such a beautiful fruit tasted so bitter. Someone behind her laughed and Anna Wulff said, "Wait until I peel it for you, then you will see how sweet it is. And here is something from me to you." She kissed Masha and handed her a small package.

Masha eagerly unwrapped the package. Inside was a little wooden doll in a red dress made of crinkled paper. She pressed it to her heart. "Thank you so much," she told Anna. "I will take good care of her. I promise she will be happy with me."

"I am quite sure she will," Anna answered seriously, giving Masha the peeled orange before running away to join her classmates.

The older pupils took turns playing on two pianos, while the rest danced around the tree or sat talking and eating sweets. Maids passed trays with biscuits and lemonade.

"Leave that doll somewhere and come to dance," Sophie urged, but Masha refused to part with her gift. After watching Sophie dance away with Katish, she found a small sofa for two in a quiet corner, and settled there with her doll and the orange to watch the tree glowing in the center of the darkened ballroom.

Soon she made a wonderful discovery. If she looked at the tree with her eyes half closed, with only the long beams of candlelight seeping through her lashes, she could see her mother sitting in place of Madame Adlerberg, with Niania at her side. She could even distinguish Mavra and Stepan standing in the shadow of the branches, and Feklusha peering over Mavra's shoulder. Trezor was there too of course, sniffing at the ornaments hanging from the lower branches.

"Are you asleep, child?"

Masha started and opened her eyes wide. Nelidova, in the same quaint gray dress, was sitting down beside her on the sofa. "No, I..." she stammered, "I was just looking at the candles and thinking about my mother, and Niania, and the others at home."

"And seeing them," Nelidova said quietly.

Masha started again. "Yes."

Nelidova did not seem to hear her. She sat, her head bent, looking at her hands, without a single ring or bracelet, lying in her lap. "When I was a small child, in my first year at Smolni," she said, "I used to play a strange game. I would stand by the window on foggy days, my chin barely reaching the windowsill, and stare at the fog, until I could see my family's faces. Sometimes I could see them very clearly. But as I grew older, they went back into the fog, never to return."

Masha listened without surprise.

Nelidova went on talking to herself rather than to Masha. "My home was in the country. I remember the river flowing under big shady trees. It was called Tzaritza-Voditza. Years have gone by, the house is no more, but the river is still flowing."

144

The name fascinated Masha. A river called Tzaritza-water sounded like magic. She longed to ask more about it, but was afraid it might not be respectful.

Nelidova suddenly turned to her. "What is your name? And this lady's?" she nodded gravely at the doll seated on Masha's knee.

Masha proudly presented the doll. "This is Anya. I gave her that name because Anna Wulff gave her to me. I am Masha, I mean Maria Fredericks." She scrambled off the settee and curtsied.

Nelidova smiled. "Anna Wulff is very kind," she said. "A little girl can be very lonely without a doll. In my time, the school provided dolls for the Brown Form. Of course, we were much younger when we entered. I was barely six and some of my classmates could not even speak properly. Do you like being a pupil at Smolni?"

"I didn't at first," Masha answered frankly. "Now I think I like it. Maybe I will love it one day. Nadia Maslova does."

Nelidova sighed. "Maybe you will, but when the day comes for you to leave, leave for good. Whatever the world may offer you, take it. Now run and dance." She rose and gave Masha a slight push toward the gay crowd.

The Browns saw Masha coming and several voices cried, "Where have you been hiding? Come quickly! What was in your bonbonniere?"

"Sweets," Masha answered, wonderingly.

Sophie laughed. "You'd better look more carefully."

Curious, Masha poked with her finger. Something small and round, wrapped in silver paper, was buried among the bonbons. She drew it out. It was a ring with a shiny green stone.

"What is it?" Natasha came running up. "Oh, a ring. I got one too. Only mine has a red stone."

"I got earrings." Sophie lifted them in the air. "And Katish has a bracelet."

Fraulein Knappe shook her finger from a distance. "Mind, those trinkets are not to be worn," she said severely. "They are only to play with."

Masha stared at the ring in her palm. "To play with? But it must be very valuable," she exclaimed.

The girls laughed. "You don't really think it is gold?" Sophie cried. "It's made of brass and the stone is glass."

Masha did not hear. The green stone caught the light of the candles and she held her breath in wonder. The soft green gleam was just like the lamp in Mamma's study. It was a magic ring. It did not matter in the least what it was made of.

The Easter Concert

T HE CHRISTMAS HOLIDAYS WERE NOT LONG. After ten days of rest and festivities, Smolni settled down again to lessons, practicing, recesses, and visiting days.

Everyone was studying hard. Examinations were looming ahead, sometime in April. The Browns had been told that after their first year the pupils with too many bad marks would not be allowed to slow down the good students. Instead they would have lessons in a separate form called "The Second Division." The Blues and the Whites also had a Second Division, or a "Dunce Class," as Sophie had promptly christened it.

"Don't let me hear that silly name again," Fraulein Knappe chided Sophie. "There is no disgrace in being in the Second Division. Not everyone learns quickly." But the name had stuck.

"It is bad enough to work all the time, and now there is fasting as well," Sophie grumbled as Lent began. She pouted at her plate of fish cakes. "Fish, fish every day, and boiled cabbage, boiled potatoes, boiled everything, or fried with that awful oil. Ugh, and the pea soup! I hate it!"

"You are not supposed to say 'ugh' about Lenten dishes," Lena Mandrika remarked with a reproachful glance. "It is a sin."

"Oh, don't preach!" Sashette snapped at Lena. "I hate Lenten food too. It reminds me of our meals at home. Oh, not for grown-ups! My stepfather is a real gourmet. But he considered that children should eat what he called 'plain food.' That was another one of his health ideas. Mother used to give us sweets in secret because my stepfather did not allow it. Once he caught my younger brother sucking a caramel. He kept him on bread and water for two days as punishment."

"How terrible!" Natasha exclaimed. "It was quite different in our house. Every week each of us children had a right to order his or her favorite dessert."

"Suppose we could order any dessert we wanted right now, what would you choose?" Sophie asked Nadia.

"Blancmange," Nadia answered promptly.

"Raspberry jelly!" Katish cried. "And you, Masha?"

Masha said "Baked apples" at random, and was glad that no one asked her anything more. She was in no mood for talking. A letter from her mother had come that morning with sad news. Olga Kirilovna's husband had died suddenly. Poor Olga Kirilovna was not feeling too well herself. Aglaya had been a great help to her during her husband's brief illness. It was unlikely that Olga Kirilovna would be coming to St. Petersburg now, or at least not for a long time. Her husband had left much less money than was expected, and Olga Kirilovna was struggling to put the estate in order.

The girls continued to grumble about the Lenten food, the long church services, and the absence of any kind of amusements. "We can't even read storybooks," Varia complained bitterly, "only the Gospels." Masha did not care. On the contrary, the darkened church and the hushed voices fitted in with the feeling of loneliness and sadness that now seemed to be constantly with her.

But as the last week of Lent dragged to an end, Masha's spirits began to rise. There was a breath of spring in the air and she was looking forward to the Easter festivities.

Good Friday was cold and rainy, but on Saturday morning the sky began to show patches of blue, and by the afternoon the sun was shining.

For the first time in her life, Masha attended the midnight Easter service. At home, the village church was too far and the spring rains often made the road impassable.

The Browns were sent to bed at five in the afternoon and awakened at eleven. The holiday aprons were edged with lace, and the girls' faces and hair shone from soap and brushing.

The service was celebrated in one of the towers of the monastery called "the children's church." Everyone carried a candle. As the pupils mounted the long stairway leading to the church, Masha glanced back and saw a moving sea of flickering lights. All through the service she stood in a daze beside Sophie, listening to the singing that seemed to fly toward the dark sky behind the windows.

Loaded tables awaited the girls as they came back to school. There were heaped dishes of colored eggs, several round loaves of sweet bread called Kulitch, as well as Pashas, made of cream cheese, shaped like pyramids and smelling of vanilla.

Maman wished the pupils a Happy Easter and the feast began.

"I used to help color eggs at home," Natasha was saying. "It was such fun! Mother scratched all kinds of designs on them with a quill."

"And we wrapped our eggs in silk rags before boiling so the colors and designs on the silk came off. It was so pretty!" Katish sighed.

"Mavra wrapped our eggs in onion skins. It was pretty too, all golden red," Masha joined in.

"That is the way poor people usually color their eggs," Sashette remarked casually to Stephanie.

Ellie and Mary Vuich protested that this was not true. They were not poor, but their cook always colored eggs with onion skins.

149

Masha said nothing. It did not really matter what Sashette thought of her, but the words hurt.

Sophie watched Sashette through narrowed eyes. "Are you all ready for the tableaux tomorrow?" she asked sweetly.

Sashette shrugged her shoulders. "My costume is ready, if that is what you mean. Of course my face and arms will have to be whitened at the last minute. I am so glad I am not going to be blackened with soot like you."

"Oh, I don't mind," Sophie answered airily. "I think it is more fun to be a chimney sweep than a statue."

"Aren't you two lucky to be in the tableaux!" Katish exclaimed. "Imagine taking part in the Easter concert! All the rest of the performers are Whites or Blues."

"Yes," Sophie agreed pensively. "It is an excellent chance."

"An excellent chance for what?" Katish wanted to know, but Sophie only laughed.

Easter Sunday was a peaceful day. The younger girls rolled eggs in the recreation hall, using them like marbles. The older students were solemnly presenting "Easter Balls" to their favorite teachers and Form Mistresses.

The art of making Easter Balls was taught to the first Smolni pupils by the nuns. They were made of silk and embroidered with intricate patterns.

"One day we will be able to make them too," said Natasha, who loved needlework.

Maria Feodorovna sent a basket of beautiful china eggs to Smolni, and each pupil received one. Masha's egg was pale blue with lilies of the valley painted on it. Lena Mandrika's egg had a little panorama of the Resurrection on one side.

On Easter Monday preparations began for the concert. There was a final rehearsal. Costumes were tried on once more and last touches put on them.

"The Empress Maria Feodorovna is expected," Nadia informed her classmates as they were tidying themselves in the dormitory.

"My cousin Zinaida wrote me that the Emperor Alexander is back from Paris and may be present too," Marie Divova announced. "Isn't it exciting? He hasn't visited Smolni since we've been here."

"He was away in Vienna for the... the Congress," Varia said. "And then he was in Paris. Isn't your cousin lucky, Marie! Imagine sitting at the same table with the Emperor! I do hope he will be able to come with Maria Feodorovna."

"But why doesn't the Emperor's wife, I mean the Empress Elizaveta Aleksievna, ever come?" Masha wondered aloud. "Why only his mother?"

"I often wondered myself," Varia answered. "Has she ever visited Smolni, Nadia?"

"Never in my time," Nadia mumbled through the pins in her mouth, as she tried to pin on a shoe ribbon. "Bother, it is off again!"

"She drives in a plain carriage with only two horses," Mary Vuich remarked. "We saw her several times when we were driving with Mother. She looks beautiful, but so sad!"

Masha thought she would have liked to see the Empress who was always sad, but soon forgot all about her in the excitement of waiting for the concert to begin.

It was late afternoon and still daylight outside, but the ballroom was darkened, with only one chandelier burning. The girls occupied the back seats. Maria Feodorovna's ostrich feather could be seen above the back of a gilt chair placed in front of the stage. Beside her loomed the white bonnet of Madame Adlerberg. The Grand Duke Nicholas had sent word that he would be in a little later.

At last the curtains parted, revealing stately Mania Suvorova in a rich costume of Russian bayards, reclining on cushions, while the dark Del Pardo, dressed like a Gypsy, was telling her fortune on cards.

In the next tableau, Anna Wulff, all in white, golden wings on her back, stood over a sleeping girl menaced by a cardboard snake. The tableau was called The Guardian Angel

Masha held her breath. Sophie's tableau was to be next. The

curtains parted once more. "How charming!" someone in the audience said.

A small black chimney sweep, with a ladder on his back, stood near the front of the stage, gazing with admiration at a white statue on a marble stand.

A ray of light, cunningly contrived to look like a moonbeam, shone on the "statue," showing five black fingers clearly imprinted on the white cheek. Laughter rippled through the ballroom and soon became uproarious.

Sashette stood without flinching, but her eyes blazed.

Masha suddenly became aware of a group of men standing near her in the aisle, laughing and applauding. She recognized the Grand Duke Nicholas. Beside him stood another man, also in the green and gold uniform, but more slender, with a round face and sparse blond hair, looking just like the big painting on the ballroom wall.

Masha seized Nadia's sleeve. "Look!" she whispered, "there on your right. Isn't it the Emperor Alexander?"

At the same moment, several servants hurried in with candelabra. The curtains that were just closing parted again, and the audience began to scramble to their feet. Madame Adlerberg came hurrying up the aisle and the Emperor smilingly went forward to meet her.

Several girls tried to leave their seats, but were sternly waved back by their Form Mistresses. The candelabra were extinguished and the performance was resumed.

There were two more tableaux, then a few minutes' intermission, during which a large piano was rolled on the stage. Two Whites played a piece, then Del Pardo sang a Spanish song. Katia Sankina played the harp, and the school's best soprano, a slight, very plain girl from the Blue Form, sang an aria from Gluck's Orfeo ed Euridice.

As a finale, the entire White Form danced a garland dance, waving wreaths of artificial flowers and forming a giant letter A in the middle of the stage.

"We were really supposed to form the initials M.F.," Anna Wulff told Masha later, "as the Emperor was not expected, but Maman asked the dance teacher to make a change. We had to have a short rehearsal behind the stage."

After the final curtain, Maman presented the performers to the Emperor. He favored each one with the famous smile that had charmed the Congress of Vienna, accompanied by a few gracious words. When Sashette and Sophie appeared, he thanked them for their "most original tableau" and his blue eyes twinkled.

The rest of the girls eagerly pressed forward, restrained only by Maman's stern gesture.

When the last performer had backed away, the Emperor turned to Maman saying, "I would like now to greet the other young ladies."

He had hardly finished speaking when the girls precipitated themselves upon him, each one eager to get as near as possible to the royal guest. Masha was almost swept off her feet, but there was too much joyous excitement to be really frightened. She simply picked herself up and joined the crowd, darting between the older girls.

It was not easy for the Emperor to leave the ballroom. The girls ran after him, waving, calling, pleading with him to stay a little longer. Someone's daring hand snatched at a button on the green uniform, but it held firm.

Maman's stern "Mesdemoiselles, you forget yourselves!" was lost in the hubbub of voices and laughter.

The Emperor laughed too and taking a handkerchief out of his pocket, threw it in the air. A forest of hands grabbed at it and a lively skirmish followed while the Emperor escaped.

When the combatants dispersed—the few lucky ones clutching bits of linen—the Emperor was gone. In the middle of the floor, Lena Mandrika lay full length, with most of the handkerchief in her hand.

"Behold the future saint!" Suvorova exclaimed, laughing.

"I could have snatched it away from her. I was right behind, only I didn't want to," Sophie boasted.

Masha suddenly remembered the tableau of the statue and the chimney sweep. "Oh, Sophie, never mind the handkerchief," she whispered anxiously, catching her friend by her apron strings. "Better think what you are going to say to Maman when she asks you about putting that black mark on Sashette's face."

"There will be no need to say anything. Sashette will see to it," Sophie answered calmly.

"I don't know what you mean," Masha said helplessly, but Sophie was right after all.

As soon as the girls were in the dormitory, Stephanie rushed to Sashette, exclaiming, "Poor dear! How terrible it must have been for you to be ridiculed on the stage. That Sophie…"

Sashette gave her friend a cold stare and interrupted her with a dry, "What's so terrible? Sophie happened to touch my face when we were taking our places on the stage. I am sure everyone realized it was an accident. I have already explained it to Maman."

"What did I tell you?" Sophie whispered into Masha's ear. "Accident indeed! I pressed my whole palm hard against her cheek when she was already on that marble stand and could not escape, but she is too proud to admit I made fun of her."

There was grudging admiration in Sophie's voice.

Reassured about her friend's fate, Masha switched her mind to another problem that had been worrying her for the last few days. Fraulein Knappe had said that tomorrow, at last, the girls would be allowed to run about the garden instead of sticking to the paths. This meant that Masha would be seeing the birch tree for the first time after the long winter months. She felt she should bring a gift to show her friend she had not forgotten even though they had been separated.

Lying in bed, her eyes half closed, Masha thought it all over again. Yes, a gift would be a wonderful idea, but "what to give? Not Anya, of course. Masha looked fondly at the doll nestled beside her under the blanket. Leaving Anya by the tree would be just like one of those human sacrifices she had read about in the history book one of the Blues left on a garden bench. Her Easter egg maybe? But a china egg tied to a branch would be sure to attract attention, and that would never do. Masha's friendship with the birch tree was a secret, a big wonderful secret. The gift should be something quite small... Small? Instinctively, Masha put her hand under the pillow and drew out her magic ring. The ring would be just the right gift. It would be hard to part with it—but could one begrudge a gift to a special friend?

When Masha woke up the next morning, she had the ring clutched in her hand and her mind was made up.

Lessons dragged that morning. The break never seemed so long in coming. Masha sprang to her feet the minute the bell rang, earning Fraulein Knappe's sharp, "Watch your manners, Fredericks."

Spring air had never tasted so good. The girls scattered all over the garden, inspecting every corner and calling to each other, "Look, the bulbs are already sprouting! No water in the fountain yet. Oh, there is Suvorova's thimble lying at the bottom. Remember how she dropped it last summer?"

To Masha's relief everyone gathered around the fountain to watch the two Whites, who were trying to get the thimble out with a long stick. She picked up her skirt and, diving between two lilac bushes, ran toward the familiar round lawn. A few more steps and she saw the birch tree. It was there, waiting for her.

"Oh, how gorgeous you look!" Masha exclaimed, admiring the small new leaves, sticky to touch, and the sturdy branches. The date on the bark was still legible, though slightly blurred.

"I am so glad to see you," Masha began, gasping after her run. "I missed you so much. I even wrote you a note once and threw it out of the window, but I suppose the wind never carried it to you. Never mind, I will visit you every day now and tell you about the Christmas tree and everything. You can't imagine how beautiful it was, but you mustn't be jealous. The Christmas tree is dead now while you are alive and happy. I know you are happy. I can see you laugh at the sun. Now look what I brought you!" Masha opened her palm and disclosed the ring. "It is magic," she whispered, "but I will give it to you because you are my best friend."

Standing on tiptoe, Masha selected a slender but strong twig well out of sight, and slipped the ring on it. "There!" she said triumphantly. "It is yours now."

The green branches swayed in the air and Masha knew it was the birch tree saying thank you. "I am so glad you like it," she said with feeling. "Do you remember the first day we met? Just think! It was almost a year ago! It is not nine years any more, only eight. Isn't it wonderful?"

Suddenly her face clouded. "It is still a long, long time!" she whispered, leaning her head against the silvery trunk.

CHAPTER SIXTEEN

The Parting

"NOBODY," SOPHIE SAID PLAINTIVELY, "IS interested in the Browns any more. The Whites hardly talk to us, the teachers hurry away before the bell rings. Even the Form Mistresses don't seem to care how we behave." She banged down the lid of her desk and sighed.

"It is because this is a graduation year," Nadia answered knowingly. "The teachers are busy coaching the Whites for the Solemn Examination and the Form Mistresses help to prepare for the ceremony."

"Already?" Lena Mandrika wondered, "But it is only the middle of September, and the graduation is next March."

"It is not too early," Nadia insisted. "Just think of the music and dances the Whites have to get ready for the examination, besides all the usual subjects."

"Making the paper roses alone will take weeks," Varia put in. "There will be a giant 1818 made of garlands at the back of the stage."

Marie Divova began to count on her fingers, "1818, 1819... Our class will have 1824 in roses."

"Oh, we will think of something else!" Sophie exclaimed. "Why be copycats?"

Masha did not care what kind of flower garlands her form was planning to have for their graduation. She was thinking sadly that Anna Wulff would be leaving. Soon there would be no one to explain a hard lesson or to hug during a break.

"Next spring there will be a new White Form," Emilia Agte said. "The Blues are excited already."

"But they won't be our Whites," Natasha remarked sadly. "I am not going to have a crush on any of them."

"You are getting too old for crushes anyhow," Sashette said briskly. "When the next school year begins we will be Blues. Remember!"

"Just fancy!" Ellie Vuich exclaimed. "No more brown dresses for us."

"And we will be allowed to wear curls!" her sister rejoiced.

"But," Masha said doubtfully, "won't the dresses be too big for us?"

"Big?" Sashette scoffed. "One would think we were still nine years old. Look at yourself."

Instinctively, Masha looked down. The skirt of her uniform that had almost touched the ground at the beginning of the third school year now barely reached her ankles. The sleeves felt tight. Her fair locks, which she had been allowed to grow for the last few months, were constantly escaping from under the round comb.

"I shall be twelve next July," she thought, almost frightened. "Two years in the Brown Form have passed so quickly after all, and now the third is flying by." With a sudden pang, she remembered the green-striped dress she had worn when she arrived at Smolni. She had already outgrown it.

The dinner bell interrupted the girls' conversations. "Come, come, girls!" Mademoiselle Souchet exclaimed, entering the classroom. "We will be late. Upstairs!"

"She is late herself, and now it is our fault," Sophie murmured rebelliously as they were leaving the classroom.

The school was assembled in the refectory and singing grace when the doors suddenly opened wide and Maria Feodorovna walked in, accompanied only by the Principal.

The strict discipline at Smolni made it impossible for the girls even to glance in the direction of the Empress before the end of the prayer. But as soon as the last note was sung, every head turned and the girls plunged into a deep curtsy.

Maria Feodorovna smiled, motioned the pupils to their seats and made a slow round of the tables, sometimes breaking a small piece of bread or tasting the food.

"Suppose I tell her the soup is watery," Sophie murmured under her breath.

"Oh, Sophie, please don't!" Masha clutched at her friend's sleeve.

Nadia grinned. "Don't you worry, Masha. She would never dare."

Varia said seriously, "I think someone else is making a complaint. Just look."

Following Varia's gaze, Masha saw one of the Whites hastily rise from the table. Pushing aside the girls who tried to restrain her, she ran into the middle of the dining room and fell on her knees in front of the Empress.

A gasp ran around the refectory, followed by a stunned silence that was broken only by Maman's stern, "Ivanova! What is the meaning of this scene?"

"It is Lisa Ivanova," Katish whispered to Masha. "She helps me sometimes with my needlework. She is a very quiet girl. I wonder why..."

Maria Feodorovna bent over the girl and tried to make her rise. "My dear, what is it? Has something happened to your family?" she was asking.

The girl did not answer. Shaking with sobs, she presented a folded sheet of paper to the Empress.

Maria Feodorovna accepted the paper with a puzzled look on her face and, holding up her lorgnette, began to read.

Madame Adlerberg touched the girl's shoulder. "Ivanova, get up. At once!" she ordered.

"Yes, Maman," Ivanova murmured, getting up. She stood breathing heavily and pressing her handkerchief to her mouth.

The Empress finished reading and lowered her lorgnette. There was a deep frown on her forehead. "I don't quite understand," she said slowly. "Your father writes that all the arrangements have been made for your marriage as soon as you graduate from Smolni. But surely he would allow you to get acquainted with... with the gentleman first. It may be a very suitable marriage for you, my dear. However, it is my opinion that..."

Lisa Ivanova backed away, her widened eyes, full of terror, fixed on the Empress's face. "No, no!" she cried violently. "I don't want to marry that man! Never! Never!" Her voice rose hysterically. "I'd rather go begging in the streets than marry him!" She slipped on her knees again, crying aloud and trying to clutch the Empress's dress. "Your Majesty, save me! Save me!"

At a sign from Maman, Mania Suvorova hurried forward with a glass of water. The Principal made the girl lift her head and held the glass to her lips.

Maria Feodorovna waited until the wild sobs quieted down, then said gently, "Get up, my dear, and tell me more about that man. Do you know him?"

Lisa Ivanova stood, swaying a little and leaning on Mania Suvorova's arm. "Yes, your Majesty," she said with an effort, "I do know him. That is, I remember him. He is my father's neighbor. I used to play with his daughter when I was small. Your Majesty, please..."

"His daughter?" the Empress interrupted. "The man has a daughter of your age?"

Ivanova murmured, "Two years older. He is a widower now. Father kept mentioning him in his letters these last few months, only I... I did not realize what he meant."

"It is disgraceful!" the Principal exclaimed. "You should have come to me at once."

Ivanova bowed her head. "I didn't dare. I thought maybe it was my duty to obey my father, but when Her Majesty arrived, I suddenly could not bear it any more!"

"I cannot imagine what your father was thinking about," Maman went on indignantly, "A widower with a daughter older than you are!"

The girl answered through her tears, "Father lost a great deal of money to him playing cards," and she blushed.

Maria Feodorovna put out her hand and gently touched Ivanova's cheek. "You need not worry any more. I shall write to your father immediately and express my displeasure at his action. Pursue your studies and when the time comes for you to graduate, we will decide whether you should go home or stay here as a student teacher. Forget the whole matter. You will not marry that man."

Ivanova rushed to kiss the Empress's hand, stammering her thanks, while Maman gave a stern order to the gaping pupils to sit down and eat their dinner.

The Empress left soon after, and the girls began to comment on what Sophie had immediately christened "The refectory tragedy."

"It almost makes me afraid to go home after I leave Smolni!" Natasha exclaimed. "Suppose my parents make me marry an old man?"

"But why should they?" Masha asked, surprised. "You always used to tell us how kind your parents were."

Natasha laid down her spoon. "You know something," she said with an unsteady little laugh, "I am not really sure any more that I remember my parents. No, no, I don't mean I have forgotten my family, but it is almost three years I've been here at Smolni. When I think of home, it is... well, vague."

"I feel the same," Emilia Agte confessed. "I haven't seen my parents since I left home."

"Am I forgetting too?" Masha asked herself. "Oh, no, I couldn't." Almost panicky, she visualized every loved face, then the house, the garden. Her memories were vivid, but... she could not remember whether the patch of violets was in the garden by the fence or in the grove beyond.

She sat silent, staring at her plate, while her classmates continued to talk about Lisa Ivanova.

"I have no fond memories of home," Sashette was saying, "but to stay here as a student teacher... No, that wouldn't appeal to me at all."

"Maybe Maria Feodorovna will make her a lady-in-waiting," Katish suggested.

"Ivanova a lady-in-waiting?" Marie Divova almost suffocated. "To be chosen for a lady-in-waiting one has to be an excellent student, and be good in music, and be pretty, like my cousin Zinaida."

"I am afraid Marie is right," Natasha said. "Ivanova is just too... colorless."

"Why doesn't she marry that old man after all?" Sashette asked unexpectedly. "If he is rich..."

She met the indignant gazes of her companions and bit her lip. "I was only joking," she muttered.

As soon as the girls were out of the refectory, Masha ran to Anna Wulff and threw herself into her arms. "Your parents won't make you marry some terrible man you don't like? Say they won't," she pleaded.

"Certainly not," Anna soothed. "My mother wouldn't dream of such a thing and I can't imagine my stepfather forcing me into a marriage. Still, it won't be too easy," she added with a little sigh. "I hardly know my stepsister and I can only hope we will be friends. She is a few years older than I am. We will be living in the country and depending upon each other for company." She kissed Masha and hugged her. "Stop worrying about me. I am sure it will be quite pleasant to be home."

"How we shall miss them all," Stephanie remarked when Anna moved on. "It is hard to believe they will be leaving in a few months."

The Browns repeated Stephanie's words over and over again' as days passed and the time for parting grew near. Even Christmas had a note of sadness in it that year. The younger girls did not want to dance or play, preferring to trail the "adored ones."

There was much excitement on the day of the Graduation Ball. The Whites, dressed in white gowns with colored sashes, their hair curled by a real hairdresser, came to the dormitory to let the Browns take a look at their grown-up selves.

Solemn Examinations began in February, then came the graduation concert, the prize-giving, the speeches. Groups of Whites began to wander all over the corridors, the classrooms, the garden, taking a last look at what had been their world for nine years.

"Here is something to remember me by," Anna Wulff told Masha, pressing into her hand a pincushion shaped like a rabbit. "Study hard, enjoy yourself as much as you can, and when you are a White yourself, remember to be kind to the little Browns."

Other Whites were also giving away small possessions to the younger girls. Clementine Del Pardo even cut off several locks of her hair and distributed them to her admirers.

The Whites left on a rainy day at the end of March. The Browns pressed their faces to the streaked windowpanes, watching the carriages roll away one after another. Stephanie was the first to start crying and was soon joined by most of the girls.

Masha did not cry. She stood numbly beside Sophie, wondering how one could hear the rumble of wheels through the double panes. It was such a loud rumble too, echoing through and through her heart.

Faithful to Anna's request, she did her best to be friendly with the new little Browns who soon started to appear in small batches, brought from every part of Russia. It seemed to her that the small newcomers looked more frightened and ill at ease than she and her classmates had been. Madame Legarpe, having led her flock through the school, was now the Browns' Form Mistress and ruled them with an iron hand. The second Form Mistress, a mild, sickly German woman, looked as if she herself was afraid of Madame Legarpe.

Passing the Browns' dormitory one evening, Masha heard a

stifled sobbing. She stepped inside and saw a little girl, her face to the wall, smothering her sobs with a corner of her sheet.

Sitting down on the edge of the bed and feeling suddenly very grown up, Masha put her arm around the child. "Are you feeling homesick?" she asked.

The little girl shook her head. "No... I haven't a real home. I lived with my uncle and aunt before coming here. My aunt hoped my little sister would be accepted too, but they wouldn't take her because she is only three. I always dressed her and played with her. I... I miss her so much."

The small, thin face looked so grieved that Masha felt her own throat tighten. "I will be back in a minute," she promised, hurrying out.

She returned a few minutes later carrying Anya. "Here," she said, thrusting the doll into the little girl's hands. "This is not the same as having your sister with you, but it may help you to feel less lonely. Her name is Anya. Be kind to her."

Without waiting for the child's answer, Masha turned and headed for the door, telling herself that she was getting too big to play with dolls. Outside, in the corridor, something made her stop for a moment. She stood rigid, listening to the strange silence around her and feeling that somehow parting with Anya meant the end of her childhood.

BLUE

CHAPTER SEVENTEEN

In the Winter Palace

NOTHING NICE HAS HAPPENED SINCE THE Whites left" Stephanie complained, putting down the handkerchief she was hemming. "It is not much fun being in the Blue Form after all."

The girls were sitting under the lime trees. Their old domain by the lilac bushes was now occupied by the new Brown Form.

Sophie threw her needlework into the air and caught it again. "Stephanie is right," she declared. "What fun did we have this year? Even the Browns are having a better time than we. Whenever Maria Feodorovna visits us, she spends all her time with them, asking their names and petting them. To whom did she send bonbons last week? To the Browns. And of course the Whites are having all the honors and pleasures."

"Oh, Sophie, you exaggerate," Natasha protested.

Sophie bristled, "Do I? Remember the dance at Christmas? Who was dancing? The White Form. Who was looking on? The Blue Form."

"But it was not a real dance," Masha said, trying to calm Sophie down. "They were just dancing among themselves."

"Well, let's say they were moving," Sophie retorted. "We had to sit still, and the veal sandwiches were stale."

"Wait!" Varia interrupted. "What's happening? Look how Mademoiselle is waving to us."

"Maman wishes to see all of you in the recreation hall immediately," Mademoiselle Souchet panted, appearing before the girls. "Vite!"

"I am sure Maman is going to announce that practicing time is being doubled," Sophie told Masha gloomily as they walked along the corridor.

"Or maybe we are to get up one hour earlier," Emilia Agte suggested. "Or maybe it is something worse."

"Nothing could be worse," Sashette grumbled behind them.

The Whites were already assembled in the recreation hall. The Brown Form was evidently not invited. Soon Maman appeared and the girls stood at attention.

As she spoke, the anxious faces cleared. The news was really exciting. The Grand Duke Nicholas was going to be married. His fiancée, Princess Charlotte, daughter of the King of Prussia, was to arrive in St. Petersburg around the twentieth of June.

"There will be a big parade on the Palace Square," Maman said. She paused and went on, "I am happy to tell you that Her Majesty, the Empress Maria Feodorovna, has graciously invited a certain number of Smolni pupils to the Winter Palace for that solemn occasion. The five Blues and the five Whites with the highest marks for study and conduct" the Principal underlined the last word, "will have the honor of being guests at the Palace. You have two weeks to prove yourselves."

"I have no hope, of course," Nadia said cheerfully, when the girls returned to their classrooms. "My marks for lessons are terrible and I was sent to Neigardt for impertinence only two days ago. Never mind, I had my share of parades when I was a small and pathetic orphan."

"I think it is going to be wonderful," Natasha said. "I do hope I may go."

"What are you worrying about? You are the first in the class," Varia said peevishly.

"You could be too," Natasha returned, "if you just read lesson books instead of stories."

Stephanie was already crying in her handkerchief. "In my French school..." she sobbed.

"Oh, who cares about your French school?" Sophie spoke crossly. "Neither you nor I are going, and that's all that matters."

"Oh, Sophie, do try," Masha pleaded. "You know you can study when you want to."

Sophie yawned. "No. See, even the thought of studying hard makes me feel tired. No parade is worth it!"

"I don't want to go," Lena Mandrika declared. "It is too worldly."

The girls went on discussing which of them might be among the five invited. Masha felt quite excited. Her marks were good. If only she could go! What a wonderful letter she would be able to write home. Mamma would read it to Niania, and Niania would tell the others. With a resolute air, she reached for her arithmetic book.

By the end of the week everyone's marks had improved. Even Sophie made a feeble attempt to study, only to abandon it almost immediately. "Too strenuous," she declared. "I don't care really!"

On the eve of the big day, the names of the five lucky ones were read by Fraulein Knappe. The girls sat at their desks, tense, their eyes on the list in Fraulein's hands.

Natasha came first, then came Varia, followed by Masha, Ellie Vuich, and finally Sashette.

Masha was too delirious with joy to hear Sashette's whispered, "So our little Fredericks did creep high after all."

But Sophie heard her. A deftly thrown paper ball hit Sashette in the eye and made her squeak with indignation.

"Try to express your pleasure in a more ladylike way, Rossett," Fraulein Knappe, who did not see the ball, reproved. "I warn you," she added grimly, "should there be any misbehavior between today and tomorrow, the culprit's name will be removed from the list and another pupil will take her place."

Ellie Vuich looked up, her eyes full of tears. "My name can be removed right now. I am not going without my sister. She worked hard too."

"Then don't go," Sashette cried from her desk. "Stephanie here will be happy to take your place."

"Stephanie indeed!" Katish cried, her voice trembling. "What about Lena Mandrika and me? We tied for the sixth place. It is we who..."

Fraulein tapped on the desk. "Silence!" she thundered. "If there are changes to be made, it is Maman who will make them and there will be no discussion about it. Mademoiselle Souchet will be in charge of you tomorrow. Mind you behave. I can't go with my bad cold." She sneezed violently and wiped her watering eyes. "Oh, yes! The music teacher wants to try several of you for a part in the play the Whites are preparing for Maman's birthday in September. It calls for some singing. Mademoiselle Souchet will take care of it. I have made a few suggestions..." Fraulein sneezed again and at the same time the lesson bell rang.

All through the morning Masha kept glancing at the window, savoring in advance the excitement of telling the wonderful news to the birch tree. If only Sophie had been going too everything would have been perfect.

It surprised Masha to find her friend gayer than usual after the lessons. "One must study for the sake of learning and not for the reward," she informed Marie Divova loftily at supper, making the whole table gasp.

As the girls were undressing in the evening, Natasha worried, "Suppose it rains tomorrow? Wouldn't it be terrible?"

"Fraulein said we will be going anyway, but the parade won't look the same," Sashette answered. "But it won't rain. The sky is quite clear."

Stephanie promptly started to weep again. "It's going to be a beautiful day and I'm going to be locked up in the classroom..." she sobbed.

"Oh, dear! I didn't mean to upset you," Sashette exclaimed, while Sophie said sweetly, "Let's not talk about tomorrow. It is really very hard for us who are not going."

The girls seemed to accept Sophie's advice, for no one said a word more about the palace or the parade until the next morning that dawned fair and warm.

"Oh, I do hope nothing is going to happen at the last moment," Masha whispered to Katish, as she sat down for breakfast.

"I was so sure I would be among the five," Katish sighed. "My marks have always been above Sashette's, but she is the lucky one this time."

"Will there be military music and flags?" Lena Mandrika asked. There was a wistfulness in her voice.

The girls were just getting up from the table when Sashette made an awkward movement and sent her empty cup flying off the table. "How could it happen! I am never so clumsy!" she exclaimed wrathfully, gathering up the pieces and glaring at each girl in turn.

"Why are you so worried about it?" Varia asked. "You know that we are never punished if we happen to break something by accident. It won't be counted against you."

"Everything counts today," Sashette answered sharply, turning her back on Varia.

"Sashette is quite right. Everything counts today," Sophie remarked in such a grave and sympathetic tone that Masha stared in wonder.

The Blues had hardly entered the classroom when Mademoiselle Souchet, in a rustling blue gown, began to give orders. "Those who are not going to the palace take your seats. A student teacher will be in charge of you while I am away. The five on the list go upstairs and get ready. Let's see." She picked up a list from the desk and read, "Meller..."

Masha held her breath until her name was read, but instead of Ellie Vuich and Sashette, Mademoiselle calmly read, "Mandrika, Muffle," and put the list down.

The form looked stupefied. "I knew they could not make me go," Ellie Vuich said behind Masha. Lena Mandrika muttered something about committing a sin, but her face shone. Mademoiselle, however, was not listening to the comments. She glanced at the clock on the wall and hustled the five girls upstairs.

Looking over her shoulder, Masha saw Sashette, her hand on her heart, repeating, "For breaking a cup! For breaking a cup!"

Katish, all smiles, pulled Masha's hand. "Come on! Quick! I am so glad I'm going! There must have been a mistake in the marks after all. Oh, isn't it exciting!"

"Yes," Masha thought, "it is exciting." Even walking down the steps toward the waiting carriages was exhilarating. Suddenly, Masha realized she was outside Smolni for the first time in almost four years.

All the way to the Winter Palace the girls pressed their faces to the windows. The streets, the people, everything looked new.

When the greenish walls and the white columns of the palace came into view, Mademoiselle Souchet lifted her finger. "Remember you are the pupils of Smolni Institute and behave as such," she reminded the girls. The chattering stopped immediately and faces became serious.

It was a very quiet and orderly procession of blue and white girls, walking two by two, with demurely folded hands, and patrolled by Form Mistresses, that mounted the wide marble stairway of the palace.

Madame Adlerberg, without a bonnet this time, her hair dressed high, St. Catherine's Cross of Merit pinned to her shoulder, met her flock on the threshold of an immense room filled with courtiers and other guests. In a low voice she reminded the girls not to talk loudly, discreetly smoothed a few heads, and smiled encouragement.

Feeling slightly dizzy, Masha gazed at the painted ceilings, the statues, the mirrors, the glittering uniforms, the precious stones on the ladies' bare necks and shoulders. Suddenly, she felt a slight touch on her arm. "Fredericks, close your mouth. Immediately!" Maman ordered. Masha caught her breath and obeyed.

Everyone was waiting for the cannons to announce Princess Charlotte's arrival. Voices were kept low.

Among the uniforms and elegant civilian clothes, Masha noticed a thin man dressed in an old-fashioned, long black frock coat with a white silk tie knotted under his chin. There was a severe expression on his clean-shaven face. He was not taking part in the conversations, only bowing his head in greeting.

"Who is he?" Masha whispered to a White who was standing near her.

"Hush," the older girl whispered back. "He is a priest, and he is going to prepare the Princess to embrace the Greek-Orthodox faith. She is a Protestant."

"A priest?" Masha repeated, astonished. "But he has no beard and no robes."

"Hush," the White repeated again. "Princess Charlotte is not used to our priests. In his ordinary clothes, he resembles a Protestant pastor. It will make the Princess feel more at ease."

Perplexed, Masha remained silent. She looked around and saw Nelidova in a heavy, tight-waisted dress of yellow brocade that made a strange contrast to the filmy loose gowns of the other ladies.

It was becoming very warm. Fans started to wave. Suddenly, the cannons boomed.

A low rumble sounded behind the windows, swelling into a roar. Watching eagerly, Masha saw the Palace Square swarming with crowds that policemen were trying to keep back. People watched from rooftops, windows, even lampposts.

The roar swelled again and broke into crashing cheers as a gilded landau appeared, drawn by six horses and escorted by mounted pages, feathers waving on their three-cornered hats.

"Look," Mademoiselle Souchet said, "the Princess!"

BLUE

Masha saw a young girl seated with the two empresses. Dressed in a simple gray dress, a big gray hat with white roses, she smiled at the crowd and timidly waved her hand. The Emperor Alexander and the Grand Duke Nicholas followed the carriage on horseback. Several carriages with retinue passed by, then the troops came, marching to the sound of military music.

Delirious crowds surged from all sides, flags waved, and the thunderous hurrahs drowned out the ringing of bells.

Masha's heart made a plunge and turned over. She seized Lena's hand and stood still, every nerve taut. It seemed to her that the whole palace was rocking.

Katish Muffle asked, "Why are you crying?" and Masha answered in all sincerity, "I didn't know I was crying."

Natasha was openly sobbing into her handkerchief. "It is too... too beautiful," she murmured.

Lena Mandrika solemnly crossed herself.

There was a movement behind the girls. Masha felt Maman's hand on her shoulder and turned around. Everyone was looking toward the door. For a moment deep silence reigned, then a ripple seemed to pass across the room as the ladies sank into a deep curtsy and the men bowed low.

A wide space suddenly cleared in the middle of the floor. Masha saw the Grand Duke Nicholas and his bride. They moved slowly as the Duke presented the Princess to various courtiers and dignitaries. Just for a second, as they came abreast of the girls, Masha caught a glimpse of a pretty, flushed face with big blue eyes, golden ringlets waving from under the upturned brim of the hat. The girls' deep curtsy made their skirts swish around them. When they straightened up, the Grand Duke and his fiancée had already passed on.

The parade followed. The imperial family stood on the balcony watching the troops march. The sun shone on the bayonets, on the silver and gold of the epaulets, on the bright armor of the Chevaliers of the Guard, on the gleaming brass of the trumpets of the military orchestra. The music and the sound of marching steps made one powerful melody.

"That is the Empress Elizaveta. Look," Mademoiselle Souchet whispered, with a discreet nod.

Masha looked at the Empress's beautiful but sad face, her head bent as if under a burden of grief. Beside her, the Dowager Empress, with her pink dimpled cheeks and stout waist, seemed even sturdier and more debonaire than ever.

The girls were made to leave before the end of the parade. "We must get back to Smolni quickly or the streets will be impassable," Mademoiselle Souchet explained in answer to the girls' pleas to stay for a while longer.

There was a general scramble, in which both forms became mixed. Masha tried to join her classmates, but they were too far away from her. To her dismay, she found herself bundled into a carriage with the Principal, Mademoiselle Neigardt, and two Whites she barely knew.

It was very disappointing not to be able to talk to her friends about all the wonders they had seen. Masha sat in a corner, looking out of the window. The two Whites ignored her, deep in whispered conversation.

Maman and Mademoiselle Neigardt were talking too. They spoke in rapid German and in low voices, but Masha caught a few sentences.

"Beautiful and sweet," Maman was saying, "but I am afraid somewhat inclined to judge people by appearance. It seems that she found Nelidova very plain. I believe she actually said 'ugly' and she has made similar remarks about other persons."

Somehow, the conversation remained in Masha's memory. She was planning to tell Sophie about it, but when they reached Smolni, Sophie seemed to have disappeared. Masha found her at last in one of the small music rooms, her back to the wall, Natasha standing over her.

"Confess! Confess!" Natasha was saying sternly. "I didn't want to spoil things for Katish and Lena. They both work hard all year through, and they certainly deserve the treat more than Sashette who puts on a spurt only when there is a reward in view. Ellie Vuich wouldn't have gone anyway. She is devoted to her sister. So I kept quiet, but now I want the truth. What did you do with that list?"

"Really, Natasha," Sophie pouted. "I simply happened to glance at the names Fraulein had jotted down for the music teacher. Is it my fault that they were almost the same? I may have put that sheet on top of the palace list—neither of them had headings—but Mademoiselle should have noticed it." She began to giggle. "Now Ellie will be tried for that singing part, and she can't carry a tune."

"Fraulein will find out soon enough and then you will see what she will do to you," Natasha threatened.

But luck was with Sophie. Fraulein's cold was a heavy one and when she returned two weeks later, the visit to the palace was only a memory.

No one else found out the mystery of the lists and for years the story was told at Smolni of how Sasha Rossett was deprived of seeing the Princess just because she broke a teacup.

Dinner with Maman

THE NEEDLEWORK LESSON WAS ALMOST over. Her tongue inside her cheek, Masha labored over an apron. The rounded hem just wouldn't come out right. She sighed and went over to Frau Udam to ask for help.

"Make a small fold from time to time. This is not a straight hem. You should know better," Frau Udam scolded. Then, just as Masha had expected, she added, "You should see the beautiful work being done in the 'other half.'"

Masha murmured, "I will try to do better next time, Frau Udarn," and returned to her seat. She smiled as she remembered that when she was a small Brown she had believed for a long time that by the "other half" Frau Udam meant the angels in heaven. It seemed quite natural that they should do better work than school-girls. She liked to imagine them sitting on white clouds and sewing with a golden thread. It had been quite a shock to discover that the name actually applied to another school also housed in the immense building of Smolni. It was almost as big as the Institute for Noble Girls and took in the daughters of lower ranking officers, of tradesmen, servants, and even peasants, provided they were not serfs. The course there was only six years instead of nine.

"Maybe it would have been better for me to be in the 'other half,'" Masha thought, trying to make small folds and pricking her fingers. "I would be almost finished now instead of being in my second Blue year. On the other hand, needlework is considered the most important subject there..." It was difficult to decide.

She sucked her finger and heard with relief the bell announcing the end of the lesson.

The girls were putting their work away when there was a familiar light step outside the door.

"Neigardt! Neigardt!" passed across the classroom. The girls were hurriedly smoothing their hair and shaking bits of thread off their aprons. Mademoiselle Souchet, who was sprinkling perfume on a long letter she had just finished writing, jumped and hastily pushed both the letter and the perfume bottle into her desk drawer.

"Do you have any idea why your aunt is paying us a visit?" Sophie asked Emilia Agte, who hissed back, "She is not my aunt."

The girls scrambled to their feet as the Inspectress entered. She gave a frosty bow to Mademoiselle Souchet and, stepping in front of the class, swept the rows of girls with a keen look of her pale blue eyes.

"Are you feeling poorly?"

The question was addressed to Lena Mandrika, who stood holding on to the edge of the desk.

Lena blinked. "No, Mademoiselle Neigardt."

"In that case, you do not need a prop."

Lena let go the desk as if it had suddenly become red-hot.

Nadia gave a hysterical giggle, tried to smother it, and ended in a splutter. The Inspectress ignored her. Turning to Mademoiselle Souchet's desk, she sniffed the air.

"What a strange smell," she said. A long pause followed, during which the Form Mistress's face changed several times from white to red.

Mademoiselle Neigardt addressed the form. "Starting this week," she said, "you will all take turns in dining at the table of Madame Adlerberg, your kind Maman. Your table manners will be observed and corrections made when necessary. I will now read the names of the girls who will attend today." She glanced at a sheet of paper in her hand.

"Vuich sisters, Meller, Brozina, Muffle..." Masha was just beginning to rejoice when the Inspectress read, "Fredericks," and then addressed Mademoiselle Souchet. "You will, please, accompany these pupils," she ordered. "Madame Adlerberg is expecting you at noon." Then she swept out of the classroom.

"Some invitation!" Sophie cried. "But I suppose that the food is good. What happens if I ask for a second helping?"

Katish gasped. "You would never dare!"

Natasha, her mole very black against her suddenly pale cheek, appealed to Nadia. "Is it very bad? You must have gone through this several times already."

"Only once," Nadia answered cheerfully. "I was four and in a high chair. It all ended by my throwing a sticky spoon at Maman. I was removed and never invited again."

"Attention! Attention!" Mademoiselle Souchet cried. "To the dormitory. You, the girls who are dining with Maman, be sure to wash your hands properly. Scrub! Scrub hard! I will inspect your nails before we start. Vite!"

Sophie pulled Masha's sleeve. "Let's try to sit at the very end of the table, away from Maman. Shall we?"

But when the six victims, scrubbed and brushed, arrived in the Principal's rooms, they were faced with a round table that left no possibility of escape.

Much to her distress, Masha found herself seated at Maman's left hand. Sophie, with the air of a martyr, took the place on the right, Natasha next to her. Mademoiselle Neigardt sat opposite the Principal, flanked by the Vuich sisters. Beside Ellie, Katish Muffle looked desperately across the table at Mademoiselle Souchet, who kept whispering to Natasha to please sit up straight.

The table was set as for a real dinner party, with crystal and flowers. Masha looked with dismay at the array of forks and spoons, hoping she would know which to use when. She was trying to remember Mademoiselle Souchet's instructions, when she suddenly realized that the Principal was asking her something in French. Completely unprepared, Masha failed to get even the gist of the question. She answered, "Yes, Maman, I do," at random. It seemed safer to say yes than no. But it immediately became clear that she had made a bad guess, for Sophie's eyes popped and Madame Adlerberg said with a displeased air, "I am very sorry to hear it."

Mademoiselle Souchet came to Masha's rescue. "Fredericks misunderstood you, Madame. She really practices hard and is making good progress in music."

"Maman said 'I hope you are not neglecting your practicing,'" Katish whispered, and Masha became scarlet.

Mademoiselle Neigardt said something about Napoleon and Maman excitedly lapsed into her native German. "That terrible man, der schrecklicher Mann, will never shed any more blood," she declared. "St. Helena is not Elba and there is no escape for him, though there's talk of a conspiracy."

"We will soon have more news," Maman added, "when Her Majesty, the Empress Maria Feodorovna, returns from Moscow."

Mademoiselle Souchet politely inquired when Her Majesty was expected back, and Maman answered that die Hebe Maria Feodorovna was due to arrive in St. Petersburg by the end of the next week and would probably honor Smolni with her visit soon after. Still talking, the Principal turned to Sophie and gently patted her between the shoulder blades. Sophie sat up straight as a rod.

Glad to have the attention diverted from her blunder, Masha ate the delicate cream soup and enjoyed it until Mademoiselle Souchet signaled to her across the table not to bend over her plate. Masha promptly obeyed but the soup became tasteless.

Veal chops with white sauce and asparagus followed the soup.

A maid removed the plates and Katish Muffle reached for her glass of water.

"Use your napkin first."

At the sound of Mademoiselle Neigardt's cold voice, Katish jerked back her hand and snatched at her napkin only to discover that it had slid off her lap onto the floor. She dived under the table and emerged red-faced, with a trembling chin, her blonde eyelashes already wet.

Maman gave her a moment to recover and to take a big gulp of water before saying calmly, "Should you ever happen to drop your napkin in society, do not try to retrieve it from under the table. Never. Make a discreet sign to the footman to give you a fresh one, or in an emergency, use your handkerchief, as unnoticeably as you can. Now eat your chop."

Mademoiselle Neigardt looked as if she had found the lecture much too mild. She frowned and told Natasha not to play with the silverware.

Masha finished her chop and sat looking at the bone on her plate. It was a nice juicy one, with lots of meat on it, but, of course, nibbling was out of the question. She thought how Trezor would have enjoyed that bone. He would carry it out on the terrace, play with it, then eat it and bury the remains in the garden.

Maman glanced at Masha's dreamy face and smiled. "What are you thinking about, my dear?"

Masha's thoughts were still with Trezor. "About the bone," she answered in a faraway voice.

Mademoiselle Souchet swayed in agony. Madame Adlerberg seemed disconcerted. "The bone..." she repeated, "I don't quite understand." She had no time to say anything more because at that moment a real catastrophe took place.

Natasha, out of sheer nervousness, was tracing a design on her plate with a fork. The Form Mistress noticed it and promptly stepped on what she thought was Natasha's foot. Only, in her agitation, she stepped on the foot of Ellie Vuich, who was just carrying to her mouth a forkful of asparagus. The girl jumped and the asparagus landed on the tablecloth.

Mademoiselle Neigardt began, "You may leave..." but a glance from the Principal stopped her. The culprit burst into tears, her face in her napkin, and her sister immediately joined her.

Sophie looked amused, but the rest of the girls gasped with terror. Mademoiselle Souchet kept repeating with growing hysteria in her voice, "It is my fault, I startled her."

The Principal had to speak loudly to be heard above the lamentations. "It is really of no importance just what startled her, Mademoiselle," she said. "Pray, calm yourself."

The maid was summoned to cover the offending place with a napkin. The two sisters stopped crying and faced Maman, expecting a scolding. But she only said, "A lady never makes a display of her emotions, no matter how much provoked. If you have been upset and have to cry, wait until you are alone. You may finish your food."

After Maman's speech, every face around the table became wooden. The dessert, a tempting-looking mold of crème brûlée, arrived in the midst of gloomy silence. Mademoiselle Neigardt sat frowning and biting her lip. Mademoiselle Souchet drank water thirstily and made poor efforts to respond to Maman's remarks about winter being very mild this year.

The Vuich sisters choked over their portions. Natasha's spoon clinked against her plate, drawing a glare from the Inspectress. Katish was holding on to her napkin for dear life.

Loyalty toward her classmates made Masha gulp her crème brûlée instead of letting it melt in her mouth. She laid down her spoon and hoped the uncomfortable meal was over.

Katish immediately put down her spoon too, followed by the rest of the girls.

"May I have some more, please?"

At the sound of Sophie's calm voice, every girl jumped. Then the unexpected happened—Maman began to laugh. "We will all have a second helping of this excellent crème brûlée," she said gaily.

CHAPTER NINETEEN

Dark Days at Smolni

"I HAVE RECEIVED A LETTER FROM MY COUSIN Zinaida. The court is back from Moscow," Marie Divova announced a few days after the memorable dinner with Maman.

It was early in the morning, and the girls were getting out of bed, shivering, and looking with distaste at the dark windows where snowflakes clung to the glass. The two oil lamps were lighted, and a sleepy-looking maid was trying to adjust the smoking wicks.

"She has never had such a wonderful time," Marie went on. "Balls, receptions. There was a man, a nephew of the Governor... Zinaida writes she couldn't imagine anyone more handsome. He danced with her quite often, and..." Marie paused and lowered her voice dramatically, "at the last ball he asked her to give him the rose she was wearing in her hair. You know what that may mean, don't you?"

Usually Marie's story would have provoked a storm of excited comments. Instead, only a few girls murmured, "Did he really?" and "How wonderful for her."

"I have a headache," Stephanie whimpered, sitting down on her bed.

"Me too. Me too." Several voices echoed, and Varia declared that the mere thought of breakfast made her feel sick.

"That's from getting up so early," Sophie grumbled, groping around for a lost shoe. "The idea of waking us up at seven in winter!"

"In the time of Empress Catherine, the pupils rose at six," Nadia remarked.

"What's all this talking? Get dressed, all of you. The bell for prayers is about to ring," Mademoiselle Souchet ordered, coming into the dormitory.

Masha noticed that the Form Mistress looked pale and did not move as briskly as usual.

The recreation hall looked strangely deserted when the Blue Form arrived for prayers. "It's funny," Katish whispered to Masha, "the Brown Form is not here."

"They couldn't all have overslept, could they?" Sashette wondered.

"Something must have happened!" There was a quiver of fright in Nadia's voice. "Just look at Maman!"

Madame Adlerberg entered, followed by the Inspectress. Masha saw with astonishment that the Principal's collar was pinned on crookedly and the rest of her clothing seemed to have been just thrown on. Her voice was tired, as if she had not had much sleep.

"Mesdemoiselles, I am sorry to announce that several pupils in the Brown Form have been taken ill in the small hours of the morning. The doctor is not quite sure yet, but he thinks it is scarlet fever. The sick are of course in the hospital and the rest of the Brown Form are quarantined in their dormitory. Under no pretext may any of you go there." She looked at the frightened faces and said kindly, "Let us hope the disease will not spread. You may now go to the refectory. Please refrain from kissing and touching each other and wash your hands most carefully several times a day." She turned to the Inspectress, "Please give orders that carbolic soap be put into each lavatory."

"Have you had scarlet fever?" Katish asked Masha as they were leaving the hall. "I have."

Masha nodded. "I have too. Feklusha brought all kinds of illnesses from the village. But Mamma said I might just as well have them when I'm young."

No one ate much breakfast. Lena Mandrika added to the general gloom by suggesting that Smolni was going to be visited by Ten Plagues and that scarlet fever was the first one.

Arithmetic was the first lesson that morning. Mademoiselle Garbi, a young and very enthusiastic teacher, always brimming with energy, entered the classroom with purposeful strides and promptly ordered Natasha to the blackboard.

Natasha, usually the best in arithmetic, stumbled through a problem, broke her chalk, and had to be prompted twice before she arrived at the correct answer.

"It is so hot in here," she whispered to Masha, coming back to her seat. "I just can't think clearly in this heat."

"Heat?" Masha asked, staring at Natasha's flushed face. "It is cold in here."

"Fredericks, to the blackboard," Mademoiselle Garbi called.

Masha was getting up when someone at the back of the room said feebly, "I feel sick," and another voice answered, "I feel sick too."

There was a frightened scream from Sashette. "Stephanie has fainted!"

Mademoiselle Garbi hurried between the desks in the direction of Sashette's frantically waving hand. Several girls jumped up and everyone began to talk at once. Mademoiselle Souchet made a movement to rise, then sat down again.

The hubbub was steadily getting worse when the door opened, and Mademoiselle Neigardt appeared.

"Quiet, please!" Her brisk voice sent the pupils scurrying to their seats. "Those who are not well, remain seated. The rest of you may leave. Go to your dormitory and do not leave it without permission."

She looked at the arithmetic teacher holding Stephanie's shoulders and raised her voice. "Mademoiselle Souchet! Please help!"

But the Form Mistress could not offer any assistance. Very pale, she leaned over the table, murmuring, "I feel very poorly."

Masha, leaving the classroom with the other pupils, distinctly heard the Inspectress say under her breath, "Drat the woman!"

Fraulein Knappe promptly joined the girls in the dormitory and ordered everyone to put on outdoor clothes. "We are going out for a walk in the garden," she said. "Fresh air is best for you now."

"It is no fun being outdoors in this weather. The sky looks so white, it may snow any moment," Sophie protested.

Fraulein said gravely, "My child, be thankful you are able to be in the garden at all. These will be difficult times for all of us."

At the end of the week only eleven Blues remained sitting in the dormitory, listening to the wind rattling the window-panes.

The dormitory itself looked different, with the beds of those who were in the hospital pushed against the walls and a table with benches at the end. Though the hospital wing was completely isolated, the Principal gave orders that the pupils were to stay out of the refectory and the recreation hall for fear of contagion. All meals were served upstairs. Cold and sleet made it impossible to go outside.

"Even paper seems to smell of carbolic soap," Katish exclaimed, holding the book she was reading at arm's length. "It simply takes you by the throat."

"What's carbolic soap compared to the tar we are forced to swallow every day?" Sashette answered tartly.

Masha suppressed a nauseous feeling. Each time she was confronted with her milk, mixed with a spoonful of tar, she felt it would be easier to die than to swallow it.

"Tar is supposed to disinfect our insides," Lena Mandrika explained. "It is not too bad if you swallow it quickly."

"You may have two glasses tomorrow then," Sashette snapped. "I am not going to take any more of that nasty stuff."

"Ha, now that she is a student teacher, Lisa Ivanova will make you," Nadia contradicted.

"It is very strange having student teachers instead of Fraulein Knappe and Mademoiselle Souchet," Mary Vuich remarked.

"Well, Maman said the Form Mistresses are needed to help look after the sick," Masha joined in, "and Mademoiselle Souchet is sick herself,"

"She may die," Nadia said in a hushed voice. "It is very dangerous for grown-ups to have scarlet fever."

"Who is talking about dying?" Lisa Ivanova asked, coming into the room. "On the contrary, Mademoiselle is feeling much better. I have just asked one of the maids. Stop talking nonsense and look at the weather. It is snowing hard." She went to the window, the girls after her.

Big drifts were already forming. In the twilight, the gray silhouettes of the trees merged with the sky.

"Maybe it will be like the big snowfall the year Napoleon came to Russia. Were you here then?" Nadia asked, creeping close to Lisa.

"You mean in 1812? Yes. See those bushes?" Lisa pointed at the tall shrubs underneath the window. "They were completely buried. Passages were cut in the garden and when we walked only the tops of our bonnets were visible."

"Were you still in the Brown Form then?" Sophie wanted to know.

"Yes," Lisa answered. "It was my third year in the Browns. It was a graduation year too, but there was no ceremony and no prize-giving. The graduates could not even go home because the roads were not safe. Every day we had services in church, asking God to save Russia. The older girls made bandages for the wounded and the younger ones pulled bits of linen into shreds to be used as dressings."

"Do tell them how Smolni was evacuated," Nadia urged.

"Was to be evacuated," Lisa corrected. "It had been decided that if Napoleon should advance on St. Petersburg the whole school would be sent to Finland. But as you know, he never came here."

"But you were all prepared," Nadia urged.

Lisa smiled. "That's true. There were tremendous preparations. Each of us received a knitted cap and thick gloves. Extra warm cloaks were made and high shoes with flannel linings."

"And you never went after all," Sophie said, greatly disappointed.

"Just as well," Lisa answered with feeling. "An aunt of mine was at the Catherine Institute in Moscow at that time. They were evacuated. She wrote to me later telling how terrible it was. The carriages got stuck in the mud and broke down. The pupils and the staff had to walk for long distances and thought themselves lucky if they found a peasant willing to lend a cart. I still have that letter somewhere. One day I will find it and read it to you."

A gust of wind sent the snow whirling behind the window, and the dusk suddenly turned into darkness. A ray of light appeared under the door. A maid brought in a tall oil lamp and announced that supper would be served in half an hour.

"Wouldn't it be wonderful," Katish said dreamily, "to go downstairs and sit in the refectory with all the Whites and all the Browns, and no horrid illness around us..."

"It will be like that again soon enough," Lisa consoled. "In the meantime," she clapped her hands, "let's make some toffee. I have sugar. Who is in charge of the implements?"

"I am." Sophie dived into her bedside table, bringing out a candle and a battered spoon.

Lisa produced a shapeless lump broken off a sugar loaf and after lighting the candle, held the sugar over the flame. The girls made a ring around the table, watching the sugar melt and drop in big yellow drops on the spoon Sophie was holding.

Masha watched Lisa's serious face in the candlelight and wondered if the older girl was happy being a student teacher. She was safe from marrying the man older than her father, but somehow, it did not seem so...

"Don't eat it before supper," Lisa cautioned as the toffee-making ended and the maid appeared again with plates and silver stacked on a tray.

"Two young ladies have taken a turn for the worse," she announced, putting the tray on the table.

"I have told you before..." Lisa began, but the girls were already asking anxiously, "Who? Who?"

"Meller, I think one is called, and the other is the pretty Polish girl," the maid answered reluctantly, shooting a guilty glance at Lisa.

"Is it true? Is Stephanie really bad?" Sashette asked in a trembling voice.

"There is no sick person who hasn't a bad day sometimes," Lisa answered evasively. "Natasha and Stephanie are not very strong, so they feel the fever more than the others. The maids don't know anything really. They are not allowed near the hospital wing."

Sashette suddenly sat down and burst into tears. It was the first time Masha had ever seen the proud, self-possessed Sashette cry. Sashette must have felt Masha's eyes on her. "Don't stare!" she cried wrathfully. "I must love someone, and Stephanie is like a younger sister to me." She went on sobbing harder. "And now she is to be taken away from me."

"Don't say such a thing," Lisa Ivanova protested. "Everything is being done that can be done. Stephanie and Natasha will recover. I know they will."

"Natasha wanted so badly to see her family again," Katish lamented, "and now she may never..."

Sophie interrupted her. "I think Lisa is right," she said. "We mustn't give up hope so easily. Better say to yourself, 'They're going to get well.' "

The girls seemed to cheer up slightly, but when supper was served and Nadia remarked that macaroni and cheese was Natasha's favorite dish, spirits drooped again.

"Everything will look better in the morning," Lisa consoled her charges as they were preparing for bed. "Please don't scare each other with dark thoughts."

"Let's pray for Natasha and Stephanie," Lena Mandrika suggested as the door closed behind Lisa. "I know we promised not to get out of bed because it is cold, but we can pray lying down just as well. I know a special prayer for the sick. Just repeat after me."

It was a very long prayer and soon the voices began to die down one by one, until Lena dropped off to sleep herself.

Masha thrust her hand under her pillow and touched a sheet of paper wrapped in a handkerchief. It was a letter from her mother she had received that very day. It ended with, "I am thinking constantly about my little girl and trust that God will keep her safe."

Natasha's mother was probably thinking about her too. Stephanie had no family. Her guardian was abroad and did not even know she was sick. "Please, God, save them," Masha prayed, feeling suddenly all alone and helpless. She glanced at the window. Somewhere in the dark, snow-filled garden, the birch tree was dreaming about spring.

Feeling more peaceful, Masha curled up, turning her face away from the flickering night-light.

When she woke up it was dawn and Lisa Ivanova was saying, "Get up, you lazy things. I have good news for you. Both Natasha and Stephanie had a good night and are out of danger."

"And we did not even say the whole prayer for them!" Lena Mandrika cried joyfully.

CHAPTER TWENTY

Princess Charlotte

I T TOOK SMOLNI A LONG TIME TO GET OVER the scarlet fever. Patients were separated from their classmates for several days after they became well so that there could be no danger of contagion. At Christmas, a tree was lighted as usual, but the big ballroom was divided into two parts, with the convalescents sitting on one side, looking thin and still weak, while the healthy ones waved and called from a distance. A few faces were gone forever, two Browns and three Whites.

At last, the dining table was carried out of the Blues' dormitory, the beds put into place, and the missing girls returned, accompanied by Mademoiselle Souchet.

"I never realized how beautiful this room is," Natasha declared, sitting on the edge of her bed and casting fond glances at the bare walls and gleaming floor.

"Mademoiselle received flowers almost every day," Stephanie was telling the highly interested audience. "Just imagine—roses in winter!

She was in that little room in the hospital wing, and I could see her door from my bed."

It was the end of January when lessons began again.

"I am not sure I can study. I am not strong enough," Stephanie complained. "Maybe..." She did not finish as Fraulein Knappe came into the classroom, followed by the history teacher, Alexander Sergeivich Anikiev.

Young and shy, he always slipped through the doors sideways and made a beeline for the teacher's desk. Once seated, he allotted himself at least five minutes respite, opening and closing the register, wiping his pen, smoothing the cuffs of his blue jacket, and only then facing his pupils.

Masha watched the young teacher fidget, trying to imagine what he would do if someone said "Boo!" She became so engrossed, she almost screamed when Nadia poked her with a pencil and whispered, "Maman!"

It was not only Maman who entered. Walking beside her was Princess Charlotte. A little behind walked a tall, thin man in a long, tobacco-colored jacket, an old-fashioned lace jabot around his throat.

The girls sprang to their feet. Fraulein Knappe also rose from her chair, and Mr. Anikiev followed their example so hastily he almost fell off the dais.

Except for the five Blues who had been present when the Princess arrived in St. Petersburg, none of the other Blues had as yet seen her. The court had been away in Moscow for several months, and later Smolni was quarantined. Every pair of eyes was busily examining the graceful figure in the pale-blue silk dress that fell straight from the high waist. A velvet shawl of darker blue matched the velvet hat.

"Mesdemoiselles," Maman said, "we have the great honor of welcoming Her Imperial Highness at Smolni for the first time."

The Princess smiled, a gay smile that still had something childish in it and made her cheeks dimple. "I am looking forward to becoming Her Majesty's faithful assistant in caring for this wonderful establishment," she said in German, and added a few words about how glad she was to see the pupils in good health again. Her speech over, the Princess stepped back, leaving the floor to the gentleman in the brown jacket.

There was no need for the Principal to introduce him. Every girl knew he was Nikolai Mikhailovich Karamzin, the great historian and a member of the Smolni school council. He visited Smolni from time to time, but seldom entered the lower forms, usually going straight to the Whites.

Karamzin's long face, framed in graying sideburns, looked tired and his right hand leaned heavily on a cane with a mother-of-pearl handle. Turning to Anikiev, frozen beside the teacher's desk, he asked, "What period of history are these children studying now?"

The unfortunate young man coughed, paled, and finally managed to utter, "Pe... Peter the Great's reforms, Sir."

"Would you like to examine the pupils?" Maman offered, while the Princess murmured something about history being such an interesting subject, "so interessant."

"Just a few questions," the historian answered in a pleasant but somewhat hollow voice. His eyes swept the rows of girls from under the tired-looking lids and stopped at Sophie. "You, Mademoiselle," he said with a slight nod.

Sophie blushed and looked helplessly in the direction of Maman and the Princess seated on chairs near the dais.

"It is very important of course to know the history of your country," Karamzin said, "but it is also important to know the history of the little school world you live in. Could you tell me, Mademoiselle, just why this establishment is called 'Smolni'?"

Sophie took a deep breath. "Because years ago tar for the ships used to be stocked where the school is now standing. The name Smolni comes from the word smola, meaning tar."

"Quite correct." Karamzin bowed and made a sign for Sophie to sit down. "And what was later built on that site?" he asked Natasha, who promptly answered, "Smolni Monastery."

"And when was the school opened in the monastery?" the historian went on, his eyes on Stephanie.

Stephanie's feeble "In 1764" could hardly be heard, but the Princess smiled and murmured to Maman, "What a lovely child."

Karamzin did not seem impressed by Stephanie's angel-like beauty and turned to Varia. "Is Smolni the first school for girls founded in Russia?"

Before Varia could answer, he said with a smile, "I know we consider Smolni to be the first, but actually it is not. Anna, the daughter of Yaroslav the Wise, founded a school for girls in 1086, in Kiev. Reading, writing, singing, and needlework were taught."

Madame Adlerberg said, "A most interesting fact. Make sure you remember it, Mesdemoiselles."

Masha was beginning to think that she was going to be spared the questions, but at that moment the historian's eyes became fixed on her. "Whose august patronage is enjoyed by this establishment?" he asked.

It sounded easy. "Maman's," Masha answered, and was surprised to hear a ripple of laughter coming from the Principal and Princess Charlotte. Karamzin smiled too. "Her Majesty, the Dowager Empress Maria Feodorovna," he corrected gently, and turning to Madame Adlerberg, remarked, "Very touching devotion."

The examination seemed to be over. Maman made a movement to rise, but the Princess lingered. "I suppose," she said, "that all your pupils speak German. It would give me great pleasure to hear it. Perhaps a poem..."

"Certainly, Your Highness," Maman answered, hastily motioning to Katish Muffle to come forward,

Katish recited a short poem by Schiller, and Princess Charlotte's face shone. "Very, very good. You recited it perfectly," she told Katish, who curtsied low and became pink with pride.

A slight feeling of envy stirred in Masha's heart. She would have loved to earn praise from the Princess, who looked so kind and whose blue eyes smiled along with her lips.

The Princess said something to Madame Adlerberg, who addressed the form. "Does anyone know a poem by Uhland?" she asked.

Masha stood up. She knew several of Uhland's poems by heart and could recite well, but before she could say anything, Sashette was on her feet too.

The two girls stood waiting.

"You," Princess Charlotte said, smiling at Sashette.

Stifling her disappointment, Masha sat down and listened to Sashette who recited the poem not nearly as well as Masha could have.

But the Princess said, "Charmant" and turning to Maman, added in a low voice, "That girl will be a ravishing beauty when she grows up."

"Why didn't you hurry and get up before Sashette?" Sophie asked indignantly after the visitors were gone. "Fraulein Knappe kept making signs to you, but you did not pay attention."

"It doesn't matter," Masha answered, keeping her eyes glued to the ink blot on the lid of her desk. "I wouldn't have pleased the Princess anyhow."

"Why not?" demanded Sophie. "You can recite splendidly."

"Because I am not pretty compared to Sashette or Stephanie." Masha had difficulty keeping the tears out of her voice and at the same time trying to speak low so that the other girls couldn't hear. "That's all she cares about. Yes," she insisted, seeing Sophie's incredulous stare, "Maman said so, only I did not believe her. Now I know."

"Maman said it? To you?" Sophie exclaimed in amazement.

"Not to me," Masha felt impatient with Sophie's frank disbelief. "Do you remember when the five of us went to the Winter Palace? The day Princess Charlotte arrived in St. Petersburg? Well, coming back, I was made to sit in the carriage with Maman and Neigardt. I couldn't help hearing what they were talking about. Maman said that the Princess is ever so nice but that she doesn't like ugly people. She wants everyone to be beautiful."

"But you are not ugly," Sophie protested.

"Silence! The lesson is not over," Fraulein Knappe thundered, and Sophie had to stop arguing. After the lesson, she promptly forgot all about the Princess and went upstairs chattering with Varia.

But Masha did not forget. From that day on, whenever Princess Charlotte came to Smolni, Masha hung back and tried to avoid being seen.

CHAPTER TWENTY-ONE

The Easter Bazaar

EVERY YEAR, ON PALM THURSDAY, THE BLUE and the White Forms were taken in carriages for a glimpse of the Easter Bazaar in the Palace Square. It was considered a great treat, and the girls were counting the days.

"I do hope the weather will be fine," Natasha said longingly, watching the uncertain-looking sky from the classroom window. "Last year Maman wouldn't let us go because there was an epidemic of smallpox in the city, though I can't imagine how we could possibly catch it sitting in the carriages, and now the weather is changing every day."

"I hate early Easter," Sophie raged. "There will be a snowstorm next Thursday. You'll see!"

But no snowstorm came. Thursday turned out to be not exactly sunny, but mild and gray, with slush on the streets and icicles dripping from the roofs.

The court carriages, with the imperial coat of arms on the doors, arrived promptly at ten. The Blues and the Whites, dressed in dark green cloaks and knitted caps of scarlet wool on their heads, were assembled in the hall.

Mademoiselle Souchet, clad in a new blue cape edged with fur, was about to lead her charges out when she was stopped by the Inspectress, also very elegantly dressed, white flowers standing upright on her hat. "Please make sure that each group of Blues is accompanied by a White, Mademoiselle," the Inspectress said. "We can start now."

Sophie drew Masha back, "Don't hurry," she whispered. "Maybe if we are the last, they'll forget to put a White in with us."

Behind Sophie, Masha saw the laughing faces of Katish and Nadia also edging out of the crowd.

The carriages were filling rapidly. The Vuich sisters were making signs from the window, but Sophie continued to hold back her fellow conspirators.

"I think we might as well get in now. Not a single White in sight," Katish began and stopped in dismay as Mademoiselle Souchet appeared in front of the girls.

"What are you waiting for? Get in at once," she ordered, and led the long-faced group to the last carriage.

"You and your bright ideas," Nadia muttered in Sophie's direction as they were settling down under the Form Mistress's eye.

The carriages moved. Through the Smolni windows, the little Browns were watching disconsolately.

"Poor things," Masha said and received a scowl from Sophie.

Mademoiselle Souchet kept making bright remarks about the shops and people on the street, but received only "Oui, Mademoiselle" in answer. But little by little the girls' spirits began to rise and by the time the Palace Square was reached, they were gay again.

The vast place was swarming with people, milling around the stalls heaped with merchandise and crowding at the tents. Merry-go-rounds turned to the accompaniment of tinkling music. Garlands of small flags flapped in the breeze. Children and grown-ups shouted on the swings. Clowns stood at the entrances to the tents, joking and asking the public to come in. The buzz of voices penetrated even through the closed windows of the carriage.

The girls pushed each other trying to see as much as possible. Mademoiselle Souchet did not try to restore order. Her eyes glued to the window, an ecstatic smile on her face, she seemed to have completely forgotten her charges.

"What is she looking at?" Katish whispered to Masha.

Nadia put her finger to her lips. "Shh, you two. Move over a little and you will see."

Craning her neck, Masha saw a slim young man sauntering alongside the slow-moving carriages, indifferent to the muddy snow splashing from under the horses' hoofs and bespattering his white breeches. Masha thought he looked like a grasshopper, with the long tails of his bright green jacket flapping against his thin legs. A giant white bow billowed under his chin and almost hid his striped, yellow vest.

"Look at his head," Nadia whispered, nodding at the high, mirror-like hat balanced on the top of an enormous wavy crest of fair hair. "That style is called a la cock."

"Mademoiselle, may I open the window on our side?" Katish asked.

"Yes, my dear, very pretty," the Form Mistress answered without turning her head.

Katish, her hand already on the sash, looked bewildered. "Er..." she began.

"Oh, sit down," Sophie whispered through suppressed laughter. "She doesn't even know what you are talking about. I'm sure if I asked her for another slice of bread and butter, she would say yes. Shall I try?"

"No!" Masha protested, but the others went into a fit of giggles and urged, "Yes, do!"

The experiment was never carried out after all. There was a sudden loud crack, the carriage lurched, jerked, and stood still.

"Ah, mon Dieu! What is it?" Mademoiselle Souchet cried, while the girls shrieked and clutched at each other.

The elderly coachman jumped off his seat and, approaching the window, started to explain something to Mademoiselle Souchet.

"He is saying," the Form Mistress told the girls, as the man turned away, "that we have grazed one of the stakes of that big tent on the left and that a front wheel almost flew off. He assures me it can be repaired in about ten minutes and then we can join the other carriages on the second round. It is customary to make several rounds of the fair." With the last words she rose from her seat, opened the door, and stepped out. "Be quiet. I will only be a few steps away," she called to the girls over her shoulder.

"Well, I never!" Sophie exclaimed. "Where did she go?"

Katish thrust her head out of the window. "She is behind that booth, talking to the a la cock man! I can see her."

"Talking, is she?" Sophie asked pensively. "I have an idea."

"What?" three voices cried.

"Let's get out too. We won't go far, just walk around and look at the stalls. It is no fun watching from the window."

"I don't mind getting into trouble from time to time," Nadia said firmly, "but this is too much."

"I agree," Katish supported her. "My parents would disown me if I were expelled from Smolni. What about you, Masha? Are you going?"

"Of course not," Masha replied indignantly.

Sophie smiled broadly. "Well, in that case I am going alone. Good-bye!" She cautiously opened the carriage door and slipped out.

"She is going to get lost!" Katish cried anxiously.

"Or trampled down. She is not used to the crowds," Nadia joined in. "Masha! What are you doing?"

"I must go after Sophie," Masha murmured, clutching at the door handle. "I can't just sit here and listen to you talk about her getting lost or killed."

"Don't!" Katish cried, but Masha was already scrambling out. In her haste, she missed the carriage step and landed on the ground on all fours. Picking herself up, she looked around. The coachman, aided by a young fellow in a sheepskin jacket, was working on the wheel. Farther away, Sophie was standing on tiptoe, trying to look over the shoulders of several women crowding around a stall. She saw Masha and grinned.

"So, you have come, after all. Look at all those pretty beads and ribbons. Wish I could buy some."

"You couldn't wear them anyway," Masha said practically. "Now, Sophie, please let's go back. Mademoiselle will be simply furious if she finds out what we have done."

"Yes, yes, I'm coming. The way you talk, one would think I was running away for good," Sophie answered tartly. "Can't we even have a look around since we are here?"

"There are too many people to see anything properly," Masha implored, jumping back to avoid a man bearing down upon her, a big bag on his back.

"Let's look at those carved toys," Sophie cried, pulling Masha after her. "See that boy buying a top? Oh, and birds in cages! And prianiki! And calico! Look at the colors!"

At the sound of Sophie's voice, a woman selecting a kerchief turned around and stared at the girls. "They are from the monastery," she told the man beside her in a loud whisper, giving him a push in the ribs. "Funny they should be running loose."

Sophie heard and blushed crimson. "Very well, we might as well go back to the carriage," she said, but this time Masha was not listening. Her face shining with delight, she pointed at something. "Look!" she whispered, "Petrushka!"

Above a faded screen, surrounded by a small crowd, the puppet Petrushka was battling with a puppet policeman. His big red nose was shining, and his mouth opened in a wide grin. He had just succeeded in giving the policeman a sound blow on the ear when a figure topped with a bright red kerchief bore down upon him, and Petrushka's wife attacked him with a broom.

The two girls stood entranced, watching Petrushka's capers, indifferent to jostlings and pushes received from all sides as the crowd grew bigger.

When the performance was over, Masha drew a deep breath. "Oh, Sophie, wasn't it lovely?"

"Thrilling," Sophie agreed. "It was... Masha, what is it? You are all pale!"

"There... It is she, Annoushka! I told you about her," Masha murmured, staring with terror at a black-robed woman emerging from between two stalls. She was carrying a bag in her hand, and on her neck glistened a brass cross, just as Masha had seen her almost five years ago.

At the sight of Masha, Annoushka stopped and lifted her hand. "There you are!" she screamed, pointing at Masha. "You have grown bigger, but you have not grown brighter. You still don't believe the truth when you hear it. I will tell you again. You will live in a palace! Remember now!"

Sophie stood transfixed, looking from Masha to Annoushka.

Again, Annoushka shouted "Remember!" and made a step forward. But Masha did not wait for her to come nearer. Seizing Sophie's hand, she dashed into the midst of the crowd, dragging her friend after her, ducking under people's elbows, and taking shelter behind every tent.

"Masha, stop!" Sophie panted at last. "That woman... Annoushka... can't possibly catch us now."

Masha stopped, still shaking and glancing fearfully around. "I was so scared!" she breathed. "Sophie, are you sure she is not behind us?"

"No, no!" Sophie reassured her. "You are quite safe." She added with a feeble laugh, "I was rather scared myself. Now listen, we must get back to the carriage. Do you know which way to go?"

"Past that booth with priamki and to the left," Masha said doubtfully. "I think I remember that big prianik shaped like a heart."

After a few steps, the girls stopped. "We are not going the right way," Sophie said. "I'm sure we never passed that stall with the wicker baskets."

"Yes, we did... No... I couldn't say..." Masha looked desperate. "Sophie, we are lost. What shall we do?"

"Don't worry. We will find the carriage somehow. We couldn't have gone too far." Sophie's tone was cheerful, but there was anxiety in her eyes. "Let's try walking toward that merry-go-round. It seems familiar... somewhat."

The two girls threaded their way through the noisy throngs of people only to come to a dead-end alley, most of it taken up by an enormous tent. A roughly painted sign announced, Siege of Ochakov. Heroic play in three acts.

"We have never been here!" Masha exclaimed, doing her best not to cry. Then Sophie suddenly made a rush forward with a joyous cry, "Michael! He will help us! Come along!"

Hurrying after her friend, Masha saw a cadet of about Sophie's age, in a dark-green frock coat with bright buttons and knee-length black breeches, coming out of the tent.

"Michael!" Sophie caught the cadet by the sleeve. "Don't you recognize me? Masha, this is my cousin, Michael Panov."

The boy did not look overjoyed at the sight of his cousin. He said, "Sophie! I didn't know you were allowed out alone."

"We aren't," Sophie answered curtly. "Now listen," and she hastily told the story.

Michael whistled. "You are in hot water," he said. "I did see several carriages with Smolni pupils in them. One carriage got stuck in the mud."

"Not stuck—the wheel broke," Sophie interrupted impatiently. "Where did you see it, Michael? Where?"

"Not too far from here. I'll show you." The young cadet led the way, stepping carefully so as not to splash wet snow on his white stockings, and staring at the girls from under the long black visor of his cap.

"Will you get whipped if you are caught?" he asked.

"No!" Sophie answered crushingly. "What about yourself? What are you doing at the bazaar?"

"I am on leave for the Easter vacation," Michael explained with great dignity, "and besides I have permission."

"Why are you creeping along the back of the tents then, if you have permission to be here?" Sophie wanted to know.

"Because I don't want my friends to see me talking to girls," Michael muttered. "Here's your carriage."

"Saved!" Sophie exclaimed. "What is the matter, Masha?"

"Say what you want, Sophie," Masha said nervously, "but we have been away much too long, at least twenty minutes. Mademoiselle can't still be talking. She must be running around looking for us."

Sophie shrugged her shoulders. "Well, she isn't. I'm sure she's behind the booth with that man. All we have to do now is make a dash for the carriage."

"Hush!" Masha hissed, pushing Sophie behind a tent. Michael promptly retreated after them.

"What's wrong now?" Sophie asked.

"The coachman," Masha answered in a low voice. "Just look!"

Peeping from behind the tent, the girls saw the coachman jump off his box and begin to look around as if trying to see something.

"Do you think he may report you?" Michael asked, also peeping out.

"He probably will. He knows we are not allowed to leave the carriage," Masha said worriedly.

"Then Michael must lure him away," Sophie decided. "Do something to make him turn his back for a few seconds, Michael. Just to give us time to get into the carriage."

"I? I am to lure him away?" Michael's eyes became round. "How?"

"I don't care. Just do something to take his attention off us," Sophie answered crossly, scowling at a group of urchins who were listening to the conversation and laughing.

Something about the laughter suddenly seemed familiar to Masha. Surely she had heard that strange "Ee" sound before? "Mitia!" she cried.

The thin, pasty face on top of the long neck blossomed into a wide smile. "Ee... You haven't forgotten me then?"

"Certainly not." Masha was so pleased she forgot about their dreadful predicament. "How are you and Katerina Ivanovna? Do you still live with her?"

"Naw." Mitia shook his head. "She got married and moved to Moscow. I am doing apprenticeship in a bakery. The master is not bad. Gave me some time off today, some money too."

"Masha, we have no time for talking," Sophie broke in. Turning to Michael, she asked wrathfully, "Are you going to get that coachman out of the way, or aren't you?"

"Aw, what can he do?" Mitia looked at the cadet with a profound disdain. "You watch me!"

Putting two fingers into his mouth, Mitia whistled shrilly and dashing from behind the tent pretended to jump on the back of the carriage.

"You, rascal!" the coachman called, waving his whip, but without moving.

Mitia whistled again and shouted something. "A bad word," Sophie whispered.

"Our big fellows sometimes use it," Michael murmured with respect.

"Asking for it, aren't you?" the coachman shouted back and took a long stride in Mitia's direction. The boy promptly vanished behind the carriage, while his friends cheered. The coachman swore and rushed in hot pursuit.

"Now!" Sophie commanded. The two girls tore to the carriage. Sophie jumped on the step first and pulled the door open.

"Come right in, Mesdemoiselles," said a familiar voice.

Stifling a shriek, Masha stared at Mademoiselle Neigardt seated by the window. Opposite her, Nadia and Katish sat very straight, with lowered eyes and folded hands.

"I was going to give you another five minutes and then send the coachman to look for you," the Inspectress said dryly, consulting the watch hanging on her belt. "You may sit down." She pointed at the seat beside her, and Masha sank into it gratefully because her knees were trembling, but Sophie remained standing.

"Mademoiselle, we did not mean..."

"Any explanation you may have is to be given to Maman," Mademoiselle Neigardt cut Sophie short. Opening the window, she ordered, "To Smolni."

As the carriage moved, Masha saw Mitia's grinning face and the cadet's open mouth float past the window.

No one spoke a word until the carriage stopped at the school entrance.

"Go upstairs and take off your cloaks," the Inspectress ordered as soon as they were inside the building. "You," she addressed Katish and Nadia, "go to your classroom and remain there until the rest of your form returns from the bazaar. You, Brozina, and you, Fredericks, will report to Maman."

There was not much time for talking, but the girls made the most of it while they were mounting the stairs and removing their outdoor clothes.

"It was terrible, terrible," Katish kept repeating, taking off her bonnet. "You two were gone for about ten minutes when Neigardt arrived in a carriage to find out what had happened to us all, and she saw Mademoiselle outside, talking. We couldn't hear what she said to her, but it must have been something cruel because Mademoiselle began to cry."

"The man was not afraid though," Nadia said admiringly. "He took Mademoiselle's hand and said something that made Neigardt keep quiet."

"Then, of course, it came out that you two were missing," Katish went on. "Mademoiselle Souchet became hysterical and wanted to run after you, but Neigardt wouldn't let her. 'The less attention we draw to them, the better,' she said. 'The reputation of Smolni is at stake. They will come back soon enough.' She sent Mademoiselle off in her carriage and sat down to wait for you."

"And now she is telling the whole story to Maman," Sophie sighed, while Masha began to tremble.

The two culprits reached the Principal's door just as the Inspectress swept out. "You may go in," she flung at the girls.

Masha had never seen Maman look so angry before. Her first question was, "Do you know why the Browns are never taken to the Easter Bazaar?"

Sophie stammered something and became silent; Masha did not even try to speak.

"Because children of their age cannot always be expected to behave in public as a Smolni pupil should," Maman went on. "However, it is considered that girls who have reached the Blue Form are old enough and have learned not to disgrace their school. You have been seen running around the fair without a chaperone and even," Maman rubbed her temples with a tired gesture, "in the company of a street urchin."

Masha was tempted to say "Mitia is not a street urchin," but she did not dare to open her mouth.

Maman spoke for a long time and ended her lecture with, "It would not surprise me if from now on Her Majesty, the Empress Maria Feodorovna, restricts the Easter Bazaar outing to the White Form."

"She is not going to punish us after all, just scold us," Masha was thinking with relief when Maman suddenly said, "Come closer, both of you." Quaking, the girls obeyed.

In terrified fascination, Masha watched the Principal take a long strip of paper from her desk with "Untrustworthy" written on it in large letters and pin it to Sophie's shoulder. In another moment a similar sign was pinned on Masha.

"You may take these off only when you go to bed tonight," Maman ordered.

The rest of the day was a nightmare of shocked glances from friends and whispers and giggles from the rest of the school. The ordeal in the refectory was especially painful to both girls, as they were ordered to eat their meals standing so that everyone could see the signs.

"I was never so humiliated in my life," Sophie raged at bedtime, taking off the offensive sign and tearing it to pieces.

"Better stop pitying yourself and think about poor Mademoiselle Souchet," Natasha told Sophie reproachfully. "She never appeared at all. Perhaps she has been discharged."

"Oh, don't say it! It makes me feel like a criminal," Sophie cried, putting her hands over her ears.

The girls learned Mademoiselle's fate the next day when Maman came to their classroom after breakfast.

"Mademoiselle Souchet is not coming back to Smolni," the Principal announced. "She is going to be married shortly and is very busy with her wedding preparations. A new Form Mistress will arrive this afternoon. Her name is Mademoiselle Padua. I trust you will obey her implicitly and that the disgraceful incident of the Easter Bazaar will never be repeated."

Later in the day, Nadia, who always succeeded in finding out the news, told her classmates the rest of the story.

"Mademoiselle is marrying her a la cock man. He is a hairdresser, and she has been engaged to him for a long time. Only he could not marry her until he had enough money to open a shop of his own."

"Does he have enough money now?" Masha asked anxiously.

"Yes," Nadia assured her. "He is going to have a beautiful shop on Nevski Prospect and all the furniture will be gilded."

"We really should send a wedding present, shouldn't we?" Katish Muffle suggested, and was greeted with a chorus of "Yes, yes! What a good idea!"

After much argument, the girls decided to make a giant pincushion of pink satin, shaped like a brush and stuck with pins to represent the bristles. The idea was carried out in the sewing class; each girl put in a few stitches.

"In very bad taste," Maman said, shaking her head when the gift was shown to her for approval, "but then they mean so well, the Hebe Kinder."

The Rosy Future

MADEMOISELLE PADUA ARRIVED AND WAS greeted by respectful curtsies from the Blue Form. She was "young middle-aged," as Sophie put it, and very thin, with a long sad face and pale green eyes. Her mouth was constantly open. She resembled, Sashette said, a fish out of the water. Very near-sighted, she was constantly snatching at her tortoise-shell lorgnette and always mislaying it. It took her several days to learn her pupils' names and when she finally mastered them, she applied them to the wrong persons.

"Divova, why aren't you at your music lesson?" she would ask, intercepting Nadia in the corridor.

"But I am Maslova, Mademoiselle," Nadia would explain.

Snatching at her lorgnette, the Form Mistress would give her a vague glance and murmur, "Ah, of course. Strange how you two look alike."

"Marie Divova is blonde, and I am dark," Nadia complained to her companions. "We are not a bit alike."

209

"We all look alike to her," Natasha said resignedly. "She always calls me Fredericks, and I don't correct her any more. It is easier."

"Oh, well, at least she doesn't scold much," the peace-loving Katish Muffle remarked. "She is not severe."

"She is too vague to be severe," Sashette scoffed. "I asked her yesterday if I could stay a little longer after the study hour to find the answer to that arithmetic problem. She stared at me and answered, "Search in your desk. It may have slipped among your books."

"I still think we are lucky," Katish insisted. "She doesn't really mind if we break a rule now and then."

The Blue Form soon discovered that Katish was right. Compared to Mademoiselle Padua, even the easygoing Mademoiselle Souchet seemed a strict disciplinarian. It became common practice to munch sweets during lessons, read storybooks in study hour, and skip piano practice whenever possible.

Fraulein Knappe, on the contrary, seemed to have become stricter since Mademoiselle Padua's arrival. The girls were busy enjoying their new privileges until one day Stephanie openly passed a box of caramels to Sashette during the geography lesson.

Seated at her desk, Fraulein did not say a word, but her eyes roamed from Sashette, calmly selecting her favorite flavor, to Sophie, peeling an orange behind a book.

When the lessons were over and the girls began to get up from their desks to go to the dormitory to prepare for dinner, Fraulein made a sign for them to sit down again.

"I have noticed," she said, "that several of you, if not all, have forgotten the most elementary rules of this establishment. It is therefore necessary for you to review them." Opening her drawer, she took out a thin bound book. "I want your full attention, please. No eating and no whispering. Now listen: Rule One..."

After Rule Ten, Emilia Agte risked a timid, "Fraulein please, the dinner bell..."

"Do not be concerned about it. We are not expected in the

refectory. This is far more important than dinner," Fraulein Knappe answered calmly, turning the page. "Rule Eleven..."

There was no more eating of sweets in the classroom when Fraulein Knappe was on duty, but as far as Mademoiselle Padua was concerned, the girls decided once and for all that "you can do what you want, and Mademoiselle won't even know who you are."

"Of course, it is wicked of us to take advantage of her, but I don't think she really cares," Varia told Masha one afternoon as they sat in the classroom, watching the Form Mistress distribute mail to the pupils.

"She is doing it all wrong as usual," Varia whispered laughingly, as girl after girl returned their letters to the Form Mistress with a "It is not for me, Mademoiselle."

"Fredericks!" Mademoiselle Padua called. Masha rose and went to the desk feeling sure there was a mistake again. Her mother wrote regularly twice a month and she had received a letter last week. But to her surprise, she saw the familiar handwriting on the envelope.

With a hasty "Merci, Mademoiselle," Masha returned to her seat and opened the letter. Her hands trembled as she unfolded the sheet of paper. What could have happened? Maybe Mamma was sick, or Niania... She began to read.

The first few lines seemed blurred, but as Masha read on, the fog before her eyes cleared and her face shone with joy. At last she folded the letter again and sat quietly, thinking over the good news.

Yes, she well remembered the bare strip of land beyond the birch grove that her mother was writing about. It was a desolate-looking spot, but now it turned out to contain clay and her mother had rented it to some people who made bricks. With a smile, Masha thought about the "Story of a Brick" in Children's Reading. Renting the land did not bring a great deal of money, but a little extra on the mortgage had been paid and Mamma had put some money aside for her "special plan."

At this point, Masha unfolded the letter again and reread a page: "I've been giving a great deal of thought to your future, my darling Masha. After all, you are more than halfway through Smolni, Here is the idea that has come to me, and I am serious. How would you like to open a school of your own? There are several wealthy landowners in our part of the country. They would like to have their daughters well educated, but quite often they do not like to have a governess in the house, and at the same time they hesitate to send their girls to a boarding school. We could take three or four girls as pupils. They could live with us and at the same time be close to their families. When people hear about your Smolni diploma, we will have more pupils than we may be able to handle. I could help you to supervise the girls, maybe also teach music or singing. Wouldn't it be wonderful for us to be together instead of your earning your living among strangers? Now we have money to repair the house."

Masha put her forehead against the letter. In her dreams she was already seeing the house rejuvenated, the garden full of flowers, her future pupils walking arm in arm along the cedar avenue. In the evenings, they would gather around the piano. Her mother would play, and they would all sing. Niania... She tried not to think about the postscript in her mother's letter, "I'm sorry to say that Niania is becoming more and more strange. She seems to waver between the past and the present. A few days ago, we found her in the attic, rocking your old cradle and singing a lullaby. She keeps airing your old clothes, saying that you will need them when you come back. She loves you very much, Masha."

"I will come back and bring Niania out of the past," Masha decided. "She will recognize me, even though I will be grown up. She can still have a few happy years with us."

Varia looked at Masha's face. "You must have had happy news in that letter," she said.

"I did," Masha answered simply. "Everything is well at home." Then she frowned a little. There was something in her mother's letter that bothered her.

"I know you are trying to be a good student," her mother wrote, "but do you think you could do even better? Maybe if you worked just a little bit harder you could graduate with a silver medal? It would impress people here a great deal, and that is important for us. A silver medal is all that I want."

This would mean giving up some dreaming and reading of story-books... Masha sighed, then threw back her shoulders and snatched a sheet of paper from her desk. There was so much to tell her mother; her hand flew.

"I promise you a silver medal." She reread the written words and pressed her lips resolutely. "But dearest Mamma, please promise me something too. When I am in the White Form, will you come and see me in my uniform? Just once, Mamma! It will make me so happy."

The bell for tea rang just as Masha finished the letter.

That very evening, sitting cross-legged on Sophie's bed, Masha told her friend about her mother's wonderful plan.

Sophie was sympathetic, but not enthusiastic. "Of course, it might be nice for her, but it also means you will be away from me, buried in the country. I had hoped you would stay in St. Petersburg. Why couldn't you become a lady-in-waiting, for instance?"

"Sophie!" Masha almost fell off the bed. "You know I could never become one! Why, I've never even thought about it."

Sashette, who had overheard the whole conversation, drawled, "That's lucky. Then you will be spared the disappointment."

"Eavesdropper!..." Sophie began wrathfully, but Sashette turned away and addressed Marie Divova. "Imagine our Masha in the Winter Palace!" she said. "She would run away the minute the Emperor looked at her, or someone asked her to dance, just as she did when we were Browns and the Grand Duke Nicholas spoke to her. Imagine the consternation—a lady-in-waiting in flight! Or suddenly forgetting her French! That happens to you, Masha, doesn't it?"

Sophie was scrambling out of bed, her fists clenched, but Masha held her back. "Please, Sophie, don't pay any attention. She is only teasing. I don't care... now. I am too happy."

Fraulein Knappe's appearance put an end to Sophie's plans for revenge. Soon the girls were asleep. Only Masha stayed awake for a long time, busily planning a list of books she would need for her future school.

CHAPTER TWENTY-THREE

The Midnight Feast

THE BLUE FORM'S THIRD YEAR BEGAN WITH an unusual event. Marie Divova was allowed to go home for two days to attend her cousin Zinaida's wedding.

"I still can't believe it is true!" Marie told her class-mates, who were gathered around to say good-bye. "Pupils are only allowed to go home when there is a death in their family. But Papa came twice to ask Maman to please make an exception this time, and my cousin pleaded with the Empress Maria Feodorovna."

"You are lucky!" the girls repeated enviously, as Marie set off accompanied by Mademoiselle Padua.

She returned on the second day, just as the girls were washing their hands before afternoon tea. "It was wonderful! Splendid!" she told the excited crowd. "Zinaida is an orphan and at first Papa was supposed to give her away, but then it was decided that she was to be married from the Winter Palace and it was the Emperor himself who gave her away! The wedding was in the palace church—and oh, such, gowns, such hats! Zinaida had an heirloom veil, and the

215

Empress gave her an emerald bracelet as a gift. I like her fiancé—her husband, I mean. You should have seen how he looked at her when they exchanged rings! I only had a glimpse of her trousseau—everything was packed already—but what I saw was simply well, I just can't describe it. They are off to Italy for their honeymoon, and when they come back he is going to be a vice-governor of some province in the north of Russia, I forget which. Anyway, Zinaida will be a grand lady, give dinners, balls..." Marie paused, out of breath.

"Your cousin Zinaida must have been born under a lucky star to have found such a husband," Katish exclaimed with feeling. "Handsome, rich..."

"Lucky star has nothing to do with it," Sashette interrupted. "It all comes from being a lady-in-waiting. A girl meets the right people at court, and she can choose She is not obliged to marry the 'only neighbor's son' even if he is a hunchback, or take a husband her parents have selected for her because they happen to like him."

Stephanie, who did not seem interested in Sashette's speech, was examining a big flat cardboard box that lay on Marie's bed. "What's that?" she asked curiously.

Marie began to laugh. "It's a pirog," she announced. "Papa couldn't stop laughing when I told him I'd rather have a pirog to take to school with me than the very best bonbons." She held up the box for everyone to see. "Look how big it is! One half is filled with minced meat and the other with rice and eggs. Let's all get up tonight after lights-out and have a feast. The whole form is invited."

"Why make such a secret of it?" Natasha wanted to know. "It is not forbidden to eat our own goodies."

"Because there is a special reason," Marie answered with annoyance. She lowered her voice. "Remember how we used to talk about the Emperor Paul's assassination when we were in the Brown Form? I heard a new story when I was home. It's very exciting and frightening too. I am simply longing to tell it to you. At night no one will disturb us, and we won't get into trouble. Shall we do it?"

"Yes, yes!" the girls cried, and Marie said, "It is settled then. Tonight about eleven, after the Form Mistress on duty makes her rounds."

"The bell!" Varia cried, and the girls started to form ranks.

Standing on the outskirts of the crowd, Masha saw Marie draw Sashette close to her and whisper something into her ear. Sashette looked amused and Masha heard her whisper back, "That should be fun, but I'd better warn Stephanie."

"If you tell that little idiot I will never speak to you again," Marie whispered back fiercely, and the two girls ran to join the others.

Sophie was the last to fall in rank. "I was tying my shoe ribbon," she explained, with a mischievous smile.

Everyone was excited about the midnight feast. Giggles came from every corner of the dormitory that evening. Small groups formed and broke apart the minute Mademoiselle Padua came near. Fraulein Knappe would have been on the alert immediately, but Mademoiselle Padua only glanced vaguely through her lorgnette and remarked that the air was so heavy, there might be a thunderstorm that night.

"Don't go to sleep," Nadia whispered, leaning over from her bed and tugging at Masha's blanket.

"I won't," Masha promised. But she dozed off almost immediately and woke up two hours later only because someone was shaking her.

"Get up," Sophie was whispering urgently. "The fun is about to start."

The dormitory seemed to be darker than usual, and Masha realized that instead of two night-lights only one was burning.

"Sashette thought it would be a good idea to put one light out," Nadia explained. "She said that if anyone came in, we could get into bed before we are recognized."

"Everyone bring your stool," Marie called from the other end of the dormitory, "and a tumbler."

"I'll help you," Sophie offered, seizing Masha's stool.

Still sleepy, Masha thrust her feet into her slippers, found her tumbler, and followed Sophie.

Several shadowy figures were bustling around two bedside tables that had been placed together and covered with a sheet. Even in the flickering night-light, the spread looked magnificent. The big square pirog occupied the center of the festive board. There was fruit, a box of chocolates, and a big bottle filled with a red liquid.

"Katish contributed the chocolates," Sophie said. "Her mother sent her a box. And that is cranberry kvas a maid brought for Nadia."

"Drinking is a sin," Lena Mandrika said reprovingly.

"Drinking!" Katish cried. "Don't be silly, Lena. There are no spirits in kvas, only cranberry juice, sugar, water, and whatever it is that makes it fizz."

"Please take your seats," Marie invited, and the girls sat in a circle around the improvised table. Sashette cut the pirog with a penknife and Varia handed it around on sheets torn from an exercise book.

At first the girls talked in whispers and kept glancing in the direction of the door, but by the time the fruit and chocolates were reached everyone was chattering away.

"What are we going to do with the empty bottle?" Natasha asked.

"Bury it in the garden tomorrow," Nadia advised.

"Put in a note and lower it out of the window," Katish giggled.

"What would you write?" Stephanie asked seriously.

"She thinks I really mean it!" Katish shrieked with laughter, then checked herself. "I'm sorry!"

"Well, do you girls want to listen to Marie's story or not?" Sophie's tone was so sharp her classmates became silent.

"Why has she suddenly become so friendly with Marie?" Masha couldn't help wondering as she watched Sophie lead Marie forward. "If you stand right by the window we shall all be able to hear and see you," she said, and then slipped back to her seat beside Masha.

Marie turned out to be a good storyteller. After a few minutes there was no more whispering or yawning. Instead, the girls were following the assassins through the dark Summer Garden on a rainy night in March, 1801.

Crouched on her stool, Masha imagined the dark, cloaked figures, whipped by the wind, taking shortcuts through the shrubbery. She could almost see the gleam of their lantern and hear the croaking of hundreds of crows roosting in the ancient trees and disturbed by the intruders.

"The Emperor could have been warned by the crows' crying," Marie was saying, "but he paid no attention to it. It is strange how he seemed to play right into the hands of his enemies. That very evening he ordered his faithful guards removed because he suspected them of treason. Even the doors leading to the apartments of Maria Feodorovna were locked because he thought his wife was against him too."

A hand touched Masha's knee. "If everyone suddenly starts shrieking don't pay any attention," Sophie whispered. "Just sit tight."

"Yes, yes, I will," Masha whispered back. "Don't bother me, Sophie, I want to listen."

"There was a secret door in the Emperor's bedroom," Marie went on. "It was hidden behind a large tapestry, a present from Louis XVI and Marie Antoinette. It was said that it brought bad luck, but the Emperor Paul liked it."

Distant lightning flashed past the window and several girls shuddered.

Marie lowered her voice dramatically. "It was past midnight when the conspirators burst into the Emperor Paul's apartments and demanded that he sign the abdication in favor of his oldest son, Alexander. Paul refused. They started to threaten him, and he realized they were going to kill him. He ran toward the secret door and would have escaped, but the tapestry fell and... ah... ah...!"

Marie let out an agonized shriek as something white descended from above and covered her from head to foot. There was an answering shriek from the other end of the dormitory and at the same time the night-light went out.

Instinctively, Masha put out her hand. Sophie was no longer beside her. She scrambled to her feet and immediately became engulfed in the stream of running shadows.

A rumble of thunder shook the windowpanes, adding the last note of terror. The screaming, panic-stricken crowd of girls stampeded across the dormitory, pushed through the door, and spilled onto the landing. There were shrieks of "Oh, please stop! You are hurting me!" but no one paid any attention.

Carried across the landing, Masha stumbled on her long nightgown and only saved herself from falling by clutching at the banister. The next moment she was already slithering down the steps, dragged by the frightened crowd.

Suddenly a glimmer of light appeared at the foot of the stairway and the girls stopped short. Masha saw Maman in a gray dressing gown, a small nightcap on her head. Behind her hovered Mademoiselle Padua and several maids with candles.

For the first time in the history of Smolni, no one curtsied. The girls stood huddled together, still trembling. Several sank down and sat on the steps.

"What has happened?" The Principal's voice was strained and anxious.

There was no answer at first, then Natasha mumbled through chattering teeth, "Something w...white came from the cei...ceiling."

Maman looked relieved. "Really?" she asked. "And who saw this... er... apparition?"

Several voices shouted in protest. "We all saw it, Maman. We are not imagining it."

"It fell right over me," Marie Divova spoke from the back of the crowd.

"Fell right over you?" the Principal repeated. "Did you see what it was?"

"No," Marie muttered in a sob. "I pushed it away and ran."

Mademoiselle Padua pressed both hands against her breast. "Madame, I assure you, I made my rounds as usual. Everything seemed to be in order."

Mademoiselle Neigardt pushed her way through the group of maids and joined the headmistress. "There is no doubt in my mind that all this is simply mischief," she said. Her hair in paper curlers, a white shawl around her shoulders, she glared at the girls.

"We will find out in due time, Mademoiselle," the Principal answered calmly. "In the meantime, we should take a look at the dormitory." She gathered her dressing gown around her and started to mount the stairway, followed by the Inspectress, Mademoiselle Padua, and the maids.

Something warm trickled down Masha's knee. She saw a big scratch. "I must have hurt myself when I fell," she thought. Then, as Sophie suddenly appeared beside her, she jumped.

"Why didn't you sit quietly as I told you?" Sophie asked. "You wouldn't have been hurt then."

The pain and fright made Masha lose her patience. "How could I sit quietly with people falling over me?" she asked. "And where have you been?"

Instead of answering, Sophie blushed and went up the stairs.

Puzzled, Masha followed her friend into the dormitory. The girls stood together at the door, watching the maids light the oil lamps.

"A real battlefield," Mademoiselle Neigardt remarked sarcastically as the light revealed overturned stools, smashed tumblers, and beds pushed out of place.

Maman did not say a word. She was carefully making her way toward the window at the other side of the room. Everyone moved after her, as if drawn by a magnet.

The improvised table with the remains of pirog and the empty bottle stood intact.

"They have been drinking," Mademoiselle Padua whispered, her lorgnette trembling in her hand.

A slight smile flickered on Maman's face. "It is not wine, Mademoiselle. Judging from the bottle, it is only kvas. However, I agree with you that this is not the time nor place to drink it" She looked around. "I still don't see what could have caused the alarm. Ah, here it is!" She bent down and scooped something from the floor near the window.

The girls came nearer. Maman was holding one of the long white cambric curtains that framed the dormitory windows.

"It must have slipped off the rod," the Principal said, glancing up. "Very strange. The other half seems quite secure. Well, we can clear up this matter tomorrow. Now, I want to ask you all something." She turned around and faced the girls. Her voice became severe. "Whose idea was it to arrange this... er... gathering?"

There was silence.

The Inspectress said sharply, "Divova, you brought some fruit and other things from home. I saw you."

Marie reluctantly stepped forward. "Yes, Mademoiselle."

"Yes, what?" Maman asked impatiently. "You mean you incited your classmates to break the rules?"

"I did," Marie murmured miserably.

"I provided the kvas" Nadia chipped in, and Katish followed with, "And I brought the chocolates."

Maman waved them aside. Picking up the curtain, she showed it to Marie. "Did you use this to frighten everybody?"

"No, no!" Marie cried, backing away. "I didn't! Everyone could see that I never touched it. I was telling a story when that thing fell on me. It happened just before Sashette blew out the light. She... I..." Marie began to mumble and turned crimson.

Sashette stepped forward. "I was with Marie, Maman. I mean, I helped her."

"Helped?"

"We... we thought it would be a joke to blow out the light just as Marie reached the most frightening part of the story. I blew one night-light out before we started to eat and later the other one, but we had nothing to do with the curtain."

The Principal frowned and looked at Marie. "What was the story about?"

Marie became even more embarrassed. "Something my grandmother told me while I was home. She was at court twenty years ago and..."

The Principal lifted her hand. "That will do. I understand."

"We never intended..." Sashette began.

"I don't want any explanations now," Maman interrupted. "You, Rossett, and you, Divova, will present yourselves in my rooms tomorrow at ten. I am distressed by your behavior, and you will both be severely punished. You, Muffle and Maslova, are deprived of your aprons for three days. Now, every one of you go to bed immediately!" Turning to Mademoiselle Padua, she added, "Please see that the lights are turned out in ten minutes."

Looking highly displeased, Maman left the dormitory, a depressed silence reigning behind her.

Masha waited until everyone was asleep, then crept to Sophie's bed.

Just as she had expected, her friend was not asleep.

"What do you want?" Sophie asked gruffly.

Masha gathered her courage. "I want to ask you if you are going to Maman with Sashette and Marie tomorrow?"

"No, I am not!" Sophie pushed back the blanket and sat up in bed. "Why should I?" she asked. "Marie and Sashette started it all. I only happened to overhear how they planned to scare us. Let them pay for it. I only wanted to scare them. How could I know the silly girls would become hysterical and a stupid maid would rush and wake up Maman? All I did was loosen the curtain so that it slipped off the rod as soon as I touched it. Marie got the fright she deserved. I am not going to Maman. Why are you staring at me?"

"Because," Masha said, "I simply can't believe you will allow the others to take the blame for what you have done."

"I don't care what you believe." Sophie snuggled down and pulled the blanket to her eyes. "I'm sleepy. Good night."

Disappointed and sad, Masha went to bed. "But I mustn't think badly of Sophie," she told herself. "She is just tired now. Tomorrow morning she will be quite different."

But in the morning Sophie did not show any sign of repentance. She avoided speaking to Masha and at breakfast she sat at the other end of the table.

BLUE

As the girls entered the classroom, Masha tried once more, "Sophie," she began, "please..."

Sophie turned away. "Leave me alone. You can't force me to own up."

"No," Masha said slowly, "I can't force you, but I can despise you."

She left Sophie standing with wide eyes and went to her desk.

"Mademoiselle Garbi is ill, so there will be no arithmetic lesson today," Fraulein Knappe announced after the first class. "Study your geography until the long recess. Divova and Rossett, go to Maman. It is almost ten o'clock."

"May I go with them, please?" It was Sophie.

Masha clasped her hands tightly and waited.

Fraulein raised her eyebrows. "You, Brozina? Why?"

Sophie's voice was firm. "Because it was I who made the curtain fall on Marie. I slipped the rings to the very end of the rod beforehand, so all I had to do was pull a little. I tried to put it back later, only I couldn't do it in the dark."

The class sat frozen, every pair of eyes on Sophie. "And you never..." Marie started to say indignantly but was silenced by the Form Mistress's sharp glance.

"You may go," Fraulein Knappe told Sophie.

No one studied geography very hard after the door closed behind the trio. The girls did not even bother to lower their voices as they discussed Sophie's sudden confession.

Fraulein Knappe made no remarks. Her eyes on her knitting, she did not seem to hear.

Masha seized Nadia's hand under the desk. "Do you think they will be punished very severely?" she asked anxiously.

Nadia nodded. "Well, that's what Maman said last night. I wouldn't be much surprised if they are whipped."

"Whipped?" Masha exclaimed, alarmed. "But whipping is not allowed at Smolni."

"The Empress Catherine did not allow it," Nadia corrected. "Maria Feodorovna does, 'as a last measure.' This may be the last measure."

"I don't remember anyone being whipped," Masha insisted, hoping against hope that Nadia was simply trying to scare her.

"Not in your time," Nadia admitted. "But when I was very little two Browns had an argument in church and started slapping each other. They were both whipped, in front of the whole school too."

"And is it Maman herself who…" Masha murmured faintly.

"Oh, no! A maid administers the whipping," Nadia explained and added vehemently, "I think that they deserve it, especially Sophie. Fancy letting the other two take all the blame!"

The culprits came back just before the long recess. Marie Divova collapsed on the nearest desk, and burying her face in her hands, started to sob. Sashette brushed aside her classmates, who were asking eagerly, "What happened? What did Maman say?" Sitting down beside Stephanie, she began to whisper into her ear.

Only Sophie, her eyes flashing defiance, went straight to Fraulein Knappe. "Maman has ordered," she said in a clear voice, "that the three of us kneel in church tomorrow."

"That's almost as bad as a whipping," Nadia whispered to Masha. "They will have to remain on their knees, where everyone can see them, all through the service."

Sophie curtsied to the Form Mistress and came to Masha. "Don't you dare say you despise me now," she said coldly.

"I don't!" Masha said, ready to burst into tears. "Oh, Sophie, I wish I could help you!"

"Don't bother. I can take care of myself."

Sophie bore her punishment bravely, but nevertheless her face was crimson when she and her two companions walked up the aisle of the church to kneel in front of the altar in everyone's sight.

The ordeal was over with the end of the service, but Sophie found that there was a greater price to pay. The girls did not forgive her easily for not immediately owning up to her share in what Nadia called "the witches' night." Conversations stopped when she came near, and no one passed notes to her during lessons or came to sit on her bed in the evenings.

It was Masha who threw herself into the breach between Sophie and the rest of the form. She was constantly on the lookout to make sure Sophie was included in a game, or she chattered and laughed to cover the silence of the others.

"You don't have to fight for me," Sophie once told Masha, after overhearing an argument. "If Lena Mandrika doesn't want to walk with me, it's all right. I don't care."

"I do," Masha answered stubbornly.

But as the weeks slipped by, Masha found that she had less and less cause to defend her friend. The dormitory commotion seemed to become ancient history compared to the new excitement—the end of the school year, the end of the Blue Form. The girls were now dreaming of white uniforms.

WHITE

End of a Dream

WHITES! WHITES! WE ARE WHITES AT LAST!" Masha and her classmates danced all over the dormitory, stumbling against beds and each other. Katish Muffle was the first to sink on a stool, out of breath, and the others followed her example, only to jump up again, afraid to wrinkle the white gowns and green aprons.

Faces looked different too with hair pinned up in loose knots and curls waving on the temples. "We are really grown up now," Masha thought. "Fifteen years old!"

"Just think of all the new privileges we are going to have!" Marie Divova rejoiced. "Bedtime a whole hour later, singing lessons, theater..."

"And new subjects," Natasha joined in, "physics, geometry, heraldics!"

Sophie eyed them with disdain. "Theater happens only once a year and not all of us like to study. You are forgetting the biggest privilege—kitchen duty!"

Sashette made a face. "Helping to plan menus and going to the kitchen to see if the food is fresh? I don't care so much about that."

"Well, I do," Sophie declared. "Don't you remember how Suvorova and the others used to bring us lumps of sugar and fruit? Varia and I are on kitchen duty tomorrow; I've seen the lists. You may all expect a treat."

"You forget our new Form Mistress," Masha reminded. "She won't let you touch anything in the kitchen."

Every face fell. The vague, absent-minded Mademoiselle Padua had left, and her place had been taken by Madame Legarpe.

"You have proved yourselves to be in need of strict discipline," Maman had said. "The Blues will have a new Form Mistress, and Madame Legarpe will see that your conduct is improved."

After a few weeks with Madame Legarpe, the general opinion was, "Now we have had enough discipline to last a lifetime!"

But Sophie never gave up hope. Next morning she came running into the classroom, a bunch of carrots in her hand. "The cook slipped them to me," she panted. "If we cut them in half, there will be enough for everybody."

Masha had not seen a raw vegetable, let alone tasted one, since she entered Smolni. She bit into her carrot cautiously. Immediately, half-forgotten scenes floated into her memory. She could see the vegetable garden at home, the scarecrow's old hat high against the blue sky, and Mavra's sunflowers waving their heads. She could smell the parsley and hear the sound of Stepan's spade digging a new tomato patch.

At the same time, another feeling slowly rose in Masha's heart, a strange, deadly conviction that she would never see the dearly loved places again, except in memory. She sat still, hoping the feeling would disappear, but it stayed on, gripping her whole being with a cold certainty from which there was no escape.

"Masha!" Katish touched Masha's hand. "Has something frightened you? You look so strange."

"Frightened me?" Yes, I mean no..." Masha stammered.

"You look sad lately," Katish pursued. "Aren't you happy to be in the White Form?"

"Of course I am," Masha assured her, "only... Mamma promised to come and see me in my white uniform and now she writes that the house is being repaired and she can't leave until the work is finished. It may not be till November and the roads are so bad in late autumn."

"Not always," Katish consoled. "It is already September and we have not had a drop of rain."

In the meantime, Smolni was getting ready for a big event. The Twenty-Fifth Jubilee of Maria Feodorovna's patronage was to be celebrated at the end of November. Lessons were stopped for a month and the girls practiced dancing and singing for a concert and a short ballet staged by Monsieur Didlo, the great ballet master himself.

Masha did not have an especially good voice and she was only singing in the chorus, but she and Sophie were to perform the Shepherd's Dance.

The Jubilee was fast approaching when Masha received a short letter from home.

"I am all ready to start," Mamma wrote. "Just give me a day or two more, dearest, to recover from a cold. I suppose I couldn't help catching it with half the roof off and all the doors constantly open. Now everything is in order and the house is warm. Niania is brewing her special tea for me, and I will be well in no time."

"Mamma is coming!" Masha rejoiced.

A week later, she was sitting behind the stage, mending a hole in her stocking without taking it off. A rehearsal was to start any moment and she was pricking her fingers trying to be ready in time.

"Masha! Masha!" Sophie entered like a whirlwind. "I just met a student teacher on the stairs. She was looking for you. Maman wants to see you immediately. There is someone from your home in her rooms. It must be your mother. Hurry!"

"Mamma is here!" Masha desperately jabbed the last stitch and broke off the thread. Sophie helped her pull up the stocking and tie the shoe ribbons.

Other girls were also crowding around Masha, pleased and at the same time a little envious.

"I'd better tell Madame Legarpe," Masha murmured, fighting with impatience.

"Oh, don't waste time!" Nadia cried. "Maman sent for you and that is enough. Are you sure now, Sophie?"

"Goodness, how many times do I have to repeat it!" Sophie exclaimed. "I met the student teacher, and she asked me, 'Where is your Form Mistress? Someone from Fredericks' home is in Maman's rooms,' She has probably found Madame Legarpe by now and told her."

Masha did not wait for more explanations. She picked up the white skirts of her uniform and ran. Reaching the Principal's door, she stopped, smoothed her hair from sheer force of habit, knocked, and entered.

"Stepan!"

He was sitting sideways on a high-backed chair by the door, his toes turned in. At the sight of Masha, he rose, dropping his cap to the floor.

Masha stood, swallowing hard. It was all quite clear to her. Mamma had decided not to come and had sent Stepan instead. It was not his fault; he would be hurt if she showed her disappointment. She tried to smile.

Stepan peered into her face. Suddenly, his mouth twisted. Lifting his hand, he crossed himself. "On the ninth," he muttered.

"On the ninth? What about the ninth?" Masha cried sharply, feeling something cold creep around her heart.

Stepan's face became ashen. "I thought you knew..." he said hoarsely. "Barinia... she met our Lord on the ninth."

For a second, Masha's mind became completely blank, then something jarred her whole body and the window across the room seemed to turn smaller and smaller.

"Oh, my dear! Fredericks!" Dimly, Masha was aware of Maman's hands on her shoulders and then of Mademoiselle Neigardt's voice asking something and Maman answering, "I can't imagine why she came. I sent for her Form Mistress." Then the voices became less and less distinct and a dense gray cloud blotted out the whole world.

When Masha came to herself, she was in the school hospital and her first thought was that the pillow was much softer than the dormitory pillows. There was a screen around her bed and a smell of mint permeated the air. The smell made Masha drowsy, but she could not sleep because behind the screen someone was crying hysterically, repeating, "It is all my fault. It is all my fault." It sounded like Sophie, and Masha wondered why.

Soon it became quiet in the ward, a deadly quiet that seemed to last and last. From time to time, Masha could feel cold fingers touch her arm or face. Then the round face of Dr. Romanus, who treated all Smolni pupils, floated out of somewhere, only to disappear into the fog again. But one day the doctor's face did not fade, and she could hear his voice instead of just a faint murmur, "You've been here for ten days, young lady. It is time to get well."

"It couldn't be ten days," she told herself. "The doctor must have meant ten months, or maybe years?"

By the end of the week, she was sitting up in bed and the screen that shut out the ward was removed. Wrapped in a warm shawl, Masha sat for hours looking at the wintry sunbeams reflected in the polished hospital floor. The two other occupants of the ward were Browns and too much in awe of a White to disturb her.

There was enough time to think, to grope back to the time when she was mending her stocking and Sophie came and sent her to Maman. But why had Maman wanted her? She remembered coming to Maman's door and smoothing her hair. That was all.

It would have been simple to ask Maman herself, for she came to the hospital almost every day, but for some reason Masha found herself unable to speak.

Still, it was Maman who in the end gave her the clue. "Your man had to return home," she told Masha gently. "It was not possible for him to stay in the city and wait for you to recover."

"Stepan…"

It felt as though someone had flung the door to Maman's rooms wide open, turning time backward. She remembered it all now…. Her mother was dead…

After six years of discipline, it was impossible to cry in front of Maman, at least not in the way Masha wanted to cry, giving herself up completely to the grief. She simply sank back into her pillow, saying through clenched teeth, "Maman, I feel very tired."

As soon as Maman left, Masha flung back her blanket, swung her feet onto the floor, and began to look for her slippers.

The hospital nurse, a small elderly woman with a pale face, saw her and came running across the ward. "My dear, don't! The doctor said you may not get up yet."

Masha forced herself to speak, "Please, may I go into the garden? Just for a little while. The doctor won't even know."

"Into the garden?" the nurse cried in horror. "It is snowing outside! Now, now. What an idea!" She felt Masha's pulse and gently forced her back into bed.

Masha turned to the wall. It would have been such a comfort to cry by the birch tree. She waited impatiently for the darkness and peace, but when night came and everything grew silent, weakness took over and she fell asleep.

The next day the girls were allowed to see Masha. Sophie came first. But as soon as she began, "I am so sorry…" Masha interrupted her with such a sharp, "No! I don't want to talk about it!" that Sophie stopped in mid-sentence. She must have told the others about it because when the rest of the form came, drifting in by twos and threes, no one mentioned Masha's loss. They only asked about her health and gave her the latest school news.

A letter arrived from Olga Kirilovna. It was a kind letter, but it hurt too. "Olga Kirilovna was there," Masha thought sadly. "She saw Mamma for the last time. I wish I could have."

END OF A DREAM

One afternoon Masha was sitting up, with half-closed eyes, when she felt someone looking at her. She opened her eyes wide and almost cried out in astonishment. Nelidova was standing at the foot of her bed. Masha had seldom seen her in the past years and had never spoken to her since that faraway Christmas Eve.

Nelidova looked older. There was a net of fine lines around her big, black eyes which were fixed on Masha. For a moment there was silence as they looked at each other, and then Nelidova leaned a little forward.

"Do you remember how I told you that when I was a little girl, I could see my loved ones' faces in the fog?" she asked Masha. "I didn't tell you the rest of the story. Later, when those I loved left this life, I came to realize little by little that I had not really lost them. They are always with me, loving, just as always. More maybe—understanding, forgiving. Only, there is one difference: I can never lose them again."

"I understand," Masha breathed, feeling sudden tears mount in her throat. But this time the tears did not hurt. They brought peace. She was just about to speak to Nelidova again when there was a tap-tap of high-heeled shoes and the Empress Maria Feodorovna appeared in the ward, accompanied by the Principal. They walked straight to Masha's bed.

"She seems much stronger and is taking her grief very bravely," Maman was saying.

The Empress looked gravely and sympathetically at Masha. "I was so sorry to hear about your mother," she said in her warm voice. "However, I am sure it was a consolation for her to know that you are at Smolni, being cared for and prepared for the future."

Masha looked up, her eyes suddenly dark. "How could Mamma be glad to have me away from her when... when..." She could not bring herself to say the word. Turning her head, she fell face downward onto her pillow, sobbing.

Maman said, "Oh, my dear!" in a shocked voice, but the Empress only murmured something about "the poor child still being very weak" and taking Nelidova by the arm, moved on to the Browns' beds.

Masha cried all the rest of the afternoon. "Mamma would never have died of a neglected cold had I been with her," she kept saying, and sobbed again. Her tears left her utterly exhausted.

Maria Feodorovna's Jubilee came two days later. Masha thought about Sophie dancing the Shepherd's Dance with Katish, wondering indifferently whether Katish had mastered all the steps at such short notice.

Soon Masha was allowed to get up and at last sent back to her classes.

"You must resume your studies and all your usual occupations," Maman told her. "You are strong enough now."

Masha curtsied. "Yes, Maman."

The Principal eyed her thoughtfully. "I want to say something to you, Fredericks," she told Masha. "You must practice restraint, my dear. That outburst in the hospital was quite uncalled for and it is fortunate that Her Majesty was so understanding about it. We must restrain ourselves no matter how we feel. You will find it very useful later in life."

Masha curtsied again. "I am sorry, Maman. I promise to restrain myself... always."

The promise was easy to keep, as she found out painfully day after day. In the giant building of Smolni, there was no place to cry unobserved. Sorrow had to be kept back while one sat at lessons or at the refectory table or even lay in bed at night, because the Form Mistress making her rounds would be sure to hear sobbing. It was like a circle, going on and on.

"She is just as usual, only a little paler perhaps," the girls whispered to each other.

Masha heard them. "I am practicing restraint," she thought.

In March she was summoned again to the Principal's rooms and listened without flinching to the news of Niania's death. It seemed only natural that Niania should follow Mamma into death as she had always followed her everywhere. It also seemed natural that the old house should be sold to pay the debts. Without Mamma and

Niania the house was no longer a home. But when she received a letter from Olga Kirilovna's governess Aglaya, telling that Trezor had disappeared, she gave way to such frantic despair that Madame Legarpe became indignant.

"You don't seem to realize it is indecent to grieve so much about a dog," she told Masha.

"I am sorry, Mademoiselle," Masha answered, putting her handkerchief away.

Fraulein Knappe was more sympathetic. "Old dogs often go and hide somewhere when they feel their time has come," she told Masha kindly. "It is easier for them that way."

Masha became quieter than ever, only rarely taking part in the chattering of her classmates and sitting at her desk during lessons without listening to the teachers.

"You are getting lower and lower in the class," Natasha chided her. "You will never get a medal if you don't study harder."

"I don't need a medal now. What for?" Masha asked.

Natasha looked at her, gathered her books hastily and walked away.

As the end of the school year came near, Maman sent for Masha.

"Fredericks," the Principal said with more concern than severity, "you know of course that your marks are very poor, so poor indeed that it was decided that the work is too difficult for you. Unless you show a considerable improvement at the examinations, you will be transferred to the Second Division next year." She looked at Masha and added gently, "It will be less of a strain for you after all you've been through."

"Yes, Maman," Masha said, thinking, "What else could one say? And what did it matter?"

Maman sighed. "You may go."

Returning to the classroom, Masha sat down beside Sophie who was studying her lessons for the next day and yawning over them. "I am to be in the Second Division next year," she remarked, trying to sound offhand.

"Really?" Sophie asked in the same tone. "That's good news."

Masha jumped. "Good?"

Sophie looked unconcerned. "Yes, certainly. I always wanted to be in the Second Division—less work, fewer subjects. Only I did not want to be separated from you. Now we can both join. What fun! No use my studying this lesson then —they don't have physics in the Second Division." She closed her book with a bang and pushed it away.

When the examinations were over, Masha's name appeared in the middle of the list, slightly above the average. She was not to go to the Second Division after all.

Sophie, close to the bottom, breathed freely only after the list of the Second Division pupils was read without "Brozina" being added to it.

CHAPTER TWENTY-FIVE

The Last Years at Smolni

AS THE CLASSES STARTED AGAIN ON THE first of August, Masha and her classmates entered their second year in the White Form.

"Two more years and then home!" Natasha chanted.

The other girls immediately took up the refrain, chanting, "Home! Home!" Even those who had no parents took part.

"But then they all have uncles or aunts, or some relatives to whom to go," Masha thought, "while I... I wonder what will happen to me when the time comes to leave Smolni." She sighed with relief when the geography teacher came in and the chanting stopped. It hurt too much.

The lesson was barely over when word came from Madame Adlerberg for the pupils to assemble in the recreation hall. The news was joyful. Princess Charlotte had given birth to a girl, who was to be named Olga.

Masha helped embroider daisies on the pink silk coverlet which the Whites were going to present to the Princess. She disliked needlework, but this time she did her best. It was pleasant to think that the Princess might smile at the sight of the pretty flowers.

"You did most of the work, Fredericks, and very nicely too," Frau Udam praised Masha. "I think it is only fair that you should present the gift to Her Highness."

Masha almost paled. "Oh, no, please. I... I am not pretty enough to represent the form."

"What a ridiculous idea," Frau Udam said. "You are simply too timid for your age." But she did not insist.

Sophie put her own work down and studied Masha's face. "Do you have to strain your hair back so tightly?" she asked. "You would be much more attractive if you let it wave and curl like the rest of us."

"I don't care what the others do," Masha answered indifferently.

"I know it!" Sophie took up her needlework again and began to stitch furiously. "When did you last hear from Anna Wulff?" she asked suddenly.

Surprised at the turn of the conversation, Masha blinked. "...About a year ago. I... I did not answer her last two letters."

"I'm going to tell you something you won't like," Sophie said in a serious tone quite unusual to her. "You are losing all your old friends, and you are not gaining new ones. One day you will find yourself all alone."

Masha remained silent.

In the afternoon, when the girls were walking in the garden, she hurried to the birch tree. "Sophie spoke the truth," she said sadly, "but I can't help it. I have practiced restraint until something died in me. I don't mind being alone any more."

She knew she was becoming more and more accustomed to people talking over her head, or laughing when she alone was serious. Now she only hoped they would not try to draw her into the conversation or invite her to share a joke.

She was surprised and even displeased when one visiting day, just before Christmas, Fraulein Knappe said briskly, "You may go downstairs, Fredericks. There is a lady who wishes to see you."

"Olga Kirilovna?" Masha wondered, as she went to the ballroom.

A young woman in a green velvet cloak edged with sable, a sable muff on her lap, jumped from her chair behind the balustrade. "I knew you wouldn't recognize me!" she exclaimed laughingly.

Masha stared at the pretty, smiling face under the green velvet bonnet. "Mademoiselle Saburova?" she asked uncertainly.

Aglaya blushed prettily and lowered her eyes. "Not Mademoiselle any more, or Saburova either. It is Madame now—Madame Iliina."

Something jarred in Masha's memory. Out of the past swam a man's face, always slightly red, with arrogant eyes and just the trace of a blond, almost colorless moustache. She thought she could hear her mother's voice saying, "You may dislike Captain Iliin, Masha, but you must be polite. If you are rude to him again, I shall have to punish you."

"I didn't know you married him…" Masha murmured.

At the tone of Masha's voice, Aglaya blushed again, but this time it was a different blush. She nodded, and sitting down again began to talk, very rapidly, glancing at Masha from time to time as if she were trying to excuse herself.

"Captain Iliin came frequently to visit Olga Kirilovna," she told Masha. "He courted me a little, but I never paid much attention to him. I'm afraid I considered him old, but he is not really, just forty-six this month. Then my youngest pupil became engaged, and I had to think about finding another position. Of course, it made me very sad. I had become attached to Olga Kirilovna and to her family. Captain Iliin saw me crying one day and… he asked me to marry him. I thought it over and I agreed. It was a sensible thing to do, wasn't it?"

She smoothed her gloves and glanced at Masha's face.

"I wish you happiness," Masha said mechanically, without answering the question, and thinking all the while, "That man! How could she?"

Once over the difficult part, Aglaya chattered on gaily. Mavra and Stepan were living in the village with relatives. Feklusha was married and was bringing up her child. Olga Kirilovna's son, who was out of school by now, had no desire to live in the country. His dream was to make a career in the army, so Olga Kirilovna was planning to sell her estate and live with her oldest daughter in the south of Russia.

Masha winced. With Olga Kirilovna gone, the last thread tying her to the old house would be cut off.

Aglaya did not stay very long. She glanced at the small gold watch hanging on a chain around her neck and murmured that she must leave. Her husband was planning to stay in St. Petersburg only a couple of days and she still had most of her shopping to do. He had given her carte blanche to buy whatever she wanted. She kissed Masha lightly over the balustrade, remarkedleft she looked healthy but too serious, and left, the smell of Violette de Parme perfume trailing behind her.

"Is that what is waiting for me?" Masha thought, walking back to the classroom. "Marriage to someone I don't love just to have a roof over my head? But how can I blame Aglaya? Lisa Ivanova, who pleaded with the Empress to save her from just such a marriage, is now a Form Mistress and she is not happy. Well, whatever is to happen to me will happen soon. Our last year at Smolni is coming fast, frighteningly fast."

The other girls shared Masha's opinion about the flying time. Winter and spring flashed past, and summer began to slip away.

"The long vacation has just started and now it is almost over," Natasha complained as August drew near.

"What vacation?" Sophie grumbled. "With all that reading to do there was no vacation at all."

"It is our duty to read those books during summer to prepare ourselves for the Solemn Examination," Sashette said loftily.

Masha felt puzzled. Sashette had never been a good student. She often admitted that she disliked studying. But since becoming a White, she had started to work hard, almost vehemently. It took her only six months to catch up with Lena Mandrika who was third in the form. Then she calmly ousted Katish from the second place and stayed there for the rest of the year. After the examinations, she emerged first, displacing Natasha, who had been head of the form since the Brown days, and now she was firmly established in that exalted position.

"It is not like our Sashette to work so hard," Marie Divova commented. "She must have some special reason." Everyone agreed.

On New Year's day, the traditional raffle took place. Only the Whites drew lots, and the three prizes were sent from the Palace. The first prize, a big bonbonniere with a small bronze crown on top, was called "The Queen." The second, also a bonbonniere, but bearing a bronze rose, was "The Lady-in-waiting." The third prize, "The Secretary" was a pretty leather portfolio with writing materials.

In the two previous years, Masha had never won a prize. This time she was lucky. "Number five," Mademoiselle Neigardt, who presided at the raffle, announced, and the portfolio was placed into Masha's hands. Katish, beaming all over, was clasping the bonbonniere with the crown, and Sashette received the Lady-in-waiting prize.

"Sashette must be disappointed. I'm sure she wanted the Queen," Sophie whispered, but Sashette did not look in the least disappointed. Her face shone. "It is just what I wanted," she kept repeating happily.

The mystery of Sashette's behavior was solved after the Easter holidays when Maman began to invite the Whites to her room, one by one, to talk about their future.

No one was surprised by the summons. On becoming Whites, the girls had begun to feel that the world of Smolni was getting too small for them. Plans were already forming, hopes expressed. Some girls were happy, some anxious. The peaceful security of school life was fading away.

Sashette was the first to go to Maman. She came back with her head held high, a triumphant smile on her face.

"How was it?" the girls cried in chorus.

"Very pleasant," Sashette answered coolly. "Maman had some wonderful news for me." She held herself up very straight and addressed the form, "After graduation I am to become lady-in-waiting to Her Majesty, the Empress Elizaveta Aleksievna. I knew that prize was a good omen!"

"Oh, Sashette! Really?" The girls jumped from their desks and surrounded the chosen one, kissing and congratulating her.

Sophie waited until the excitement calmed down, then asked in a matter-of-fact tone, "Now tell us how you managed it."

But Sashette was not easily taken aback. "I managed it by working hard," she answered, underlining the offending word. "I don't want to go back home. Do you know what my stepfather wrote me only a few months ago? 'You will be welcome home, Sashette, but only on condition that you show me due respect and abide by my decisions.' Well, now he is going to show respect to me. Of course, I did not leave anything to chance. I talked to Maman as soon as I became a White. She told me that a great deal depended upon my place in the class. It would be easier for her to plead the cause of a good student. I promised to work hard, and I went as far as I could."

"Fancy living in a palace!" the girls commented excitedly. "You'll see all kinds of interesting things, maybe go abroad! With your beauty, you'll be the queen of all the balls! You'll be getting a salary!"

The last remark came from Marie Divova. "My cousin Zinaida used to tell me how nice it was to have money of her own," she explained.

Several girls gasped, and Sashette nodded seriously. "I've thought about that too. Now I am provided for until I marry. And just think how much more exciting it is to be paid for being a lady-in-waiting than for being a governess or a companion." She shrugged her shoulders with disdain.

Nadia's turn came next. She returned all agog with excitement, her always-untidy hair falling down her back, a trail of hairpins behind her. "What do you think has happened?" she shouted even before she was inside the classroom, "I am an heiress! And I was always sure I was a pauper from the way Maman doled out my pocket money."

"How? What? Tell us quickly!" The whole form surrounded Nadia, who perched herself on top of her desk and began breathlessly. "Just imagine! My father left me loads and loads of money, but I can't do what I want with it until I am of age. Maman said it is 'in trust'whatever that may mean. Oh, and something else! I have always believed that our house burned down at the same time as the theater, but it didn't. It is still standing, and Maman said it's being redecorated for me to live in later on. But first I am to travel abroad. An elderly relative was unearthed somewhere, and she is to chaperone me. We are going to Paris first, then to Rome, and maybe to London. Isn't it wonderful, just wonderful!"

Nadia jumped off her perch and began to skip and dance between the desks, her classmates after her, pleading for her to tell them more.

Lena Mandrika did not dance after she came back from her talk with the Principal. Sitting down at her desk, she announced without looking up, "I am not going to be a nun after all. At least not for some time."

No one spoke. All the girls knew that Lena had been planning to enter a convent immediately after graduation. At last Natasha said, "I'm sorry to be so blunt, Lena, but none of us knows what to say. Are you glad or unhappy about it?"

"I don't know myself," Lena murmured. "That is what made me say yes."

"Yes to what?" Varia cried.

"To my uncle's offer," Lena said slowly. "He wrote to Maman that he and my aunt are anxious to have me live with them in Moscow. They want me to help entertain, go to balls… that kind of life."

Masha listened with interest, thinking that Lena was becoming quite pretty. Her complexion was not sallow any more and her pale skin went well with her blonde hair and soft, gray eyes.

"I explained to Maman that my great wish is to become a nun,"

Lena went on, "but Maman said, 'My dear, one should not renounce life before finding out just what life is like.' I decided to obey Maman."

After Lena and Sashette, and especially after Nadia, the other girls' visits to Maman seemed flat and unexciting.

"What do you expect her to say to girls like me who are just going back to their families in the country?" Natasha laughed. "Or to those like Sophie, or the Vuich sisters, or Stephanie, who are going into society?"

"Mother is ordering our wardrobe already," Ellie and Mary Vuich informed the others, their eyes shining.

Masha was among the last ones to go. She walked listlessly along the corridors and knocked at the familiar door.

Maman went straight to the point. "It was my intention for you to become a student teacher here," she told Masha, "and later take the position of a Form Mistress. However, after talking with both Madame Legarpe and Fraulein Knappe, I have come to the conclusion that you do not possess the necessary authority to handle the pupils and enforce discipline, nor are you really suited for that kind of work. Her Majesty, the Empress Maria Feodorovna, shares my opinion."

Masha said nothing, although Maman paused, evidently expecting her to speak.

"It was decided," Maman continued, after a moment, "that it would be best for you to become a governess in a carefully selected family."

Still, Masha remained silent. Maman studied her pale, set face and went on. "There is still another alternative." Her tone became solemn. "Her Majesty has authorized me to tell you that if you feel too young to be among strangers, you may remain at Smolni for a year or two more. You will be provided with a room, meals, and suitable clothing. You may also attend the student teachers' classes without being an official member. I trust you appreciate Her Majesty's great kindness."

For a second the shelter of Smolni, even temporarily, seemed like heaven. Then suddenly into Masha's mind came Nelidova's words of so many years ago—"When you leave, leave for good."

She forced herself to speak. "I do appreciate Her Majesty's offer, Maman, but I would rather accept a place as a governess."

The Principal looked relieved. "A very wise decision," she said encouragingly. "I will talk to you again when the time comes."

The Principal's last words made Masha think that she might have some respite before the ordeal, but she was called to Maman's rooms again the very next day.

As she entered, she saw a lady in a heavy, blue silk dress, a pea-cock shawl around her shoulders, talking to Madame Adlerberg. At the sight of Masha, the lady looked up quickly. Cold, blue eyes, set in a young but already fading face, measured Masha from head to foot.

Masha curtsied.

"This is Mademoiselle Fredericks," Maman said, making a sign for Masha to come closer. "Madame Danilova is looking for a gov-erness for her small daughter," she explained.

"Do you like children?" the lady asked abruptly.

Masha became scarlet, not knowing what to answer. She had never had anything to do with very small children and wondered how old the lady's daughter might be. "I like the little Browns," she said at last.

"Our youngest pupils," Maman explained.

"Betsie is a very delicate child," the lady said. "The person in charge of her should be really devoted. I am very busy with my social engagements and naturally I can't spend much time with her. Also, I am often tired and weak." She spoke peevishly as though it was Masha's fault. "My daughter must have the best of examples in front of her eyes." the lady went on. "I mean the best in every-thing—poise, grace, conversation."

"Fredericks, my dear, please bring me that register," Maman indicated a table at the other end of the room.

Masha obeyed. The Principal opened the register at random, glanced at a page, and gave it to Masha again. "Take it back, please."

Masha realized she was made to walk up and down the room so that the lady could have a better look at her. Immediately, her feet seemed to stick to the rug, and she moved awkwardly, almost dropping the register when she was placing it on the table.

Madame Danilova asked a few more questions—Masha's age, who her parents were, where her father was killed. All the time, she kept looking at Masha's face, hands, nails. It was not a friendly gaze and Masha stammered her answers unhappily, so embarrassed and shy that she could hardly remember her mother's maiden name.

"You may go, Fredericks," Maman said at last, and Masha left.

Sophie was waiting at the Principal's door. "I guessed why Maman sent for you," she told Masha. "Have you been engaged? Oh, goodness, you're crying! Was it so bad?"

"Yes… No. I mean it was probably just as usual. It is silly of me to mind. Only it was so… so terrible being looked all over as though you were an animal."

"It is all over now. Don't think about it," Sophie was saying gently, putting her arm around Masha's waist and leading her away.

That same evening Maman called Masha again. "I'm sorry to say that you did not make a favorable impression, Fredericks," she said. "I realize you felt shy. Let us hope you will do better next time."

The next time came in a few days. A little, elderly lady with a pleasant, wrinkled face wanted a governess for her two granddaughters. She was kind to Masha, but she did not hire her. "I did not see her smile even once during our whole talk," she told the Principal even before Masha left the room. "I want someone gay and cheerful for my girls."

Two weeks passed quietly. Then Masha was invited to appear in front of a middle-aged gentleman whose military uniform made her think about her father. He did not even waste time asking questions. After one look at Masha, he said firmly that he couldn't imagine her handling his niece, a very difficult and wayward child.

After the military gentleman, Maman said to Masha kindly, "Do not be distressed, my dear. I have another plan for you. A lady, Madame Nazimova, wants a companion. She is very wealthy and I'm sure you would be very comfortable living with her. She is coming next week to see you."

"Next week?" Masha thought, quickly counting on her fingers. "Almost five days respite!"

"Being a companion sounds better than being a governess," Masha's classmates kept saying. "You'll probably like it."

Sashette shrugged her shoulders and remarked, speaking to no one in particular, "Certainly. Those old ladies are often easy enough to please. All Masha will have to do is read the same book over and over again until the old lady drops off to sleep and comb the fleas out of her pug."

"I don't really care what I do," Masha murmured listlessly.

Madame Nazimova arrived on the sixth day. Masha expected someone frail and elderly. It was a shock to see a large, fat body, almost bursting out of a bright yellow gown. Shrewd gray eyes stared at Masha from a wrinkled face that looked bizarre under the high pile of jet-black hair. Coming closer, Masha realized that her prospective employer was wearing a wig.

"Mademoiselle Fredericks has a very pleasant reading voice," Maman said after the introductions were made.

"Don't need it," Madame Nazimova answered briskly. "Never read a book in my life and don't intend to listen to one." She addressed Masha, "Well, my dear, let me ask you a few questions before I decide whether we suit, though offhand I would say you are not exactly what I am looking for."

Masha's heart gave a leap of relief, then plunged back into despair. If it were not Madame Nazimova, it would be someone else, maybe much worse.

"I like to have people around me," the old lady was saying in the same brisk tone. "My house is open day and night, so to speak. Now this doesn't mean that I want to wag my tongue all the time. Do you think you would be able to keep my guests amused, talk to them, maybe tinkle on the piano for their benefit, while I have a nice game of cards with my usual partners?"

Masha moistened her lips. "I... I will do my best, but... I don't know... my music is not very good."

"Ha," Madame Nazimova said in a voice that held a shade of contempt. "Now, do you suppose you could keep an eye on my silver and give a good scolding to my housekeeper if you should find a spoon missing?"

Masha visualized an elderly housekeeper, full of her own importance, a bunch of keys at her belt—like the housekeeper Olga Kirilovna had. She felt appalled. "No, no, I couldn't," she almost cried, and Madame Nazimova said in a satisfied tone, "Just what I thought." She looked at the Principal. "Any more girls for me to choose from?"

Madame Adlerberg pursed her lips. "Very few of our pupils take up a position after they graduate. Most of them return to their families and go into society. A few who have a teaching vocation remain as student teachers. Sometimes, one or two privileged girls become ladies-in-waiting at the court. We have no one except Mademoiselle Fredericks to offer you, Madame."

"She won't do," the lady said curtly.

Masha glanced at Maman, and having received a nod, curtsied and went out.

She was summoned back fifteen minutes later. Madame Nazimova had left, and the Principal was sitting in her chair, looking tired and annoyed.

"It is really unfortunate, my dear, that you do not have more confidence in yourself," she told Masha, "After all, Madame Nazimova was not asking the impossible. Many young girls would have been glad to take such a position." She looked at Masha and her voice softened, "But please do not take it so to heart, Fredericks. There will be more people looking for a governess or a companion just before graduation, in March. And if we cannot find a place for you, some other arrangement will be made."

The vagueness of the last sentence terrified Masha. She began to sleep badly, always haunted by the same nightmare —she was walking out of the Smolni front door and down the steps only to find that the steps ended suddenly in a black, blank void.

CHAPTER TWENTY-SIX

The Graduation Ball

W HEN I THINK ABOUT TONIGHT MY FEET dance all by themselves!"

Sophie's joyful announcement was accompanied by a smell of burning hair and a frantic, "Mademoiselle, please sit still!" from Monsieur Henri, the French hairdresser. He was rushing around the dormitory, curling irons in his hands, faced with the giant task of getting twenty-five heads ready for the Graduation Ball.

The girls sat on the stools by their beds, waiting for their turn under Monsieur's artistic hands, Two harassed maids kept running in and out, bringing pins and helping to lace the long ribbons of the dancing slippers. One maid edged her way to Sophie and hastily pressed something into her hand. "Thank you, Klavdia," Sophie said and beamed. "Girls, look what Klavdia brought me!" Opening her palm, she showed a dozen cranberries. "Two for you, Masha, two for me, and the rest for you, for you, and for you." She distributed the berries to her nearest neighbors and sat down again. "One for each cheek," she explained, crushing the berries and rubbing them into her skin.

Another maid brought in an extra oil lamp and a bunch of freshly ironed blue and deep-pink sashes.

Masha turned her face away from the light and thought she had never felt so plain. Judging by the reflection in the small mirror, the freckles on the bridge of her nose had certainly multiplied during the last half hour. She dabbed some powder at them, then put the puff down, completely discouraged.

Sashette said in a loud whisper, "Dear me! My turn comes after Masha's. She has so much hair, it will take Monsieur hours to fix it."

Stephanie promptly took up the cue. "It is hard on you, especially since Monsieur will have to invent a new style for her. You know… something that covers the forehead."

Masha felt the tips of her ears burn. She knew that her hair was lanky, and her forehead was too high. It was bad enough without being teased by the two beauties of the school.

"Did you hear about the new rule?"

Masha straightened up and turned around. Sophie stood behind her, balancing a pair of small gilt scissors on two fingers.

"What new rule?" several girls cried anxiously.

"Didn't you hear?" Sophie opened her eyes in innocent surprise. "Very short girls are not going to be allowed to dance. It does not look pretty when men have to bend in half over them." In the way of consolation she added, "But they will be allowed to watch."

Tiny, elf-like Stephanie paled, and asked in a trembling voice, "Is it true, Sophie? Do say it is not true!"

Sophie ignored her and approached Sashette. "You promised once to give us, your classmates, locks of your hair to remember you by after we graduate," she said sweetly. "I see just the curl I like. There, near your left ear. With your permission . . ," She made a sudden dash and snapped her scissors.

But Sashette would not give permission. She clutched at her

raven locks and sprang back with a wild shriek, almost upsetting Stephanie. Sophie promptly ran after her and charged again.

Sashette dived between two beds, slipped on all fours and emerged from the other side, only to find herself almost in Sophie's arms.

"Sophie, don't!" Masha cried, throwing herself between the two combatants.

"If you dare…" Sashette hissed, sitting on the floor and glaring at Sophie.

Other girls were running up, laughing and elbowing each other. The maids gaped. Monsieur Henri waved his irons and shouted something in French.

The noise was steadily becoming worse when the door opened, and Madame Legarpe sailed in. A sudden hush fell over the dormitory, broken only by the swish of Madame's blue silk gown. Without saying a word, she lifted her lorgnette and gave a slow look around. A second later, every girl was in her place, the maids ran in a flurry of blue and white striped uniforms, and Sophie sank behind the nearest bed. Turning to the Frenchman, Madame Legarpe ordered coldly, "Please proceed, Monsieur."

The remaining preparations were completed in awesome silence and with remarkable speed. At last Monsieur bowed out and the Form Mistress clapped her hands.

The girls grouped themselves around her, all alike in their high-waisted dresses of white muslin with colored sashes, curls trembling at the temples.

Madame Legarpe scrutinized every pair of hands to make sure the nails were clean, sniffed for forbidden perfume, and distributed long white gloves. "Make sure not to soil these and return them to me tomorrow morning," she instructed the girls.

"These are too big," Stephanie complained, flapping the tips of the gloves in the air.

Madame Legarpe eyed her disapprovingly. "My dear, the school cannot provide individual gloves. Just pull them up a little more. Let me see…"

"Why doesn't she finish fussing and let us go," Sophie hissed impatiently in Masha's ear.

Madame Legarpe cleared her throat, and the girls froze to attention. "Mesdemoiselles," she began, "there is no time now for me to comment on the disgraceful scene I saw when I came in. What grieves me even more than your behavior is the fact that instead of speaking French like ladies, you were all chattering in Russian like kitchen maids."

"Of course, she doesn't like us to speak Russian," Sophie muttered. "She came from Switzerland twenty years ago and she doesn't know a single Russian word."

"Hush," someone from behind hissed, "listen!"

"I'm afraid I have a disappointment for you," Madame Legarpe announced. "His Majesty the Emperor is indisposed and will not honor us with his presence tonight."

The Form Mistress paused, and whispers ran around. "However," she went on, "Her Majesty, Maria Feodorovna, graciously promised to be with us. His Highness, Grand Duke Nicholas, and the Grand Duchess are also expected."

"She means Princess Charlotte," Natasha whispered. "Of course, she's right, but to me the Grand Duchess is always Princess Charlotte."

Madame Legarpe frowned in the direction of the whispers and raised her voice. "I want to remind all of you once more to behave modestly, not to talk or laugh too loudly, not to dance twice in a row with the same partner, not to…" She went on but Masha was not listening. She was too busy imagining herself in the ballroom, awkward and tongue-tied, dancing with a strange man, or else sitting by the wall, trying to look as if she were too tired to dance.

By the time Madame Legarpe reached her last "not to…" Masha had given up deciding which of the two possibilities was the worst. If only she didn't have to go. If only she could hide, or run away, or faint, or be suddenly, miraculously, forbidden to attend the ball. Her mind searched desperately for some means of escape. She noticed a long thread hanging from the hem of her skirt. It was like an answer to a prayer. Quickly she bent down and pulled at the thread. Part of her hem now hung down, trailing on the floor.

The Form Mistress finished her speech with a menacing, "And if there is any serious breach in behavior, I will not hesitate to remove the culprit from the ballroom." Her lorgnette was fixed on Sophie, who folded her hands, dropped her eyes, and bowed her head so low that several hairpins fell out.

Then the lorgnette swept the group and trained itself on Masha's hem. "Fredericks, my poor child! How very annoying. Find a maid at once and tell her to put in a few stitches. You will join us downstairs as soon as you are ready. Now, Mesdemoiselles!" With a slight gesture, Madame Legarpe directed her white flock toward the door.

Left alone, Masha looked for a hiding place. The bare walls and rows of beds did not offer much protection. She ended by standing behind the door, pressed against the wall.

Her ear caught the strains of music. The royal guests were proceeding down the ballroom. She stared at the floorboards, imagining the rows of girls dipping into a deep curtsy.

Time passed. Masha was beginning to think herself safe when she heard a light step pass her hiding place, stop and walk back.

"Ah, here you are," Sophie said, peeping behind the door.

All Masha could say was, "How did you know I was here?"

"Because it is the darkest corner," Sophie explained. "And now come out."

Masha squeezed herself further back. "I don't want to come out. Please, Sophie, go and dance. I'm enjoying myself, really. I can hear the music and that's enough."

"No, it is not enough," Sophie said gravely. "You can't always hide in a hole and only listen. You have to get out sometime and make the others listen to you for a change."

Sophie's tone was so unlike her usual gay banter that Masha accepted the outstretched hand and let herself be led out.

"Let's see how you look." Sophie stepped back and surveyed her friend from every angle. "Not bad, considering. They really do keep the corners remarkably clean here. You're very pale, though. What did you do with those cranberries?"

"I ate them," Masha confessed. "Madame Legarpe came in just as I had them in my hand. There was no other way."

"Did you really?" Sophie laughed. "Never mind. Let me fix your skirt and then we'll do your hair."

Masha stood still while Sophie's nimble fingers shook out the folds of her dress and pinned up the hem. She looked at the dark windows streaked with sleet, at the smoking oil lamps, the scattered hairpins, discarded shoe ribbons, and she shivered.

Sophie looked up. "What is the matter? Are you cold?"

Masha shook her head without answering. She would never be able to explain to Sophie the sudden feeling of being left behind while her companions were already beyond the bend of the road. To her own surprise, she asked eagerly, "Will I do now?"

"In a minute." Sophie rolled a stray curl around her finger and then took Masha's arm.

"Now!"

The two girls ran down the wide stairway.

The strains of music became clearer. Sophie pushed the door open, and the two girls slipped into the ballroom. Masha took a few steps and shrank against a pillar. Voices, music, the smell of flowers and perfumes, the heat from hundreds of candles reflected in the mirrors and in the crystals of the chandeliers seemed to rise in waves around her.

For a second she was tempted to turn back. She had even started to edge toward the door when she became aware of a lorgnette fixed on her from behind a bank of flowers. Years of discipline made her instantly straighten up and drop a hasty curtsy in the direction of the lorgnette. It helped. The pillar behind her stopped moving and the blur in the middle of the floor became a group of dancers going through the intricate steps of a quadrille.

Absorbed in looking around, Masha did not at first notice the young cadet who appeared in front of her, bowing and muttering something. Then she saw Sophie making strange signs from a distance, and suddenly she remembered. This was Sophie's cousin whom they had met at the Easter Bazaar. It seemed years and years ago.

The music changed to a waltz. The boy suddenly lurched forward and gripped Masha's hand. Before she knew it, they were among the dancing couples, gliding on the polished floor.

The cadet turned out to be a poor dancer, though he was certainly doing his very best. His blond eyebrows drawn together, his cheeks ruddy above his high collar, he whirled Masha jerkily, counting under his breath, "One, two, one, two."

Trying not to laugh, Masha looked at the bristling blond hair on the level with her eyes and wondered how to start a conversation. How old could the boy be and what was his name? Michael... Michael something, about seventeen probably. She was groping for a suitable remark when Michael said in a deep, bass voice, "There is a fellow in my form who can turn somersaults ten times in a row."

Startled by this unexpected information, Masha missed a step and trod on her partner's foot. The music stopped and she was saved from finding an appropriate answer. Michael led her to a chair, heaved a sigh of relief, and disappeared in the crowd.

With mixed feelings, Masha watched him go. She had not exactly enjoyed his company, but she did find it enchanting to waltz across the white and gold ballroom to the crystal shower of music. She was eager to dance again, but another waltz started, then a gavotte, and nobody came to invite her.

Sitting in her corner, she watched the colorful medley of military uniforms, gold epaulets and decorations, civilians' black jackets with tails, ladies' flowing gowns of every hue, white gloves, fans, and feathers. She noticed that the pupils' simple white dresses did not lose anything in comparison with laces, streams of ribbons and flounces, but looked even more fresh and graceful.

Old ladies sat in small gilt chairs, their snuffboxes at their side, while the younger ones flirted with their partners. Groups formed, dissolved, and gathered again.

The babble of voices merged into a steady hum. The French language reigned supreme, with only occasional German or English mixing in. The native language of the immense Russian empire was banished from the drawing rooms and ballrooms.

From time to time Masha caught sight of Sophie, dancing every dance. She moved her chair a little so that Sophie could not see her being a wallflower.

Another waltz started. Masha looked at a group of her classmates, also waiting for partners. They sat just like herself, hands folded in their laps, their feet in a graceful position on the floor. Yet, one after another, they were asked to dance, while she was bypassed. Perhaps it was the smile they let play at the corners of their lips, the slight beating of lashes, all saying without words, "I am waiting for you."

"It is no use," Masha thought. "I just don't know how to do it." She looked up and saw two young men threading their way to her corner. One went to the only girl who remained sitting nearby, the other seemed to hesitate, then turned back. "I don't want the plain one," Masha heard him say to his companion before he became lost among other guests.

Masha blushed, then paled, feeling as though everyone in the ballroom was pointing at her, chanting, "The plain one! The plain one!" She rose from her chair, but sat down again, surprised by a sudden movement around her. Everyone was hastily stepping back, giving way to a tall man in a green uniform who was heading in her direction.

It took Masha a full minute to realize that she was being asked to dance by the Grand Duke Nicholas himself.

For once her shyness did not betray her. Perhaps it was the sweeping rhythm of the waltz, or the skillful way the Grand Duke led her among the dancing couples. She was aware of the glances in her direction and caught a few whispers. "She is dancing with the Grand Duke." A feeling of pride suddenly made her lift her head and smile at something the Grand Duke was saying. "Just a few more moments, just once more around the ballroom," she thought as the strains of music were dying away.

The waltz was over. Masha dared to lift her eyes at her partner. His rather severe face softened as he saw her anxious expression. To her surprise he did not lead her back to her seat.

"I want to present you to Her Highness," the Grand Duke said, and taking Masha's trembling, white-gloved hand, led her toward the group at the far end of the ballroom.

The Grand Duchess looked more beautiful than ever in her pink dress embroidered with pearls, a circle of pink pearls in her hair. But the gay, flighty manner that she had when Masha first saw her at Smolni was gone. The blue eyes were now more serious and calm.

Rising from her curtsy, Masha suffered agony as the Grand Duchess waved her to a red velvet chair at her side.

"What happens if I can't answer?" Masha thought wildly, only to forget everything else at the sound of "Princess Charlotte's" kind voice. There was genuine interest in her tone as she asked, "Graduation is coming soon. Tell me, my dear, what are your plans for the future?"

Masha's wistful "I have no plans" came out before she realized it. After that everything was easy. Masha forgot the awesome presence of Maria Feodorovna sitting with Maman and the other dignitaries grouped around and found herself talking to the Grand Duchess as she would have talked to Sophie. For the first time in almost three years, she brought herself to mention her mother's death. Only once did she stumble. When the Grand Duchess asked her who was her best friend at school, she answered quickly, "I have two, Sophie and the birch tree," and blushed scarlet.

The older woman did not laugh. She said pensively, "A birch tree? It must be a trustworthy friend, one that would never betray you." Masha thought she saw a shadow cross the lovely face.

"I will be present at the Solemn Examination," the Grand Duchess told Masha. "Try to make us all proud of you. And now," she continued with a smile, "I mustn't keep you away from your dancing."

Masha hardly had time to take a few steps before Sophie came rushing up to her. "What did Her Highness say to you? Were you talking in German or French? How... Oh, bother! Here is someone coming up to ask you for a dance. Never mind, you will have hordes of partners now. See if you don't."

Sophie was right. For the rest of the evening, Masha did not sit down.

CHAPTER TWENTY-SEVEN

The Fairy Tale

THE SOLEMN EXAMINATIONS WERE TO BEGIN on the fifth of March. Everything was ready when a message came from the palace that the Empress Maria Feodorovna was not feeling well and that the examinations were to be postponed.

"Gives us some more time for study. Not that it helps me much," Sophie remarked, yawning over her books. "Bother French history! Why did they have so many kings named Louis?"

Other girls were grumbling too. "I hate having to write to my parents that now I won't graduate till April," Natasha said, wiping away a tear.

Only Masha did not mind. She was working feverishly, waking up at dawn to study and even trying to read by candlelight. The Grand Duchess wanted to be proud of her and Masha was not going to disappoint her.

The big day came at last. Pale and tense, the Whites faced a long row of examiners. They all looked alike, in long jackets with silver buttons, and all equally alarming. But the Grand Duchess was present, sitting beside Maria Feodorovna. She smiled encouragingly at Masha. For her sake, Masha recited poetry in a clear voice instead of whispering and forced herself to answer questions without hesitating at every word.

Music and dancing examinations were considered very important. Masha was one of the four pupils playing on two pianos. She set her teeth and let her hands glide on the keys. "You were good," Katish Muffle, who was playing with Masha, said after the examination was over. There was surprise in her voice.

Dancing was easier. Masha was one of several girls who danced on the stage Le Pas de Chale, furling and unfurling silk scarves. When the music stopped, Masha suddenly discovered she was sorry to have it end.

When the results were announced all eyes were on the list in Maman's hands as she read the names of the lucky ones who were to receive prizes.

Sashette naturally headed the list. "The first chiffre," everyone murmured enviously. The chiffre was a coveted reward—a gold letter M with a crown, on a white ribbon bordered with red. The M stood for the Empress Maria Feodorovna. Natasha and Katish were to receive the second and third chiffres.

Lena Mandrika was awarded the first gold medal, Varia the second. Then came Ellie Vuich, who received the first silver medal, and… Masha couldn't believe her ears when Maman read, "Maria Fredericks—second silver medal."

It was almost too much for Masha. Red-faced, she hid herself in a corner of the classroom after the reading of awards was over. Sophie, who came out "regrettably low," as Maman put it, rejoiced so loudly over her friend's achievement that several people congratulated her instead of Masha.

The prize-giving itself came several days later. It was an impressive ceremony in the large ballroom. The Grand Duchess came with

Maria Feodorovna. There were also several dignitaries and some of the court ladies who had once been Smolni pupils themselves.

All in white, every curl in place, the girls stood in ranks, not even daring to whisper, while Form Mistresses walked up and down the aisle.

Maman made a short speech, wishing the girls happiness in their future life and asking them not to forget their years at the Smolni Institute.

"Attention!" Madame Legarpe whispered when the speech was over, and Fraulein Knappe echoed the word, farther on.

A quiver passed across the ranks of Whites as Sashette walked up the aisle to receive the chiffre.

Mademoiselle Neigardt stepped out, holding the tray with prizes, and stood beside Maria Feodorovna, who was seated in a gilt chair.

Sashette knelt on a red velvet cushion. Maria Feodorovna pinned the chiffre to the girl's left shoulder and kissed her cheek. Sashette touched with her lips the extended hand, rose, curtsied low, and backed into her place.

Natasha and Katish followed.

The medals were distributed next. Masha braced herself and tried to remember all Madame Legarpe's instructions. Three steps and curtsy, another three steps and curtsy again. Through a haze, she saw the Dowager Empress take a medal from the tray and place it in her cupped hands. Instead of moving on, she stood still, staring at the silver circle, hardly believing it was hers.

Maman said, "Fredericks!" in a warning tone. Masha dropped her final curtsy and backed into the ranks.

Diplomas were given out and more speeches made. As soon as the signal came to break ranks, the younger girls rushed to the graduates, offering congratulations and begging for souvenirs.

Thoughtful Natasha had brought an old hair ribbon and was giving pieces of it to the small girls. Sophie generously sacrificed a few strands of her bronze hair. Sashette defended her chiffre from the curious hands, screaming shrilly, "Don't touch!"

A small Brown asked to see Masha's medal. "It is beautiful," she murmured shyly, caressing the medal. "Your mother must be proud of you."

To her own surprise, Masha said with sudden conviction, "Yes, she is very proud." At the same time, another thought came—the Grand Duchess had not spoken to her or congratulated her. From where she stood Masha could see her talking to the Principal and to Mademoiselle Neigardt. Feeling suddenly very disheartened, Masha went to join the rest of her form, just in time to hear Natasha say, "I hope... to live happily with my family, help my mother around the house, and teach my younger brother and sister."

Masha shrank back. Her companions were playing the traditional game of the graduating class, each girl beginning with, "I hope..." But it was too late to escape. She stood a little aside, trying not to draw attention to herself.

Sophie was speaking now. "I hope... to sleep late every morning, never wash in cold water again, and dance every evening. Oh, I forgot! I also hope to have a pale blue ball gown."

Sashette said bitingly, "How modest! With your father's wealth, you can afford a different colored gown every day."

"When my turn comes," Masha thought, "I will have to say I hope to become a governess." It sounded funny, only she did not feel like laughing.

"You, Stephanie!" Katish cried,

"I hope..." Stephanie's fluty voice faltered and stopped. Everyone looked up. The Grand Duchess stood beside the group of girls, dressed in a silvery-gray gown, a bunch of violets pinned at her throat.

"This sounds like a very interesting game," she said gaily, "I think I will join. Let me see now..." She half closed her eyes and smiled. "I hope... I hope to have a very special lady-in-waiting soon, all for myself. Her name is Masha Fredericks."

There was a sudden silence, like a thunderclap.

Masha stood with clasped hands, her eyes fixed on the kind face smiling at her, sweetly, almost... yes, lovingly.

"Masha, don't you understand?" Katish seized her arm.

"Say something," Sophie hissed into her ear.

"Wait…" Masha murmured. "Wait…" She wanted to explain that she could not find words that would express the wonderful warm feeling of "belonging" that was slowly spreading all over her. The most important part of her happiness was that she was not one of those "privileged ones" Maman had spoken about, who were chosen because of their beauty or their high marks. The Grand Duchess wanted her because she liked her, plain Masha Fredericks.

Abandoning the hope of ever finding the right words, Masha gave one long look of gratitude and devotion to the Grand Duchess and sank into a deep curtsy, her head almost touching the floor.

CHAPTER TWENTY-EIGHT

There Was a Beggar Maid...

OR THE REST OF THE MORNING, MASHA found herself showered with congratulations and advice from the girls and the staff. She answered, "Thank you" and "Yes" to everything. It was the easiest way to be left alone to get used to her new vast horizons.

Only in the afternoon did she find herself free to run along the familiar path toward the birch tree.

When she reached her friend, standing tall and graceful, the April breeze moving the slender branches, her heart was so full she could hardly speak. "Listen," she murmured, leaning her head against the trunk. "Listen, I am going to tell you a fairy tale. Once upon a time, a beautiful princess came from a faraway land to Russia to marry a handsome prince. There was a big wedding, bells rang, and people cheered. The prince and the princess went to live in a beautiful palace, they had children and were very happy." She paused, then went on in the best Niania tradition, "But this is not the end of the tale. One day, driving in her gilded coach, the princess saw a beggar

269

maid standing by the roadside in ragged clothes. The maid had no family, no home, nowhere to go... The princess took pity on the poor girl and took her to the palace to become her lady-in-waiting."

Masha's voice trailed away. Overcome by dreams, she stood looking upward at the branch, now high among the leaves, on which she had once placed the "magic ring." The metal had long since rotted and fallen away, but the green glass was still there, embedded in the bark, shining softly like Mamma's lamp, as if sending Masha a blessing for her new life.

With a sudden carefree laugh, Masha flung her arms around the birch tree. "It is not a fairy tale at all," she whispered. "I am the beggar maid, but I am not going to be a governess in some stranger's house. I am going to live with a beautiful princess and be her faithful lady-in-waiting."

ANCILLARIES

Photos

THE SMOLNI INSTITUTE FOR NOBLE GIRLS

VISITING HOUR AT SMOLNI INSTITUTE

A DANCE LESSON IN THE MAIN HALL

EMPRESS CATHERINE THE GREAT

CATHERINE II VISITING THE SMOLNI
INSTITUTE FOR NOBLE MAIDENS.

MADAME ADLERBERG

EMPRESS MARIA FEODOROVNA

Cast of Characters

Akulina, Niania (Masha's nurse; called Niania)

Feklusha (maid)

Kirilovna, Olga (Barinia Antonova; friend of Masha's family)

Mamma (Masha's mother, Maria Borisovna Fredericks, widow of Colonel Vasili Fredericks; called Maria Borisovna and Barinia*)

Masha (9 years old 1814–15, 18 years old 1823–24)

Mavra (cook)

Max (horse)

Papa (Masha's father; killed at Borodino)

Saburova, Aglaya (called Aglaya; governess for Olga Kirilovna's children; marries, becomes Madame Iliina)

Stepan (manservant)

Trezor (Masha's dog)

---

* A term of respect used for a married woman of the upper class

CAST OF CHARACTERS

PERSONS AT ST. PETERSBURG

Alexander I, Emperor (married to Empress Elizaveta Aleksievna)

Annoushka (witch)

Anya (doll given to Masha by Anna Wulff)

Catherine the Great, Empress (founder of the Smolni Institute)

Charlotte, Princess, Grand Duchess (wife of Nicholas)

Elizaveta Aleksievna, Empress (wife of Alexander I)

Feodorovna, Maria (Her Majesty, the Dowager Empress; widow of Emperor Paul I; patroness of the Smolni Institute)

Iziumova, Katerina Ivanovna (called Katerina Ivanovna; rents furnished rooms; the widow Iziumova)

Karamzin, Nikolai Mikhailovich (historian)

Mitia (boy servant of Katerina Ivanovna)

Nicholas, Grand Duke

Panov, Michael (Sophie Brozina's cousin)

Paul, Emperor (first wife: Natalya Aleksievna; second wife: Maria Feodorovna; assassinated)

Riabov, Boris (Michael Panov's classmate)

Rose, Madame (Rose Bonnets hat shop)

Zinaida (lady-in-waiting; cousin of Marie Divova)

CAST OF CHARACTERS

PERSONS AT SMOLNI INSTITUTE

Note: students and teachers are often called by only their last names.

Students in Masha's Form

Ellie and Mary Vuich

Emilia Agte

Katish Muffle

Lena Mandrika

Marie Divova

Masha (Maria) Fredericks

Nadia Maslova

Natasha Meller

Sasha Rossett (called Sashette)

Sophie Brozina

Stephanie Radzivill

Varia Bikova

Students in the White Form

Anna Wulff

Clementine Del Pardo

Katia Sankina

Lisa Ivanova

Mania Suvorova

Teachers and Personnel

Absolom, Mademoiselle (music teacher)

Adlerberg, Madame (Principal of Smolni; called Maman)

Anikiev, Alexander Sergeivich (history teacher)

Aranov, Monsieur (Russian teacher)

Didlo, Monsieur (ballet)

Garbi, Mademoiselle (arithmetic teacher)

Henri, Monsieur (hairdresser)

Klavdia (maid)

Knappe, Fraulein (Brown Form Mistress)

CAST OF CHARACTERS

Legarpe, Madame (White Form Mistress and later third Form Mistress for Masha's group)

Neigardt, Mademoiselle (Inspectress; called Neigardt; distant relative of student Emilia Agte)

Nelidova, Katerina (called Nelidova)

Padua, Mademoiselle (second Form Mistress for Masha's group, replaces Mademoiselle Souchet)

Romanus, Dr. (medical doctor at Smolni)

Souchet, Mademoiselle (first Form Mistress of Masha's group)

Udam, Frau (needlework teacher)

www.ingramcontent.com/pod-product-compliance
Lightning Source LLC
Chambersburg PA
CBHW051103030726
47504CB00006B/1762